BEFORE THE FACT

by FRANCIS ILES

"One of the finest studies of murder ever written. It is a masterpiece of cruelty and wit."
—Christopher Morley

"Astonishingly intimate is Francis Iles's knowledge of the emotions of a murderer." —*News Chronicle*

Also available in Perennial Library:

MALICE AFORETHOUGHT by Francis Iles

FRANCIS ILES

BEFORE THE FACT

PERENNIAL LIBRARY
Harper & Row, Publishers
New York, Cambridge, Hagerstown, Philadelphia, San Francisco
London, Mexico City, São Paulo, Sydney

First PERENNIAL LIBRARY edition published 1980.

ISBN: 0-06-080517-X

82 83 84 10 9 8 7 6 5 4 3 2

FOR
HELEN

BEFORE THE FACT

by FRANCIS ILES

CONTENTS

PART ONE

CHAPTER I

SOME women give birth to murderers, some go to bed with them, and some marry them. Lina Aysgarth had lived with her husband for nearly eight years before she realized that she was married to a murderer.

Suspicion is a tenuous thing, so impalpable that the exact moment of its birth is not easy to determine. But looking back over the series of little pictures which composed the memory of her married life, Lina found later that certain of them—a small incident here, its significance quite unnoticed at the time, an unimportant action there, perhaps just a chance word of her husband's—had become illuminated by her fear so that they stood out like a row of street-lamps along a dark, straight road: a road which looks so easy in the daytime but so sinister by night.

Even her very first meeting with Johnnie seemed, in this later illumination, a red triangle of danger whose warning she had deliberately ignored.

It had been at a picnic got up by the Cotherstone girls.

The Cotherstone girls were always getting up picnics and asking the participants to bring friends: a fatal thing to do, for the friends of our friends are often so very unexpected. Lina McLaidlaw lived then in Abbot Monckford, which is a small hamlet in Dorsetshire seven miles from the nearest railway station, so that even a picnic got up by the Cotherstone girls was an event.

The objective of the picnic was a well known beauty spot in the neighbourhood, containing a View. Lina, who had seen the View a hundred times already, went because there was a chance of meeting strangers. She often felt that in the country the only thing worth living for was strangers.

On this particular picnic there was only one stranger.

"My dear," Lina said to the elder Cotherstone girl, under cover of the View, "who is that *rather* attractive man with the Barnards?"

"*Very* attractive man," corrected the elder Cotherstone girl with enthusiasm. "Isn't he simply divine? It's Johnnie Aysgarth. You know. He's a cousin of the Middlehams."

"I know." Lina looked at the young man with increased interest. So that was Johnnie Aysgarth.

"You've heard about the Aysgarths?" said the elder Cotherstone girl disappointedly.

"Of course," Lina nodded. Naturally she had heard about the Aysgarths. Everyone who knew the Middlehams had heard about the Aysgarths. Sir Thomas Aysgarth was Lord Middleham's first cousin. Lord Middleham had somehow managed to retain his estates, unlike most of his brother peers, and even enough money to keep them up. Sir Thomas Aysgarth had not. He now lived partly in an upper maisonette in Hampstead, and partly with such of his relations and old friends as he could induce to invite him for long visits. Of his four sons, one had been killed in the war, one was in Australia, nominally sheep-farming, one was on the stage, and Johnnie, the youngest, was—well, no one quite knew what Johnnie was. But when the Aysgarth name was mentioned at all, Johnnie invariably came into the conversation at once.

"He's staying at Penshaze," Miss Cotherstone volunteered. Lord Middleham, at Penshaze, still ruled Abbot Monckford and its attendant hamlets of Abbot Tarrantington and Abbot Blansford, as firmly in fact if not in theory as his feudal ancestors had done five hundred years ago.

"But what's he doing with the Barnards?" Lina wanted to know.

Miss Cotherstone shrugged her shoulders. "I should put it, what are the Barnards doing with him? And that's pretty obvious, isn't it? I don't want to be catty, but Jessie and Alice *are* getting on, aren't they? And the Barnards have got money and the Aysgarths haven't. I should say it's quite obvious."

"Poor man," Lina laughed, "if he's booked for Jessie or Alice. How old is he?"

"I don't know. But no doubt the Barnards could tell you, if you're interested."

"Interested!" said Lina.

But she was interested.

She was interested to know if Johnnie Aysgarth was as fascinating as he was supposed to be. She was interested to know if he was as attractive as he looked. She was interested to know why all the women who knew him spoke his name in tones of mingled rapture and guardedness. She was interested to know whether he was really just another of the horsey, doggy, shooting, fishing, hunting nincompoops with which her path seemed to be strewn, or whether for once something a little more civilized had come out of Penshaze. She was interested to know whether he resented the Barnard girls calling him "Johnnie" already. She was interested to know whether he was interested in one of the Barnard girls.

In fact, Lina told herself, Johnnie Aysgarth was a stranger and she was therefore automatically interested in him.

"At any rate, his manners are charming," she thought, covertly watching him; and her interest grew.

It was gratified.

Before they had settled down for lunch Mrs. Barnard (and obviously reluctant Mrs. Barnard, Lina saw with hidden amusement) appeared at her side, Mr. Aysgarth in tow.

"Oh, Lina dear, may I introduce . . . Mr. Aysgarth, Miss McLaidlaw. Mr. Aysgarth is staying at Penshaze."

"Oh, yes?" Lina said brightly. "You know the Middlehams, then, Mr. Aysgarth?" What a ridiculous thing to say, she thought. Of course he knows the Middlehams if he's staying there. And of course he knows perfectly well that I know he's a cousin.

Johnnie Aysgarth was still holding her hand in its pigskin gauntlet. "Yes," he smiled, "I know the Middlehams. In fact, Charlie Middleham's some sort of a cousin of mine. But they evidently don't know me, or I shouldn't be staying there."

"Now, where . . . ?" said Mrs. Barnard, and wandered distrustfully away.

Johnnie Aysgarth was still smiling at Lina. It was an infectious, intimate smile, which seemed to imply that out of all the people there only they two really had the right to smile at each other. And his eyes did twinkle.

Lina smiled back. He *was* fascinating.

She withdrew her hand. Nobody had ever retained it so long on an introduction before.

She saw now that Johnnie was shorter than she had thought, not more than five feet eight at most; but his chest was broad, and he was evidently well muscled and athletic. His hair was very dark, with little tight curls over the temples, and his eyes a light gray. Lina thought his face the merriest she had ever seen.

"I had an awful job to get the old girl to introduce me to you," he said. "She didn't want to one little bit."

"Oh?" said Lina, a little taken aback. "Why?" she added feebly.

Johnnie laughed. "Oh, she's got me booked in her mind for one of her comic daughters, of course," he said, without self-consciousness. "She didn't want me to meet the opposition."

If Johnnie Aysgarth was not self-conscious, Lina was. "Opposition?" she said, as frigidly as she could.

"Local opposition," he replied with another smile. "Who'd look at the Barnards when you're on the same picnic?"

Lina felt herself colouring and was correspondingly annoyed. She was not used to these direct methods. This Johnnie Aysgarth needed putting in his place.

"What," she said, as deliberately as she could, "do you think of our View, Mr. Aysgarth?" It was a question she had thought out the moment she saw Johnnie at her side. It was to be said with a little smile, which would convey that this was the stereotyped question that every other girl in the county would put to him in similar circumstances, and that he was going to be judged on his answer to it. If he had any intelligence he would interpret the smile rightly; if not . . .

But she now forgot to smile.

"Damn the view," replied Mr. Aysgarth simply. "It's you I want to look at, not the view."

Lina's colour deepened.

Then she laughed. It was really impossible to take the man seriously. What idiots other women were. She realized suddenly of what Johnnie's expression had reminded her. It was that of a small boy participating in some joyful, small-boyish crime, smiling at his accomplice.

He must be met on his own ground.

"If you're trying to tell me I'm pretty, I'm afraid

you're wasting your time. I've had it far too well rubbed into me by my family that I'm nothing of the sort. Ask Mrs. Barnard, if you want an unprejudiced opinion."

Johnnie Aysgarth's eyes began to twinkle again. "Oh, Mrs. Barnard said something quite different about you."

"What?"

"That you were clever."

Lina made a grimace. "Anybody would be clever by the Barnard standard."

"So you see, I thought if you were clever you'd like to be told you were pretty; whereas, of course, if you'd only been pretty I should have told you you were clever."

"Oh," Lina laughed. "Those are your methods, are they? But why bother to tell me anything at all?"

Johnnie suddenly looked serious. "Because I'd decided as soon as I saw you that you were the only person in this outfit worth talking to for more than two minutes at a time."

"Had you?" Lina said feebly. Aysgarth's sudden earnestness had again robbed her of confidence.

"Yes," he said with conviction. "And aren't you? Of course, you know perfectly well you are."

He smiled at her once more, the same intimate, knowledgeable smile. But this time it made Lina uneasy.

She thought: he looks as if he knows me down to the most secret detail. And I believe he does.

She felt stripped.

Johnnie hardly left her side for the rest of the afternoon.

2

Lina went up to her bedroom in a temper of resentment. She had been cold, she had been actually rude, but she had been unable to shake Johnnie off until they reached her own front door. She had refused to ask him in.

She pulled off her hat and stared at her face in the mirror. Her cheeks were still flushed with annoyance.

She was angry that at first she had enjoyed Johnnie's company. She was angry at the realization that for a moment she had really believed that he did think her pretty, and at the pleasure the belief had given her. She had known that she was looking her best when Mrs. Barnard brought him up to her. The wind had whipped some colour into her usually rather pale cheeks, and the cocky little blue hat which exactly matched her eyes, dipping its brim over one and lifting over the other, was the prettiest she had. She had been delighted that someone found her good to look at.

And he had just been playing with her: experimenting, as he apparently did with every woman or girl he met: saying the things he thought she would like to hear, with his tongue in his cheek and a mocking twinkle in his eye that all the others were too foolish to read.

But she had read it. And very bitterly she now resented it.

She began to change for dinner, trying to reason herself into calm.

She was twenty-eight, she reminded herself; not eighteen. What on earth did it matter that a man should have tried on her the hackneyed methods which appeared to be successful with others—and had failed? Nothing. But it *was* annoying, for all that. He should have had the intelligence to realize that she was not the same as other women.

Her nervous exasperation grew.

Johnnie Aysgarth was intolerable. Women had told him for so long that he was irresistible that he believed it. He took it for granted. He traded on it. He considered it made him fascinating to say things which anyone else would not say: to walk up to a girl and talk to her as if he had known her all his life. Did other women really fall for such crude methods? Lina felt herself a Pharisee among her own sex.

" 'It's you I want to look at, not the view.' "

Insufferable!

" 'I decided as soon as I saw you that you were the only person here——,' " No!—" 'in this outfit, worth talking to.' "

As she dressed, Lina went over and over the conversation.

It was perfectly clear to her now. What a fool she was to have been taken in at the time. At first he had called her pretty, because he thought she would like that; then he had shifted his attack and said she was interesting to talk to. And that really had got home. Right until after lunch she had been taken in by that. Interesting to talk to!

She could picture Johnnie recounting the scene to a friend.

She did picture it. "Oh, they've all got their weakness. I made a bit of a false start, but I soon got round that. I just let her think she was interesting. That's the line, my boy. If they're not pretty, they always think they're interesting. Good Lord, they'll believe anything you tell 'em in that line; and love you for it."

She pictured too what the Barnards must have said to him.

"Oh, Lina McLaidlaw. She's terribly clever. We're all terrified of her. Her sister married Cecil Witton, you know. Yes, the author. Lina often goes to stay there. She knows all sorts of writers and people. We always feel terribly out of it when she talks about Wells and Edgar Wallace and all those clever people. She's far too clever for us." In the country it is the worst social misdemeanour to be clever.

And Johnnie had said: "You watch. She'll be flirting with me before tea-time."

He had probably made a bet on it. Hadn't someone once told her that Johnnie Aysgarth was always ready to make a bet about anything?

Lina pulled her second stocking off with a tug that was positively vicious.

Well, if he had made a bet on it, he had lost. She had not flirted with him. And he had not had the sense to see that she was not of the kind that likes flirting, that she detested the idea of flirting, that she never had flirted in her life. He was just a fool, like the rest of the young men. Rather a different kind of fool, perhaps, but a fool all the same.

Well, what did it matter? He was going to marry one of the rich Barnards. Good luck to him—and her! She would probably never see him again.

She did not see him for so long that she began seriously to fear that she really never would see him again.

3

As she had reminded herself, Lina was twenty-eight. As she found out, among other things, during the next few days, Johnnie Aysgarth was twenty-seven.

She had said nothing less than the truth when she told him that she knew she was not pretty. She did know it. Her family had informed her of that fact so often and so earnestly that not even the toughest doubt could remain with her. To underline it, they not infrequently called her "Letter-box," in pleasant allusion to her mouth.

Lina's younger sister, Joyce, was the pretty one. That had been rubbed into both girls from a very early age. There were no brothers. Joyce, rather against her father's wish, had married an author who was also a dilettante, or a dilettante who was also an author. At any rate, he had plenty of money of his own besides what Joyce would bring him. Since marrying Joyce he had become quite famous, whether as a result of Joyce's prettiness or not. Joyce and he lived in London, in a big house in Hampstead, and Lina envied her sister whole-heartedly.

"No, my dear," had been the burden of Mrs. Mc-Laidlaw's observations to her elder daughter ever since the latter was out of her 'teens. "No, Joyce has got the looks, and one can't expect two pretty ones in the same family. You've got nothing but your hair and your eyelashes, so you'll just have to rely on your brains." Mrs. McLaidlaw belonged to the era when a girl's assets were reckoned entirely in terms of husband-catching.

Lina had always known that she was supposed to be intelligent.

At eighteen she had been extremely pleased with herself about it. She had joined feminist movements, taken them, as well as herself, very seriously, read a great many pamphlets and even written some, and despised her family and her neighbours in by no means a quiet way. She had despised mere prettiness too, she had despised men, she had despised most things except Lina McLaidlaw.

By twenty-eight her views had very much changed.

Bored at home, longing for escape, and yet never quite able to take the drastic step of leaving it on her own initiative, she had found that her values had been, for a woman, mistaken ones. Her mother's firm ideas about feminine objectives, and still more her family's outspoken comments, had had their effect. Lina, always impressionable, arrived at the other extreme. She came, quite imperceptibly, to despise her mind, which was very much above the feminine average, and embraced the idea that the only thing worth having for a woman was looks. Not being pretty she was therefore, as a woman, a failure.

Indeed, not only did she now despise her brains: she often wished heartily that she had none.

Intelligence, she had very soon discovered, was in her set the thing above all others which was not done. In a woman it amounted to the unforgivable crime. Kleptomania could always be excused; intelligence never. The rumour of her unfortunate brains frightened the young men away from Lina as effectually as if she had scared them off with a police rattle. The only times she had ever felt glad that she was not a complete fool were on her short and very occasional visits to Joyce, whose circle held to a table of values very different from that prevailing in Abbot Monckford; but she disliked Joyce's literary young men so heartily that she might just as well have stayed at home.

These families . . .

What her family had never troubled to tell Lina was that her face, if not conventionally pretty, was a hauntingly attractive one. Among our friends, even among our loves, there are very few faces which we can re-create before the eye of the mind in their fleshly absence. Lina's was one of these.

It was a very small face with, except for her mouth, small features: an elfish, puckish little face, which is rare among fair women. Her hair, which even her mother admitted to be a good point, was a pale, silvered gold, and her eyes a vivid blue with very long lashes, curling up at the tip. Her mouth was very red and was only thrown into prominence by the miniature effect of her other features. Her upper lip was short, and her chin very delicate and narrow, though only just holding its own against recession. She was not tall, and her undiluted Scottish ancestry had ensured that her bones, while fine, should be definite; it would have been an exaggeration to call her figure sturdy, but it was certainly not slight. Her hands were very small and very soft. She did not care for games and was no good at them, but she could walk most men off their feet.

She came of a family of soldiers. Her father was the first McLaidlaw for heaven knew how many generations who had failed to produce a son for the army. Though a genial man, there were times when General McLaidlaw looked gloomily upon his two daughters. Lina knew and quite understood. She was no more of a snob than was good for her, but she was naïvely glad that she was descended in the direct line on her father's side from Robert the Bruce. The fact would not, however, have deterred her from marrying a man, if she had been in love with him, before whom her parents would have thrown up their hands in horror.

Women have not the class feeling of men. It is environment rather than instinct which sets their standard. A chorus girl who marries into the peerage can out-dowager any duchess, and a duke's daughter can be, and frequently is, more vulgar than any shop assistant. If Lina had hesitated at all over an intimacy with a man whom her father would have called an outsider, it would have been only to make sure that there was enough in common between them to make marriage possible; that settled, she would have thought no more about it.

For Lina now very much wanted to be married.

She no longer despised men at all. She respected them profoundly.

She was not happy, and she longed for happiness. She knew herself well enough to realize that she could never be happy alone. And in spite of her brains, Lina at twenty-eight was, in her heart, old-fashioned enough to take it for granted that happiness for a woman lay only in a happy marriage. Having lived all her life in the country, where people do not talk about these things, she had never realized that the percentage of happy marriages among the population of Great Britain is probably something under .0001.

Lina now wanted to be married very much indeed.

She nearly had been married, two years ago.

What Lina had then considered the first, and latterly the only, love affair of her life had then dragged to an ignominious close. It had been with a man of whom her father heartily approved, a solid young landowner in a neighbouring county, of impeccable parentage and equally impeccable reputation. Indeed, the only trifling blot on his perfection was the fact that mentally he resembled one of his own prize bulls, except that the landowner could hardly recognize the significance of a piece of red rag when he saw it; but that of course did not worry General McLaidlaw, and even Lina was able to keep her eyes shut to it. For even the blot had a silver margin: the young man was as solid as one of his own bulls too. For the first time in her life Lina found herself able to lean on someone, morally, at any rate, if perhaps not spiritually; and she found the process singularly restful.

She had fancied herself very much in love with this rock of gentility.

When she was away from him she invested him with all sorts of qualities which secretly, though she refused to admit the doubt, she was not at all sure that he possessed. She also put into his mouth certain passionate speeches which she did quite well know that he would never utter. He would, in fact, have gone as deep a red as one of his own Devon cows at the very thought of speech at all on such topics : topics that are obviously undiscussable at all until one is decently married, and probably not to be discussed even then, only performed. When she was with him, it surprised her to find herself at times yawning with boredom.

His attitude towards her was completely correct. He was kind, if a little obtuse, and most respectful. Lina wished he would not always be quite so respectful. A woman in love, even a young woman, does not want respect. She wants something a good deal warmer. And if she does not get it, she will descend from the pedestal on which she has been unwillingly placed and astonish her worshipper with a totally irrational fit of hysterics.

Slowly Lina realized that a pillar of any sort, even of respect, though it may be solid, can be incredibly dull. Finding that she had mistaken leaning for love, she allowed the affair to fizzle out. Matters had not even reached the point of a formal engagement, for the pillar was a slow mover. He went back to his pigs and his apple trees, and Lina shed a great number of tears into her pillow, not for what had been but for what had not.

Lina was no Samson. Within a couple of months the pillar, quite unshattered, had announced his engagement to another, and plainly a more determined, girl ; and Lina had resigned herself to perpetual spinsterhood.

During the last two years nothing had happened to shake her resignation.

4

It was actually ten days before Lina saw Johnnie Aysgarth again.

The day was Sunday, and of the kind that only early April can produce. Lina, having left the *Observer* to her parents indoors, had taken the *Sunday Times* out onto the flagged terrace and settled herself in a deck chair in the sun.

Unfortunately a part of the terrace was under observation from the drive, and though General McLaidlaw had talked for years of running a hedge of *lonicera nitida* across the vulnerable gap, nothing had ever been done about it. Lina looked up from James Agate's column to find herself surrounded by Frasers.

The Frasers were very gay, very modern, very jolly. Everyone always said: "And we must have the Frasers, of course. They make anything go." Lina found them unbearable.

"Get your hat on, my dear," Mrs. Fraser said gaily. "We've come to drag you to church."

"Oh!" said Lina, jumping up. "I didn't see you coming."

"We wanted to go to the front door," giggled the eldest Miss Fraser, "but Johnnie saw you out here and insisted on coming round."

"Johnnie?" Lina echoed stupidly.

Among the Frasers she now saw Johnnie Aysgarth, twinkling at her confusion. Lina blushed and hated everyone.

Her mind groped with difficulty from James Agate,

through Johnnie's unbearably knowledgeable smile, to Mrs. Fraser.

"Church?" she said, and felt that her conversation lacked sparkle.

"Place where they pray, dear," explained the youngest Miss Fraser succinctly. "You must have heard of it. Where they park the parson." Nobody could say that the Frasers' conversation lacked sparkle.

"Hush, dear," smiled Mrs. Fraser mechanically. And then to Lina: "Yes, really, Lina. The girls absolutely insist on your coming with us."

"But—I wasn't thinking about going to church this morning," Lina stammered.

"Then think about it now," said the middle Miss Fraser. "You've got to come, so you may as well make up your mind to it."

Johnnie Aysgarth said nothing. He just stood there and grinned at her. But his grin was eloquent. Every line of his face told Lina that she was going to join the party, and that he knew she was going to join the party, and she was going to join the party simply because he wished her to do so.

Lina tried to speak calmly. "In any case, I couldn't go to church in this frock." Against her will she caught Johnnie's eye. It was openly derisive. Lina's flush deepened. Certainly the implication contained in her banality, that her Creator could bear to be worshipped by Miss McLaidlaw only in her best frock, hardly did credit to one who out of twenty-four persons had been the only one worth talking to.

"Then change," said the middle Miss Fraser crisply.

"And buck up about it," added her younger sister.

Mrs. Fraser sank into the deck chair.

Lina went upstairs in a fury. She knew quite well who

was responsible for this preposterous invasion. The "girls" absolutely insisted, did they? Exceedingly likely! And what right had anyone to "insist"? It was insufferable.

Besides, everyone would see her there, sitting next to Johnnie Aysgarth. Probably he would try to hold her hand during the sermon, or something equally impossible. And everyone would know why she was there, and there would be talk, and people would say the most ridiculous things.

But what made her most angry of all, as she tore off her frock, was the fact that she simply had not had the strength of mind to refuse.

"My dear, where are you going?" asked her mother with simple wonder, encountered on the stairs five minutes later.

Lina held out her prayer book as if it had been a snake. "To church," she said bitterly.

"What, all alone?"

"No, with the Frasers."

"The Frasers? But I thought you didn't like them?"

"I loathe them," replied Lina with conviction.

"Well, thank you, dearest, at any rate. It was quite time one of us went," said her parent.

Life in the country has its obligations.

Lina walked the half mile along the dusty road between Johnnie and Mrs. Fraser in angry silence. She refused to be appeased even by the precocity of the hedges, and allowed her neighbours to exchange comments on them over her head. Johnnie hardly spoke to her at all.

At the church door she felt his hand on her arm. She tried to shake it off, but it held her too fast. She found herself being detained while the Frasers filed inside. Then, to her unspeakable indignation, she was turned about and marched back along the path, Johnnie's hand tightly gripping her elbow, right under the eyes of certain other late-comers.

"Mr. Aysgarth!" she gasped. "What in the world . . . ?"

Johnnie's eyes twinkled at her, just like those of a schoolboy who has brought off a successful prank. "You didn't think we were really going to church, did you? We're going for a nice long country walk—on which you're going to apologize for being so infernally rude to me last week."

"I'll do nothing of the sort!" exploded Lina. "Please let go of my arm at once."

"You will, and I won't. Come along, Lina."

They went.

5

"Well, dear, who was at church?"

"I didn't go after all," Lina said, helping herself to horseradish sauce from the tray at her side. "I went for a walk."

"With the Frasers?" asked Mrs. McLaidlaw in surprise.

"No, with Johnnie Aysgarth." It gave her a little thrill of excitement just to speak his name so casually.

General McLaidlaw drew his bushy brows down over the bridge of his nose in an effort of memory. "Johnnie Aysgarth? That's Tom Aysgarth's youngest boy, isn't it? Pity he's turned out a rotter. Rough luck on Tom. Tom may have been a fool, but he was always as straight as a die. What's this, eh? Horseradish? Didn't know horseradish was in season now. Is it out of a bottle, eh?" asked the General suspiciously.

"Of course not, dear," replied Mrs. McLaidlaw, with placid untruth.

The General helped himself and tasted a portion. "No, this is the real stuff. Tell the difference at once. Can't stand things out of bottles. Never taste the same."

"Never, dear," agreed Mrs. McLaidlaw.

"Why do you say Johnnie Aysgarth is a rotter, Father?" Lina asked, quite calmly.

"Because he is a rotter. Turned out of some club for cheating at cards, wasn't he? Or ought to have been turned out. Something unpleasant, anyway. What's he doing down here?"

"He's staying at Penshaze. I shouldn't have thought Lord Middleham would have had him there if he'd ever been turned out of a club for cheating at cards." Lina's heart was beating so fast that she could hardly swallow.

"Well, it might have been a woman. Something ugly, I'm sure. Good heavens," grumbled General McLaidlaw, "can't expect me to remember every detail about everybody, can you? Anyhow, it was something to do with a woman. Co-respondent, or something. Or ought to have been co-respondent, or something. It may have been hushed up, but——"

"*Méfie-toi*," said Lina, with a militant sparkle in her eye, "*les oreilles domestiques t'écoutent.*"

"Ah! Hum!" said the General and subsided. He always subsided when his daughter addressed him in French. Lina had been at school in Paris, and the General had not.

Lina did her best to go on with her lunch just as if this was as ordinary a Sunday as all the Sundays of her life before.

Johnnie Aysgarth had explained everything.

Lina saw now that she had misjudged him, quite heartlessly. The details were perhaps not quite so clear still, but Johnnie had made it perfectly plain. She had misjudged him.

He had clung to her so closely on the day of the picnic because never in his life before had he met a girl who had attracted him so much at first sight!

That had been very interesting to hear. And it was not blarney. Lina, skeptical, very skeptical at first, had gradually become sure that it was not blarney. Then he had avoided her afterwards because he was so afraid he had offended her. He had been afraid—yes, afraid of her. Really afraid. She had alarmed him. She was so poised, so confident, so sure of herself and her ability to handle men. She! Lina had simply had to laugh.

Johnnie had apologized; he had explained, he had begged for forgiveness. And Lina had forgiven him. For what, had been rather glossed over; but nevertheless, with some ceremony, Johnnie had been forgiven.

After that the morning had become almost impossibly delightful.

Lina was to meet him again that afternoon. He was to bring his car, and they were going for a long run, with tea at some charming little inn, wherever they found a charming little inn. There would of course be no difficulty in finding a charming little inn. It was that sort of day.

At half-past two Johnnie rang through to say that he was terribly, *terribly* sorry, but his cousins had arranged something or other for the afternoon and it would be quite impossible for him to take Lina out.

She went upstairs, feeling that life held nothing more for her.

She did not see Johnnie again for a fortnight. By the

end of that time she would have gone to meet him along
a mile of public road on her knees.

6

Actually, they became engaged about two months later.
So far as Lina was concerned, it was not a happy engagement.

At first she was almost unbalanced with happiness.
That she, Lina McLaidlaw, Letter-box McLaidlaw,
could have fascinated a man so experienced, so witty, so
good-looking, so accomplished, so everything a man
ought to be, as Johnnie Aysgarth seemed quite incredible.
But she had fascinated him. He adored her. He told her
so repeatedly, with a mischievous smile at her incredulity.
And his kisses carried conviction. Never had Lina
dreamed that kisses could be so convincing. Johnnie
kissed her till her jaw ached quite painfully. She was en-
raptured.

All her life Lina had felt the need of someone on a pedestal in front of her, to whom she could look up as in-
fallible. Hitherto her father had occupied this position,
with a brief deposition in favour of the head mistress of
her first school. Now Johnnie was firmly installed, on a
bigger, brighter, and better pedestal than had ever been
in use before.

Everything Johnnie did was right.

To Lina's horrified joy, he treated her not at all re-
spectfully; hardly even politely. She was clearly very
much of a woman to him. It was Lina's first experience
of being a woman. Johnnie, she knew, was the first man
who had found her exciting; and prim though she was,
almost to prudishness, it had always disturbed her vanity and something deeper than her vanity, that other

women, far less intelligent than herself and sometimes downright plain, should to her knowledge have received advances of a kind that she had never encountered. Now she was having them thrust upon her; and though there was layer upon layer of primness to be broken through before she could relish them, so that delight and repulsion were continually at war in her mind, she knew she would be very upset if they were to cease. Besides, if Johnnie made them, they were right. So that though she repulsed the more obvious of them, she did so laughingly and lightly, for all that she was, sometimes, very shocked indeed. She felt that Johnnie would despise her for being shocked.

But they did cease, spasmodically.

After the first fortnight or so Lina was sure that Johnnie's ardour was cooling. He left the neighbourhood, he hardly wrote a line to her when he was away, and when he came back, as he did every now and then for two or three days at a time, he was seldom so hair-raisingly bold with her as he had been.

Lina wept nightly into her pillow and tried to find the reason. Had she been too cold with him? Had she been idiot enough not to have hidden that she was shocked, and put him off? Had she been too outspoken in their last little quarrel? She so often said things on impulse that she would have given her right hand afterwards to recall. Had she allowed that nervous irritation of hers to fly out with even less cause than usual? It did, so often. Or had she—hopeless thought!—simply ceased to attract him?

She wondered desperately whether it would not be better, the next time he really seemed to want her, to "give herself to him" (she used the cant phrase in her thought) once and for all, marriage or no marriage. She wanted to, really. But it had been impressed on both the Miss McLaidlaws, with all a mother's earnestness, that once a man has "got what he wants" he wants nothing more; and Lina could not bear to think that Johnnie should want nothing more of her than that—so it seemed better not to risk it.

Both General and Mrs. McLaidlaw seemed to think that Johnnie wanted a good deal more of her.

That was another trouble. The General voiced it with soldierly conciseness; Mrs. McLaidlaw was more inclined to hint it in solicitous questions. But her purport was just as plain as her husband's: both Lina's parents had conceived the preposterous fear that what Johnnie wanted really was not so much Lina herself as the fifty thousand pounds which would come to Lina, as under their grandmother's will another equal sum would come to Joyce, on the death of their father. Lina became almost speechless with anger against her parents; but not so speechless that she was unable to say things which no daughter should even think.

Undeterred, the General gave it as his flat, and undemanded, opinion that all the Aysgarth stock was rotten, that Johnnie was as rotten as the rest, if not a bit rottener, and whether he was after her money or not, if Lina could not do better for herself than marry an Aysgarth, then she should preferably take the veil or whatever it is that women do take when they take anything.

Lina stood up to her father and brushed angrily aside her mother's insinuating questions, but they made her very miserable. Not, of course, that there could be anything in them. Whatever Johnnie had been, and by his own boast he had been a bit of a rip, which Lina vaguely deplored and yet felt a little proud of—whatever Johnnie might have been, he was not that sort. Lina knew that.

She *knew* it. And yet—*why* was he often so cold and uninterested with her nowadays?

And then she would be sure that Johnnie was beginning to see through her at last. She was not what he had thought her. She was dull, for a man so used to the most accomplished and fascinating women; dull, prim, silly, provincial. Johnnie was beginning to see through her.

Then she would cry. And having cried, she would set her teeth and say, out loud: "Well, anyhow, I'm not going to let any other woman get him. Never!" Then she would cry again.

Then, two days later, Johnnie would kiss her so hard, and make love to her so entrancingly, and teasingly try to do such terrifyingly improper things to her, that she would forget for half-a-dozen hours all her trouble.

The upshot was, of course, that Lina adored him so madly that not all the generals in the world, drawn up in a solid, glittering phalanx between herself and the altar, could have prevented Lina from getting to Johnnie there. Lina admitted humbly to herself that she did not know men; it did not occur to her quite how well Johnnie might know women.

The spectre of housekeeping brooded over her. Lina, who invariably worried over her troubles in advance, was convinced that she would never make an efficient housekeeper. She would make Johnnie uncomfortable; she would forget the blacking; she would omit to order the cream for the strawberries; there would never be enough of anything in the house. She vowed passionately that she would *always* look through Johnnie's shirts when they came back from the laundry. Never should a stentorian bellow echo through her house that there was a blank button missing from some blank garment. But she knew there would be.

Then she would fall to brooding again over Johnnie's new coldness, and ask herself for the millionth time whether he really did love her still after all or was just being chivalrous after giving his promise, and if so, whether any measures were not better tried, however desperate, and whether when a girl has lost that she really has lost all.

Lina was a great trial to her family and her friends during her engagement. She was a great trial to herself too.

And in any case Johnnie must have loved her after all.

He must have loved her, because, just three months after their engagement, in early September, he married her.

In a passion of gratitude Lina was formally bestowed on Johnnie Aysgarth, before God's altar, by a resigned but still indignant General McLaidlaw.

CHAPTER II

"Darling," Lina said tentatively, "surely it was a 50-franc note you gave the waiter, not a 100-franc one?"

Johnnie grinned at her as he shovelled the change away into his trouser-pocket. "It was. We put one over on him there. Don't often catch a French waiter making that sort of mistake, do you? Let's get on before he realizes."

"But—you aren't going to keep it?"

"Of course I'm going to keep it," Johnnie said, in genuine surprise, and stood up.

Lina picked up her gloves and bag and followed him. She was surprised too, and bewildered. Surely it was downright dishonest to keep the extra fifty francs without saying anything? Yet Johnnie seemed to think it only an excellent joke.

She walked in silence beside him along the boulevard. She felt somehow hurt, as if Johnnie had cheated her instead of an obscure waiter in the Café de la Paix. Because it *was* cheating: there was no getting away from it.

Or wasn't it? Johnnie would not conceivably cheat consciously, so evidently he did not consider it cheating at all. And yet . . .

Her mind went back to that rather curious incident after lunch yesterday. They had sat on talking for hours, as they often did still, although the honeymoon was now in its seventh, and last, week; and one by one the waiters had disappeared, till at last they had the room to themselves as Johnnie had marked by kissing her across the table. It was twenty minutes to four when at last she went to powder her nose, and certainly Johnnie had not paid the bill then.

When she came back Johnnie was still alone, but with his hat and gloves in his hand; he had risen at once, and they had gone downstairs. Just as they were going out a waiter had come up to Johnnie and said something. Lina was already halfway through the door, and she had not heard very distinctly, but she had thought he was asking Johnnie if he had paid; Johnnie answered something carelessly, and followed her outside, where they had stepped straight into a taxi by the curb. Lina had happened to look back just as the taxi was starting, and had seen the waiter looking through the glass door at them with a very odd expression, certainly of doubt, almost one might have said of suspicion; he had seemed to be trying to make up his mind, in the half-second at his disposal, whether to run out onto the pavement after them or not.

It was ridiculous, of course, because Johnnie must have paid while she was powdering her nose, but the waiter's expression had been so strange that she asked Johnnie herself in the taxi whether he had paid, and Johnnie had said, in some surprise, that of course he had. She had thought no more about it.

She told herself that it was ridiculous to think any more about it now.

They were walking towards the Madeleine after their *apéritif*, to lunch at Voisin's. Johnnie was finding amusement, as he always did, in the people who passed them.

"Darling, do look at what's coming towards us. No, this one with the fuzzy hair. What is he, do you think? An artist, or something escaped from a home? I mean, if he wants to wear a mauve tie with a scarlet shirt I suppose that's all right, but do you think he ought to be allowed to wear purple socks too? Shall I call a gendarme, darling? I really think we ought to give him in charge for assaulting our eyesight. Hullo, hasn't that girl's posterior slipped from its moorings? Shall we stop her and tell her? She'd probably be grateful. I'm sure it ought to be looped up again. You tell her, darling; it's a woman's job."

"Johnnie," said Lina, "*please* come back to the Café de la Paix with me and give that waiter those fifty francs back. To please me."

Johnnie laughed and tucked her hand under his arm. "You funny little thing! Aren't you delighted at having put one over on those thieves for a change? I am, I can tell you. They're simply out to rob us at every turn; it gives me a lot of pleasure to get our own back for once."

"But it—it's dishonest, darling," Lina said, really distressed.

"Dishonest my hat! I've been robbed of a good deal more than fifty francs since we came here. That's a little back, on account." He looked down at her, with the mischievous schoolboy's smile that so peculiarly belonged to him. "You mustn't be so punctilious, you infant. Besides, it makes me feel good."

"To cheat a waiter out of fifty francs?"

"You funny little thing!" said Johnnie indulgently.

But Lina did not smile back.

After lunch Johnnie took her to the best shoe shop in Paris and bought her the most expensive pair of mules in the place, decorated with absurd and delectable flame-coloured feathers. She had mentioned, just by chance, in their bedroom that morning that she really must get a pair of mules before they left Paris.

She had forgotten all about the fifty francs before they left the shop.

Johnnie was wonderful.

2

On the whole Lina blissfully enjoyed her honeymoon. Johnnie was perfect: attentive, affectionate, and patient. They did not have a single cross word, and they laughed and talked inordinately. For the first time in her life Lina found herself able to talk without reserve, and she poured herself out in a flood of words which Johnnie received with at any rate apparently close attention; though from some of his irrelevancies which occasionally followed, Lina was not quite sure whether he had altogether appreciated all the subtler points she had been trying to make. But the mere talking cleared her mind of a lot of lumber that had been accumulating for years.

For the first week or two she had tortured herself with doubt as to whether she would ever make a satisfactory wife at all.

She was desperately anxious to find, and to give, complete fulfilment in marriage; but, try as she might at first, she simply could not see what all the fuss was about. It all seemed to her, to say the least, remarkably overrated. With characteristic despair she had decided within the first three days that she never would be satisfactory; that there was something lacking in her which would make her always useless as a wife. It never occurred to her that the conflicting emotions which possessed her might be something that she was sharing with every other bride that had ever been. Her case was unique. No one before could ever have experienced feelings so bewilderingly contradictory and so intense.

Johnnie was very kind to her, and very gentle, and her adoration for him increased in ratio with the conviction of her own insufficiency. The knowledge that he must be finding her so inadequate, though he never even hinted as much, distressed her unbearably. When he was asleep she lay and cried for hours by his side. Always she had supposed herself passionate; now, put to the test, it appeared that she was not; worse, she could not even begin to understand what passion was. It became clear to her that she had not distinguished between mental and physical passion, taking it for granted that the presence of the one implied the possession of the other. As a wife it was plain that she could never be a success.

Previous experience reinforced this pessimism. She thought she realized now why she had never been approached in this way before. Other men had instinctively recognized her inadequacy. Only Johnnie had been chivalrously mistaken.

She tried to say something of all this to Johnnie, and to apologize for her shortcomings; but Johnnie did not seem to understand what was worrying her. It was borne in upon her that Johnnie could not be quite so perceptive, nor even quite so sensitive, as she had imagined. The ideal lover should know the inside of his mistress's mind as well as he knows his own; for how otherwise can he anticipate her thoughts and fulfil her wishes in advance? Johnnie either did not realize the immensity of the trouble that overshadowed them both, or else was inclined to laugh it away, which Lina could not bear.

In the same way she was secretly a good deal upset by Johnnie's proficiency in his love-making. She told herself, and she had told Johnnie too, that it did not matter to her in the least what he had done before he met her. But it did matter. She found herself jealous, sometimes bitterly jealous, of all the women Johnnie had loved before he loved her.

"I'm being ridiculous," she told herself, with tears in her eyes. "It's a fatal mistake to be proprietary. I won't be proprietary."

But she was proprietary. She felt proprietary. Johnnie was hers now, as she was his; and she wished fervently that he could have come to her clean, as she had to him. And yet all the time she could not help thinking how wonderful it was of him to have had so much success and experience.

Johnnie thought so too.

On the whole, however, Lina enjoyed her honeymoon.

Of one thing it was impossible to accuse Johnnie, and that was niggardliness. He spent with an unconscious prodigality that left Lina quite aghast.

It was Johnnie's instinct, as it was his upbringing, to go only to the most expensive restaurants and hotels, as it was his instinct to order the most expensive dishes and wines when he got there. He probably did not realize it, but to Lina he seemed to take it for granted that the most expensive things had been prepared for him personally, and it simply never occurred to him to put up with the second best.

In the same way nothing was too good for Johnnie's wife. A sheaf of fresh flowers arrived every morning at their suite for her; she had only to mention the most passing wish for a thing and the thing was hers at the first opportunity. Lina, whose own tastes were simple, did not know whether to cry over Johnnie's extravagance, or smile at the unconscious arrogance that prompted it. Johnnie seemed more boyish to her than ever in his prodigality.

She remonstrated with him continually, but he only laughed and called her a little provincial; and Lina, who was very conscious of her provincialism in Johnnie's presence, had to laugh too. Johnnie could always make her laugh. That, Lina knew, is the greatest bond of all between two people, to be ready to laugh at the same things. And they did laugh, enormously. Lina told Johnnie that he had laughed his way through their honeymoon from beginning to end; as indeed he did, and sometimes in the wrong places.

Once or twice Lina did persuade him to let her take him to some unpretentious little restaurant on the left bank that she remembered from her schooldays, where, in her own private opinion, the food was just as good as in the expensive places and just about ten times less in price; but Johnnie never seemed at home there. In return Johnnie taught her a great deal about drink. Lina thought she drank more on her honeymoon than in all her life before. Sometimes, too, she felt she needed it.

In public, to Lina's delight, he was just as attentive and affectionate to her as in private. Any qualms Lina had felt by her wedding day that Johnnie might not be really in love with her, vanished before this open love-making, so Johnnie-like and so un-English. Obviously he adored her, and did not mind the world knowing so. Lina felt little curls of joy twisting through her body when he took her hand across a restaurant table and kissed it right under the waiter's nose. Nobody but Johnnie could have done a thing like that.

Already he had a pet name for her. "Monkeyface," he called her sometimes, because he said that when she was eating she made faces exactly like a monkey; and he would always sit on the opposite side of the table so that he could watch her and crow with delight.

"Your little jaw pounces on every mouthful as if it hadn't seen food for a week. Do you know you eat in little snaps? You do. You funny little monkeyface!"

"My family used to call me 'letter-box,' " Lina would feel constrained to point out, in the way that one is forced to mention something derogatory about one's self before another person's praise.

" 'Letter-box!' " Johnnie would echo indignantly. "You've got the sweetest, most adorable, wickedest little mouth any woman ever had—and what's more, I'm going to kiss it this instant."

"Johnnie, you *can't*. Not here!"

"Can't I?" Johnnie would retort with his most mischievous smile; and it was made plain that he could.

Then Lina would vow passionately to herself that she would be an adequate wife, if only Johnnie would go on loving her like this.

And almost before she knew it had happened, she found that she was an adequate wife after all. It just happened, like that. Johnnie congratulated his pupil, and Lina found herself so happy that it seemed almost sinful; as if one were snatching all the happiness there was in the world, and leaving none over for anyone else.

After that the honeymoon wildly surpassed even the most entrancing versions of itself that Lina had lived through, when her fancies took that turn, for the last dozen years.

They got back to England in the last week of October.

CHAPTER III

JOHNNIE leaned back in his chair, crossed one leg over
the other, rubbed its silk-covered ankle, and laughed as
if this was all the greatest joke in the world. "Not a
cent!" he repeated. "I thought you'd better know," he
added.

"Well, I should hope so," Lina said tartly. And after
a pause, as calmly as she could: "What do you intend
to do about it?" Already she saw them begging their
bread, from house to house.

"Oh, I don't know. I expect something will turn up. It
always does."

Lina was too upset even to retort with Mr. Micawber.

Johnnie had just broken the news to her that, after six
weeks in their new home, he had no money left: not a
penny, for them to live on.

"But why did you take this house? It's far bigger
than we need. What on earth possessed you?" In her
voice dismay was sharpening rapidly into irritation.

"I told you, darling," Johnnie said, in hurt tones.
"You'll have plenty of money one day. It seemed silly
to wait to be comfortable; I thought we might just as
well be comfortable from the beginning."

"One doesn't necessarily have to have eight bedrooms, for comfort."

"I like plenty of rooms," Johnnie retorted nonchalantly.

Lina stared at him, her chin on her hand.

Such complete irresponsibility dumbfounded her. She

had always known that Johnnie was irresponsible, but she had never imagined that even he would go to the length of taking a house twice as large as they needed, with no funds of his own at all with which to keep it up. General McLaidlaw was making his daughter an allowance of five hundred a year since her marriage, but that was supposed to be for her own personal use; in any case, more than double that sum was needed to keep up Dellfield.

And Johnnie had taken a house with eight bedrooms just because he liked plenty of room. How like Johnnie. It just would not have occurred to him to wait for plenty of rooms until he could afford to pay for them.

"How much money did you have?" Lina asked. She and Johnnie had never discussed money before. She had taken it for granted that Johnnie, though hard up like all the Aysgarths, must have enough for them to live on, though she had expected to have to supplement her housekeeping money out of her father's allowance. Now it seemed that he simply had no income at all.

"Oh," Johnnie smiled, "I borrowed a thousand to marry you on, darling."

"A thousand! Oh, well, I suppose that isn't too bad." Lina tried to be optimistic, though it was bad enough that Johnnie should have borrowed at all. "Considering we've furnished out of it and had those alterations done."

"Those?" Johnnie repeated in surprise. "Those aren't paid for. Nor the furniture."

"Then what have you spent the thousand on?" Lina asked sharply.

"Why, our honeymoon, sweetheart. As a matter of fact, I thought I'd done rather well. I didn't expect anything over by the time we got back, but there was enough to keep us for six weeks into the bargain."

"I think," said Lina slowly, "you must be mad." To her Scotch mind there was something almost blasphemous in pouring out money like that—and borrowed money!

Johnnie jumped to his feet, looking just like a guilty but not very penitent schoolboy, and came over to her chair. "My little monkeyface, it was the sanest thing I ever did in my life, to marry you. I shouldn't wonder if it wasn't the only sane thing. You couldn't grudge me a bit of a splash to celebrate it."

He bent down, but Lina turned her face away. "No, Johnnie. No, I don't want you to kiss me. I'm upset. I didn't think even you could be so silly. No, Johnnie, don't, please." Johnnie had dropped on his knees beside her chair and put his arms round her.

But for once he had lost his power to charm; and when the maid came in for the coffee tray a few moments later, causing him to jump hurriedly to his feet, the thread of his persuasiveness was definitely broken.

Almost before the door was safely closed Lina had burst out, as if it had only needed the interruption to bring her resentment to full pitch.

"Well, what do you propose to do? You can't leave things like this. We've got to live, I suppose." It was almost incredible to her that Johnnie could have plunged into marriage without any income at all, or any prospect of making one.

"What about your father?" Johnnie said hopefully. "He could easily make you a bigger allowance, if he wanted to."

"He wouldn't want to. And I shouldn't dream of asking him." Lina could well imagine what General Mc-Laidlaw's reply would be to such a request, and pride would never have allowed her to hear it. She looked with distrustful resentment at Johnnie, all her parents' hints and warnings sounding again in her ears. "Besides," she added tartly, "you wouldn't want to live on your wife's allowance, would you? At least, I hope not."

"No, darling, of course not," Johnnie said quickly, though to Lina's suspicious ears his tone was not altogether one of conviction. He scratched his curly head, looking at her with comical perplexity. "Well, I expect if the worst comes to the worst I can always borrow a spot somewhere. As a matter of fact, I've never touched old Middleham yet. I know," he went on with enthusiasm. "I'll take the car and run over to-morrow morning to Abbot Monckford. It's only about sixty miles. Old Middleham ought to be good for a month or two's housekeeping. Dash it, he's a cousin; and what's the use of a cousin if you can't touch him occasionally? You'd better come too, and we'll take a lunch off them."

Lina looked at her husband with angry exasperation. "No! I don't know what sort of a life you've led up to now, my lad, but you needn't think you're going on with it. I'm not accustomed to living in this haphazard way, and I'm not going to begin now. You've got to pull yourself together. There's going to be no more borrowing." It was the first time in her relations with him that Lina had ever taken a decision that was opposed to Johnnie's. It marked the beginning of a new era, had either of them realized it.

Johnnie, who had never heard his wife address him in such a tone before, looked mildly astonished. "But what else is there to do?"

The new responsibility that had been forming in Lina for the last twenty minutes came suddenly to birth in another burst of irritation. In face of such fecklessness, she must have responsibility for two. For the first time she was fully conscious of being the elder of the two of them; and not merely by one year, but by all the difference between an adult and a silly, irritating boy.

"What else is there to do? I wonder you dare stand there and ask such a thing. What do other people with no money do? Hasn't such a thing ever entered your head? You've got to work, my lad. W-o-r-k! That's what there is to do."

"Work?" Johnnie turned the word over doubtfully in the air, as if distrusting its implications. "I'd work all right, darling, if there was anything to work at. But what could I do?"

"Oh, good heavens, what does that matter? You can find something, surely. Don't tell me you're no use to anybody. Though I must say you haven't shown signs of being much use at anything so far, except borrowing."

"All right, all right," Johnnie said sulkily. "I've said I'll work, if there's anything to work at. There's no need for you to speak like that."

"There's every need, I should think," Lina retorted, her nervous exasperation growing. "In fact, it's quite time somebody did speak to you like that. I suppose you know what everyone says about you? That you're a waster."

"And you agreed with them, I suppose?" Johnnie sneered.

"I didn't believe them; and I married you to prove it. But what do you expect me to believe now? A man who can borrow a thousand pounds, with no prospect of repaying it, and then expect his wife's father to keep him for the rest of his life . . ." Lina was scarcely less astonished than Johnnie to hear the words issuing from her mouth. They seemed to come out of their own accord, and all she could do was to sit and listen to them.

Johnnie's sulky lines deepened. "Go on. You'll be telling me next I married you for your money."

"If I did, I should only be saying what plenty of people have said to me," said Lina, and burst into tears.

It was their first quarrel, and it was a bad one.

2

An hour later it had subsided into a more or less acrimonious discussion.

What was Johnnie to do?

Johnnie, it seemed, had no views on that point, beyond a scarcely hidden reluctance to do anything at all. However, he intimated handsomely enough that if Lina could find anything suitable for him to do, he would very probably, in view of her strange ideas, go so far as to do it. Unfortunately he at once vetoed every suggestion she made, as unsuitable.

Lina wept, now with rage and now with frustration, and Johnnie stood sulkily by.

The maid brought in the tray of whisky and soda, and two generous portions were poured out, for the soothing of frayed nerves.

The discussion continued, on rather more mellow lines. Lina wept again and this time was comforted. More whisky was poured out, and still the discussion went on.

What was Johnnie to do?

With characteristic ineptitude on the part of the Aysgarth parents, none of the Aysgarth boys had been trained to any profession or useful occupation whatever. Each of them had been brought up to expect as much money as he would want, and extravagance had been rather encouraged as a gentleman's prerogative than condemned as the act nowadays of a fool. The only subject Johnnie knew really intimately was horses, their training, their ailments, and their breeding; but to Lina's suggestion that he should breed them he pointed out that considerable capital was necessary; the same objection applied still more forcibly to the opening of a stable, and Lina herself vetoed the idea of a little gentlemanly horse-dealing as an insufficient and too spasmodic occupation. But why should not Johnnie become a vet? Why, because years of training were necessary, and one has to know about all sorts of animals besides horses; moreover, Johnnie did not wish to become a vet.

So what was Johnnie to do?

Gradually Lina found herself talking more and more peremptorily. Johnnie had got over his sulkiness and was now charmingly penitent, but Lina remained hard and practical, waving him away whenever he tried to embrace her, or else suffering his kisses in abstracted silence, her mind busy with the theme of the moment.

"Darling, don't you love me any more because I decided to make sure of you first and see about keeping you later?" Johnnie would ask, rubbing his cheek against hers.

"What about engineering?" Lina would reply abruptly. "You know all about cars. Couldn't you do something with that?"

And Johnnie would have to break off his conciliatory love-making to point out that except for the job of mechanic in a garage, a knowledge of cars is of little profitable use.

"Well, if I were a man," Lina would retort, not without bitterness, "I'd sooner take a job as mechanic in a garage than live on my wife's father."

"Darling," Johnnie would answer reproachfully, "you

know I wouldn't live on your father for good. I only thought he might help us over this gap. Something's bound to turn up soon."

Johnnie continued to reiterate this comfortable creed all the evening. There was no need to worry. Something would certainly turn up. Something always did.

It was clear to Lina that he was quite content to wait until something did. She would never be able to shame him into active search for a job. Johnnie had made what was to him the supreme concession of not refusing work if work fell into his lap, and he obviously felt extremely virtuous in consequence. Lina realized that if Johnnie was ever to shoulder his job of keeping the roof of Dellfield over their heads, it must be she and she alone who would have to find the means; and the knowledge gave her an odd feeling of superiority. Johnnie might be this and that, and the most charming man in the world, and she loved him very much indeed; but in practical matters he was simply hopeless.

They did not find that evening the answer to the problem of what Johnnie was to do.

3

Lina had had ideals about marriage.

In spite of the flaw that had developed in Johnnie's perfection, the ideals remained. They were, in fact, encouraged; for, being Lina, her ideals were naturally practical ones.

A wife, Lina had felt, can do a great deal for her husband. The fact that most wives do nothing was beside the point. They should. Lina had always sworn to herself that, should she ever marry, she would never let things rest at the usual wife's idea of wifely perfection, that of running her husband's house efficiently for him and not withholding her arms whenever he happened to want her embraces. She would do a great deal more than that. She would actively help her husband in his work. Whatever a man's work may be, Lina was sure that there are ways in which a woman can solidly help him.

The fact that Johnnie had no work, and did not welcome any, only made Lina's assistance more valuable. She would now not only help him with the work when it had been obtained; she would find it for him first. A wife can do a very great deal for her husband, even against that husband's will.

After a good deal more discussion, Johnnie's line of work was decided upon at last: he was to look after somebody's large estate. It was now up to Lina to find someone with a large estate who wanted it looked after, and who would pay Johnnie a sufficiently important sum of money to do so. Athirst with eagerness, Lina hurled herself into the task.

She and Johnnie had settled in a part of the country that was new to her. It was in Dorsetshire, but on the further side of the county from Abbot Monckford, nearer London. Lina knew nobody in the neighbourhood when she arrived there, but she now began to trace out such friends of her friends as lived within reasonable distance and establish relations with them. There was little difficulty in getting into touch with the important landowning families. Johnnie, who was related to half the peerage, was himself dragooned into resuscitating half-forgotten acquaintanceships and getting into touch with extremely distant but unmistakable cousins. Lina, busily sifting the likelies from the unlikelies, entertained the former to dinner.

At first she suffered agonies of shyness, as she sat at

the foot of her own dinner table; and to her horror found herself adopting to cover it a hard, artificial brightness. She knew that this manner paralyzed her less self-confident guests, and their paralysis in turn infected her; but she was quite unable to shake it off. She saw Johnnie watching her from the other end of the table with a whimsically lifted eyebrow. Johnnie, of course, was a born host from the very beginning.

It took Lina several months to learn to be natural, and by that time her end had been accomplished.

A certain Captain Melbeck, a distant connection of Johnnie's, who had recently inherited an estate of nearly twelve thousand acres including a dozen farms, and had not the faintest idea what to do about it, quite thankfully undertook to pay Johnnie five hundred a year to do it for him.

Lina, after some difficulty, succeeded in borrowing from her father enough capital to pay off Johnnie's debts, dismissed two of her servants, and settled down to run Dellfield, as economically as possible, on a thousand a year.

And Johnnie departed every morning, with resignation but with punctuality, on the twenty-mile run that separated him from his office on the Bradstowe estate.

Lina watched him go with affectionate pride. Johnnie, in his new rôle as world's worker, was completely reinstated as the perfection of mankind.

CHAPTER IV

"In the country," said Lina brightly, "one doesn't choose one's friends; one accepts gratefully those whom providence has put there." She laughed, a little self-consciously, as she always did when she thought she had said something rather smart in the presence of her brother-in-law.

Cecil was stirring his coffee, and looking into the depths of the cup as if hopeful of learning the secrets of the universe in it. "I do think you are so right, Lina," he said sadly.

"Well, whom has providence been pleased to bestow on us this afternoon?" asked Joyce, very cool and smart in a white silk frock, and absurdly young for a mother of two children.

Lina enumerated the guests who were coming to her tennis party that afternoon. "I'm afraid you'll find them a terribly dull lot," she apologized to Cecil.

"It isn't other people who are ever dull," Cecil replied dreamily. "It's we who are dull, when we find them so."

"Don't hold your cup like that, darling," adjured Joyce. "You'll spill the coffee over your trousers."

Cecil looked in a pained way at his coffee cup and then at his white trousers, before adjusting the angle of the former.

"You are so right, dear," he murmured.

Lina wished that Johnnie's work did not take him away from home for lunch. She enjoyed having Cecil

and Joyce to stay, and it was wonderful to have someone with whom she could rasp brains again, but undoubtedly Johnnie did lighten the atmosphere. Cecil was
charming, but he was at times a little heavy.

As soon as she reasonably could, Lina suggested that
Cecil and Joyce should go out to the court and have a
practice single, while she herself went upstairs to change.
Cecil fell in with the suggestion at once, as he fell in
with almost any suggestion that was made to him; and
Joyce demurred only enough to make her acquiescence
of value.

Standing by the big, low window in her bedroom, Lina
watched for a few minutes Joyce's dark, fluffy head
moving rapidly over the green of the court, and Cecil's
lanky form twisting into sudden and unexpected angles
on the further side of the net. It was odd that Cecil
should be so good at tennis. One would not have expected
it. Joyce, who had been reckoned a really excellent player
at Abbot Monckford, was only just good enough to give
him a game. Lina herself was hopelessly outclassed by
both of them.

But Johnnie could give Cecil fifteen a game and beat
him. Johnnie was almost first class.

Lina finished her dressing, put on her rubber-soled
shoes, and went downstairs. It was nearly half-past three.
People would be arriving at any moment.

The chairs and tables had all been taken out in the
morning, for by the mercy of heaven it was a lovely day.
Lina went into the kitchen to make sure that the lemon-
ade and cider cup were ready, and then into the drawing
room to collect the silver cigarette box. By the time she
reached the garden Joyce and Cecil had finished their set
and were sitting under the big cedar at the side of the
court. She joined them, and they sat in the comfortable

silence of people who know each other well enough not to have to bother to say things that are not worth saying.

Lina was a little anxious.

During the two years since she was married, Joyce had been to stay with her several times, but this was the first time that Cecil had come with her. Everybody who was coming that afternoon knew Cecil by name and reputation, and all were, or had professed to be, most anxious to meet him. But Cecil detested being lionized, and Lina hoped anxiously that no one would try to lionize him. It was a mistake, she decided now, to have asked Edith Farroway. How could she have been so silly? Edith would almost certainly say the wrong things. And if she didn't, her sister Mary would. And if neither Edith nor Mary did, Bob Farroway could be practically relied upon to do so. What on earth had made her ask the Farroways, any of them? It had been an inane thing to do. They would make Cecil most uncomfortable. Wild ideas rushed through her mind of going to the telephone and putting the Farroways off on some ingenious pretext or other.

She had almost found the exactly right pretext when Ella, the parlourmaid, appeared from the house and announced the Misses and Mr. Farroway.

"Oh, how are you?" Lina said effusively. "I *am* so pleased you could come."

2

The tennis party was in full swing.

But it was not being a success. Lina could feel that in every nerve, and it perplexed as well as worried her, because her parties usually were a success. She had learnt a great deal about the art of entertaining since those early and rather desperate little dinners. Johnnie had actually told her, not three months ago, that she was now one of the best hostesses he knew; and Johnnie's standard of hostess-ship was a high one.

On the court Cecil was partnering Winnie Treacher, a plump young woman who did her best and perspired freely but unfortunately with little effect in the effort, against Edith Farroway and Martin Caddis, an earnest young product of Eton who aspired to write novels and was so much in awe of Cecil that he seemed hardly to like to send him a really hard serve. It was an uninspiring set, and the latter pair were getting much the worse of it.

The chairs at the side of the court were filled with a dozen or so listless onlookers, more or less torpid after tea and strawberries-and-cream, and Lina herself was engaged in a laborious conversation with Lady Fortnum, a hard, bright little woman with beady eyes and fuzzy hair, who did not play tennis, and so far as Lina knew never had played tennis, but was not in the least deterred thereby from instructing others how tennis should be played. She was the daughter of a Lancashire cotton-mill owner, and her grandfather had been an operative in one of the mills which her father was later to own. She seemed to take considerable pride in these facts.

"Aldous Huxley?" she said sharply, in reply to an inadvertent observation of Lina's. The conversation, in view of the company, had taken a literary turn. "No, my dear, I do *not* like Aldous Huxley. I really can't understand why people make such a fuss about him. I read one of his books, and one only. I don't mind its being indecent in the least; I hope I'm broad-minded, whatever I may be; but I simply couldn't make head or tail of it—and I don't believe he could either. I'm quite sure your brother-in-law will agree with me: Aldous Huxley is *no good.*"

Lina murmured something noncommittal, wondering vaguely why Lady Fortnum should think it necessary to wear a diamond pendant as big as a broad bean at a tennis party.

Her companion's views on Mr. Aldous Huxley did not surprise her. She had long since ceased to be distressed by the calm dogmatizing upon artistic subjects which takes the place in country circles of intelligent criticism. If one did not happen to like a certain book, picture, or piece of music, one took it for granted that the book, picture, or piece of music was just bad; and the people who thought it was good were, quite simply and plainly, mistaken. It never occurred to any female critic that a book might possibly be above her own level of intelligence (the men of course read only detective stories).

"My dear Mrs. Aysgarth—really! I mean, the Sitwells! Isn't Osbert Sitwell the man who speaks his poetry while his sister plays a trumpet? Well, I mean . . ."

Exit Mr. Osbert Sitwell as a subject for discussion.

Probably the critic would add: "I mean, why *write* about unpleasant things, when there's so much unpleasantness in the world already? What I like is a nice, clever story, with real people in it. Gilbert Frankau, you know. Or Michael Arlen. I know some people think Michael Arlen rather highbrow, but I *like* him."

And Lina would murmur feebly something to the effect of Michael Arlen being a very popular author, which was undeniably true and committed her to nothing.

She suddenly felt now that she could bear Lady Fortnum no longer. She rose, with a bright little excuse which she felt must sound as insincere as it was, and abandoned Lady Fortnum and her literary views to Harry Newsham, who was sitting on the other side of her.

She hoped, maliciously, that Harry would entertain her with his favourite subject, politics.

She looked down the line of chairs. Freda Newsham was sitting next to a middle-aged major, and both looked as bored with each other as they probably were. Evidently, thought Lina, Major Scargill was more interested in the play than in his companion: an unforgivable sin, from Freda's point of view. Freda always expected attentions as well as attention, even at a tennis party.

Lina exchanged a smile with Janet Caldwell, who was nobly listening to Bob Farroway's stories of the prodigious feats performed by his elderly Morris car on the neighbouring hills. Janet had the sense not to play tennis, since she did not play well enough. Lina often envied her her courage.

Janet liked good deeds. Lina did not.

There were two chairs vacant, one beside Mary Farroway and one beside Joyce.

"A somewhat sticky lot, your friends this afternoon," commented Joyce with sisterly frankness, as Lina dropped into the chair beside her.

Lina agreed. "And yet some of them would probably be quite amusing at one of your cocktail parties," she added. "I think they're rather overawed by Cecil."

"Cecil does have that effect. I can't imagine why."

Lina could imagine it. The mildest of men, as she quite well knew, Cecil had exactly that effect upon herself. And she knew that she herself had that effect upon other people, which was odder still.

"Perhaps it's his beard," she said, with a feeble giggle.

The set came to an end, and Lina arranged another.
The players drifted towards the chairs, Winnie
Treacher alone, and Cecil, looking even more melan-
choly than usual, between Edith Farroway and Martin
Caddis. Lina saw a literary light kindling in Mrs.
Newsham's eyes and heard Edith Farroway saying: "Of
course, I often think *I* could write a book, if only I could
spare the time." She hurried to Cecil's rescue.

It seemed to her that Cecil's melancholy was spreading. Faces grew more and more listless and occasionally
yawned; even Bob Farroway's horse-laugh ceased to
ring out. Harry Newsham had given up Lady Fortnum
in his turn, and was watching the play with an expression
of concentrated interest. Lina, looking helplessly round,
felt that of all the dismal parties she had ever attended,
this was quite the worst.

And then, suddenly, the whole atmosphere changed.

Harry ceased watching the play and grinned; Lady
Fortnum sat up with a jerk and visibly preened herself;
Winnie Treacher's dull eye brightened; Mary Farroway's gentle smile of resignation changed to one of
welcome; her sister frankly stood up and waved; the
players on the court stopped the game to brandish their
rackets—and Lina herself jumped up and almost ran
towards the figure in white flannels who had emerged
from the house and was coming towards them.

The mere appearance of Johnnie had been enough to
turn disaster into triumph.

3

"It will turn up, Lady Fortnum," Lina repeated
helplessly. "It's bound to turn up. I mean, it can't be
far, can it?"

"Bound to turn up," Major Scargill repeated robustly. "Can't possibly be far."

"Yes, it's bound to turn up," chorused half-a-dozen other voices, with the greatest conviction.

"I had it when I came out from tea," Lady Fortnum said firmly, looking at her hostess with what Lina resentfully felt to be a positively suspicious eye. "I remember quite distinctly."

"You had it when I was sitting next to you," Lina said, and would have liked to add: "I remember wondering why the hell you wanted to wear it at a tennis party."

"Yes," agreed Lady Fortnum. "I had it when you were sitting next to me." No doubt she did not say it in the least pointedly, but her words sounded pointed to Lina.

"Johnnie," she said, a little impatiently, "are you sure you've looked everywhere?"

"I've personally turned over every blade of grass within twenty yards," Johnnie said, with complete cheerfulness. "Do you know what I think, Lady Fortnum? That you'll find it when you undress."

"I hope so," Lady Fortnum agreed drily. "I don't want to insist on its value, among friends, but I shouldn't at all care to lose it permanently."

Lina reddened angrily, but Johnnie, with a quite unabashed grin, said: "Are you sure you wouldn't like to make sure in the house here? I'll come and see fair play."

Somebody guffawed, and Lady Fortnum's highly powdered cheeks took on a slightly more violet tinge. "Thank you, but I can't agree that *that* is the place where one had better look."

Lina said, coldly and distinctly: "I thought, Johnnie

you were going to say: Isn't Lady Fortnum sure she wouldn't like all of us to turn out our pockets?"

There was a moment's horrified silence, during which Lina, furious as she was, was yet able to wonder whether it was really she who had spoken those words which she had heard dropped into the gathering so calmly.

Then Major Scargill, extremely red and clucking like an old hen, said the right things and smoothed down Lady Fortnum's very ruffled feathers; and Johnnie, with a comical grimace over his shoulders to the others which somehow managed to transform that lady from the aggrieved into the aggrieving party, conducted her to her car.

Lina, still angry, but very conscious of the responsibility on her shoulders for the finding of a diamond worth five thousand pounds, watched him hold her in conversation for a couple of minutes before she got inside it, and watched during that short time Lady Fortnum's face change from stony suspicion, through affability, to something extremely like apology. Johnnie really was marvellous.

The search continued with serious energy. Everyone else stayed behind to help with it. Even Freda Newsham pretended to look, and Janet Caldwell seemed almost as perturbed as Lina herself. They tumbled over each other in the intensity of their efforts; for since Lady Fortnum had not moved more than a dozen yards between the time when she was certainly wearing the pendant and the moment when she discovered its disappearance, the area of useful search was small.

Sympathy, at first silent and then gradually more and more outspoken, was entirely with Lina and Johnnie. It was felt that anyone who arrived at a tennis party wearing a great fat diamond thoroughly deserved to go away without it. But this sentiment, reasonable though it might be, did not blind those who voiced it to the extremely delicate position in which their host and hostess found themselves. For unless Johnnie was right in saying that Lady Fortnum would find the thing when she undressed, it certainly was very difficult to see how it could have disappeared, in that very small space, altogether of its own volition.

Martin Caddis did, in fact, try to get Lina's suggestion taken seriously that the men should turn out their pockets; but Johnnie, obviously distressed, would not hear of it. The utmost that could be permitted was that they should examine the turn-ups of their trousers; but these yielded nothing but fluff.

When at last Lina, with a rather high-pitched laugh, insisted an hour later in calling the search off, the diamond had not been found.

"And now it's gone for good," observed Joyce, as they watched the last of the cars swing round the circular drive and out of the gates. "I wonder which of them had it."

"Joyce, I won't believe it," Lina said stoutly. "It must have got trodden into the ground. We shall find it tomorrow morning."

"Of course we shall, darling," said Johnnie confidently, and put an arm round his wife's waist. "Don't you bother your little monkey head any more about it."

"Well, I wish I had your simple faith," Joyce retorted. "I invariably believe the worst of people."

"My dear, you are so right," said Cecil, sadly smoothing his beard.

Lina gave the hand on her waist a little quick squeeze. "Well, anyhow," she said, "let's go in and get ready for dinner."

"I'll just let down the net and collect the balls," said Johnnie. "You can have first bath, monkeyface, if you jump to it."

4

Actually the diamond was found, that same evening. Lina found it, in a pocket of Johnnie's white trousers.

Johnnie had gone down to mix the cocktails (in spite of having second bath, Johnnie was always dressed first), and Lina, when she was ready, had just looked into Johnnie's dressing room to see that everything was in order. Johnnie's flannels lay sprawling on the floor where he had flung them, as he always did; not even Lina had been able to induce him ever to put anything away. She picked them up mechanically, and noticed a long green smudge on one knee, where Johnnie had slipped. Obviously they could not be worn again, and Lina felt in the pockets before putting the trousers in the washing basket. In the left-hand pocket was nothing, in the right-hand one was the diamond pendant. Lina almost cried with relief.

"Johnnie," she burst out as soon as she got inside the drawing room, where the other three were already sipping their cocktails. "Johnnie, you really are the limit. Why didn't you tell me you'd found that wretched diamond?"

Johnnie, bringing her cocktail to meet her, stopped dead. "What?" he said, almost stupidly.

"Why didn't you tell me you found that diamond when you went back to let the net down?" Lina repeated quite crossly. "You knew how worried I was." She took the cocktail and finished it at a gulp. Johnnie really was very exasperating sometimes.

"What's that?" said Joyce. "The diamond found?"

"Yes. Johnnie found it when he went back to let the

net down. It was in the pocket of his white trousers."

"She searches my pockets, you see," Johnnie threw over his shoulder to Cecil. "Does yours?"

"Why on earth didn't you tell me?" Lina persisted.

Johnnie looked at her with his most mischievous smile. "I thought it would give the hag a lesson if we pretended for a day or two that we couldn't find it. Of course I didn't tell you, monkeyface. You'd have given the show away in two minutes." He laughed.

"I don't think it's at all funny," Lina said coldly. "Give me another cocktail, please."

Lina had not a very good sense of humour.

All through dinner Johnnie was in the most uproarious spirits and teased Cecil unmercifully.

5

Oddly enough it was, in the end, Lina herself and not Lady Fortnum who lost a piece of valuable jewelry.

About a week after Cecil and Joyce had gone, Lina became aware that a diamond-and-emerald ring was missing from her jewel case. It was not a ring she wore very much, for the setting was old-fashioned and cumbersome, and she had never had it reset, but the stones were good. She had worn it, she remembered, one evening towards the end of Joyce's visit, and was almost sure she had put it back in the little suède case in which she kept her jewels and trinkets, and which always lay, unlocked, in the top left-hand drawer of her dressing table; but in the case the ring certainly was not.

Her room, and the whole house, was searched, and searched again and again; for, apart from the ring's value, Lina had a strong sense of possession, and the mere feeling of loss in itself distressed her. However, no sign was ever found of it.

Johnnie was most sympathetic and pointed out with evident glee that, on his own recommendation, all Lina's jewels had been insured for their full value, only six months or so ago; she would therefore suffer no monetary loss. He helped her make out the claim to the insurance company, and the money duly arrived.

Johnnie was rather urgent that she should lend it to him, for some scheme of his which he assured her would be of immense profit to both of them but about whose details he was a little vague when pressed; but Lina, who could be very obstinate where her own money was concerned, distrusted such nebulousness and bought another and more modern ring.

She remained, however, not a little uneasy about the way in which her old ring had disappeared; and since it boiled down to the fact that nobody but Ella, the house-parlourmaid, could possibly have stolen it if it had been stolen at all, she played for safety by getting rid of Ella. She was the more ready to do so, as she had noticed that the girl had been getting a little pert with her of late, and seemed to resent the very mild and almost smiling reprimands which were all that Lina ever dealt out to her maids.

"I can't understand what's happened to her," Lina complained to Johnnie when they talked it over. "She used to be so good-natured. I suppose really she's too pretty. She must have had her head turned by some man in the village. Whether she took my ring or not, it's quite time she did go."

And Johnnie agreed that it was quite time Ella did go.

So Ella went; and very soon was as completely forgotten as the loss of the ring for which she came to be held responsible.

CHAPTER V

ONE of the incidents in her married life which Lina always remembered afterwards was the first visit of Mr. Thwaite.

"Mr. Thwaite," announced Ethel, the new parlour-maid, and left it at that.

Mr. Thwaite was very tall. His nose was large and curved, and his hair sat in little tight curls round his head.

"Hullo," said Mr. Thwaite loudly. "Hullo, hullo. What?" Mr. Thwaite seemed to think that he had now explained himself.

"Hullo," said Lina, trying not to laugh and feeling that her visitor must have escaped from the pages of Mr. P. G. Wodehouse.

"So you're old Johnnie's wife?" accused Mr. Thwaite, shaking hands.

"I am, yes."

"Poor old bird, what?" said Mr. Thwaite surprisingly, and then laughed with much amusement. "Didn't mean that. Putting my foot in it as usual, what? I mean —well, how is the old bean?"

Lina rang for tea and with some difficulty induced her visitor to seat himself. She replied that Johnnie's health was excellent. He was not in at the moment, but she expected him back for tea.

"Still mugging it in that estate office, eh? Hates it as much as ever, I suppose. What?"

"Yes, he still works there. Do you live near here, Mr. Thwaite?" Lina asked politely.

For some reason Mr. Thwaite seemed to consider this an admirable joke. He laughed heartily. "Good God, no! What? I mean . . . Near here? My goodness, no. My place is in Yorkshire. Oh, I see what you mean. No, I was at school with Johnnie. Shared a study. Bosom pals and all that sort of rot. Only seen him about twice since we left. Ran into him at Newbury last year. He'd dropped a packet. Still following the gees, I expect?"

"Johnnie?" said Lina. "No, I don't think he ever goes racing now." She thought idly that it was odd that she should not have heard of this visit to Newbury.

"What? Oh, rot. Fact? Good God, poor old bean. Must have changed a bit, what? Marriage, I expect, eh? Told me he was married last time I saw him. 'Oh, rot,' I said. 'Not come down to that, old bean, have you?' 'Don't you worry,' he said. 'She'll be worth a packet one day.' 'Oh,' I said, 'that's different.' Hullo! P'raps I ought not to have said that. What? Putting my foot in it, was I?"

"Not in the least," Lina said, concealing her surprise. "Johnnie and I quite understand one another." But she did not think it very nice that Johnnie should have boasted of the money that would come to her.

"That's the scheme," Mr. Thwaite said with enthusiasm. "Makes marriage almost bearable if you can do that, what? I remember Johnnie said what a topper you were, too. What ho! Well, how is the old bean, anyhow? Estate agent, or something equally ghastly, isn't he? Good God! What?"

"I didn't say anything," Lina said faintly.

"No, of course you didn't. Expect I said 'what,' what? Always saying 'what.' God knows why. Silly habit, really.

Well, anyhow, how is the old bean? Fit and hearty? I haven't seen him for ages. Oh, I told you that. Yes, I was passing through, or as near as dash it, so thought I'd get off and give the old bean a call. I say, I'm not butting in or anything, am I? You haven't got a tea fight on, or a bazaar to open, or what not, what? What?"

"Of course not," Lina said, as brightly as she could manage. "I'm always delighted to see any of Johnnie's old friends. Tea will be coming in a minute. Of course you must stop and see him. I know he'll be back for it to-day."

"Will he, by Jove! Same old slacker, I'll bet. What?"

Ethel, entering with the tea tray, saved Lina from replying. The interruption did not, however, disconcert Mr. Thwaite. He boomed away through the clatter as merrily as any bittern.

Lina had hardly poured out the tea when she heard Johnnie's key in the front door. Excusing herself, she ran out to intercept him.

"Johnnie, I thought I'd better warn you. There's a most extraordinary man here called Thwaite, who says he was at school with you."

"What, old Beaky Thwaite? Whatever brought him here?"

"He says he was passing, so got off to see you," Lina explained. "Is he quite mad?"

"Not quite," Johnnie grinned. "Pretty nearly, perhaps. Won't say a word, eh?"

"Won't say a word? Won't he! Come and listen to him."

"That's funny. He used to be painfully shy, as a boy. He stayed with us once or twice in the holidays, and my people used to say he never uttered a word from the moment he entered the house to the moment he left it."

"Well, he's making up for lost time now," Lina giggled. "Hurry up and wash, darling, and help me out. I can't *bear* it any longer alone."

Johnnie looked back at her over his shoulder as he mounted the stairs. "Be kind to him, monkeyface, anyhow."

"I have been. Why particularly?"

"He's got more money than he knows what to do with. I always feel one should be kind to people like that."

"He might get you a better job," Lina said, promptly and hopefully.

Johnnie shrugged his shoulders and went on upstairs.

Three minutes later Lina was witnessing the hearty meeting of two old school friends. An American film producer would have been disappointed. Instead of putting an arm round each other's necks and massaging the middle of each other's backs, they merely hit each other violently in the chest.

"Well, Beaky, you old sinner, this is great. How the devil are you, and all that kind of thing?"

"You're getting fat, old bean," pronounced Mr. Thwaite in return. "Deuced fat. What? You'll have to knock his oats off a bit, Mrs. Aysgarth. Here, what's your wife's name, old bean? Can't go on calling her 'Mrs. Aysgarth,' I mean. Sounds too damned formal, and all that sort of rot. What?"

Lina stifled an insane request to be called Mrs. Old Bean.

"Her name's Lina."

"Lina, what? Damned good name, too," adjudged Mr. Thwaite loudly. "Call you 'Lina' then, may I?"

"Of course," Lina said, producing a rather forced

smile. She had ideas about whom she permitted to use her Christian name and how long they must have known her first.

She dispensed tea and listened, with wandering interest, to the reminiscences of the two men.

For some time these were confined to old This and old That, and what had happened to old Thing. Then Mr. Thwaite's memories took a more personal turn.

"Remember how you won the Isaiah prize, what? Good God, I shan't forget that in a hurry. I'll bet he hasn't told you about that, Lina, what?"

"No." Lina roused herself from the worried consideration of a possible menu should unexpected Mr. Thwaite stay to dinner, as Johnnie, most hospitable of men and untroubled by a larder outlook, would certainly invite him to do. "No, I don't believe he has. What was that?"

"Why, the Chief was deuced keen on Isaiah, and all that sort of rot, and he offered a special prize one term when the Sixth were mugging it up. This old bean, being a school-pre., was in his study one day and saw the paper on the Chief's desk. So he took a copy of it. Never done a stroke of work, of course. Never did. But he got the prize all right. What about that?"

"Really, Johnnie." Lina laughed, but her strict code made her amusement sound forced. The incident reminded her dimly of something that had happened in Paris, on their honeymoon: something to do with a waiter and wrong change, and not by any means creditable to Johnnie. "But of course he didn't keep the prize, Mr. Thwaite?"

"Didn't he just! I see you don't know Johnnie yet. And the dirty old dog never told me till afterwards that he knew what the questions were going to be." Mr. Thwaite laughed hugely.

Lina wondered if this were the public-school code of honour about which she had heard so much.

Johnnie laughed too. "Yes, I put it across you all that time." He caught Lina's pained gaze and added quickly: "Don't look so tragic, monkeyface. The Isaiah exam. wasn't taken very seriously."

"Not that it would have mattered to you, old bean, if it had been," retorted Mr. Thwaite. "Old Johnnie was supposed to be the finest cribber ever known at the place, Lina. He never did a stroke of work all the time he was there; but he got a prize every year, and ended up in the Sixth. I'll bet he'd have cribbed his way to a schol. at Oxford, wouldn't you, old bean, if they hadn't cut your career a trifle short by——"

"Look here, Beaky, aren't you being a bit tactless? You ought to know that women don't understand the what-d'you-call-'ems—what's the word, monkeyface?"

"Ethics?"

"I expect so. Well, the ethics of cribbing. You'll be giving Lina all sorts of funny ideas about her poor husband."

"What?" said Mr. Thwaite. "Oh, I see what you mean. Sorry, old bean. Putting my foot in it again, what? All rot, Lina, anyhow. Cribbing as a fine art, and all that sort of thing. Everyone does it. No good at it myself, but a trier. Sorry, old bean, what?"

"Well, anyhow, what are you doing with yourself in these days, Beaky?"

"Me, eh? Oh, tooling around, you know. Nothing much."

"Lucky old cad, aren't you, with so much money?"

"Oh, come. Here, I say. Not so much as all that, you know. Draw it mild. Just enough, that's all."

"It would certainly be enough for me," Johnnie grinned.

Johnnie did not ask Mr. Thwaite to dinner.

Lina was so relieved that she quite forgot to pursue some inquiries she had intended into the art of cribbing.

She did not see Mr. Thwaite again for four years.

2

By the time she had lived in Upcottery three years, Lina was able to congratulate herself on two things.

The first was that Johnnie, who before he met her had never done a stroke of work in his life and apparently had never contemplated doing one, should have really settled down to his job. More, he was now taking it for granted that he should have a job.

Every morning still, with perhaps rather less punctuality but now without any resignation at all, Johnnie went forth to deal with estimates for repairs to labourers' cottages, quotations for slates, and all the multifarious petty bargaining that his work entailed; and every morning Lina, having got up early in order to breakfast with him, kissed him good-bye on the doorstep just like any suburban wife.

Johnnie, in fact, was altogether a reformed rake. Even General McLaidlaw acknowledged that Lina had turned him from whatever he had been into a useful member of society. It was a revolution of which Lina was quite aware, and for which she took full credit.

She was still not sure how she had done it.

She looked back on that evening when the revolution had been effected, with a kind of wonder. Something had seemed to take possession of her then: something which had given her a strength of character which she normally imagined she lacked, and which had certainly been greater for the moment than Johnnie's. The odd thing was that, so far as Johnnie was concerned, its effects remained. On that evening Lina had established a moral superiority to which, as she realized vaguely, Johnnie still paid tribute. It was absurd, of course, for after that one effort Lina had quite reverted to her former perfectly contented moral dependence upon Johnnie; and it irked her to find Johnnie at times trying to placate or cajole her, instead of giving her the peremptory orders that she would much have preferred; though she did understand, in an indefinite way, that this was not Johnnie's method of gaining his ends. She still adored Johnnie for the grown-up schoolboy he was; but she did not like being considered his schoolmistress.

The other matter on which she was able to congratulate herself was that after three years' residence in an English rural district, she was not yet a member of the Women's Institutes, had never had a fête in the grounds of Dellfield, and had allowed herself to be persuaded into joining no body, secular or lay, for the dragooning of people into doing things they did not want for the benefit of institutions in which they had no interest.

That is not to say that Lina did not admire those whose bent lay in such directions. Her closest friend in Upcottery, Janet Caldwell, actually ran the village branch of the Women's Institutes; but Lina did not for a moment allow this fact to interfere with their friendship.

On the contrary, she envied Janet her power of enjoying her duties.

Lina knew herself to be lazy.

At home this laziness of hers had been actually encouraged. "Oh," they said, when it was a question of something practical, "it's no good relying on Lina to do *that*. She couldn't. Lina's always up in the clouds." And as Lina invariably did not at all want to do whatever it was that required doing, she took good care to foster the idea that she always was up in the clouds. It had been a quite mistaken idea, but nobody except Lina ever knew that.

At home that had been all very well. In her own house it was impossible for Lina to shelter in the clouds. Joyce was always most surprised that Lina's house should be as efficiently run as her own.

But Lina's mental laziness remained.

It was not a good, hearty laziness, that was proud of itself and informed the rest of the world that it could go hang. It was the nagging kind. Lina felt all the time that really she ought to be getting up and doing something useful, but that, on the other hand, she simply could not bear, just for the moment, to be mixed up in all these horrible village activities. And the moment when she might feel she could bear it never seemed to arrive.

So that she very much admired Janet, who was always getting up and doing useful things.

For Janet Caldwell was a serious soul. So, in her way, was Lina, though it was a different way. There was, however, an intellectual bond between them which was quite strong enough to allow such deviations without weakening. Lina had not been in Upcottery two months before she realized that Janet Caldwell was the only person in the place with any real intelligence whatsoever—not excepting Johnnie.

Lina still did not know whether to be disappointed with Johnnie in that respect or not. While they were still engaged she had persuaded herself that Johnnie had a Mind, undeveloped though it might be, which under her ministrations would bud and flower after marriage into as capable a blossom as any in Joyce's own set. It appeared that she had been wrong. If Johnnie had a Mind, he did not encourage it. Lina felt that it was a pity. She had seen herself in the rôle of mental horticulturist, and she had liked it.

It did, she felt, leave a gap not to be able to discuss passionately with Johnnie the new books or get pleasantly excited over completely academic topics; for Johnnie did not even read the new books, unless they happened to be detective stories, and would have seen nothing to get passionate about in them if he had; while as for academic topics, Johnnie simply could not understand his wife's interest in them—and where Johnnie did not understand, he laughed. But then Lina got so much from Johnnie, so much that was red-blooded and vital, that a pallid intellectualism super-imposed might have seemed positively out of place: for contrasted with the things for which Johnnie stood to her, intellectualism did look pallid.

In the passionately protective love with which she now surrounded everything that was Johnnie and Johnnie's, Lina not only sympathized with, but at times even envied, his simple philistinism. Johnnie was her child; and what have children to do with abstractions? Food and drink and love and bodies, the raw meat of life, those are their concerns; not its civilized complexities.

But since Lina herself did not happen to be constituted that way, Janet Caldwell adequately filled the gap, which might otherwise have become a serious one.

Janet was a graduate of St. Hugh's, Oxford.

She had taken a third in Honour Mods. and a second

in History. Contrary to the practice of so many otherwise intelligent women, she did not consider it necessary to impair her appearance in order to prove her intellectual capacity. This was the more fortunate since she was something rather more than good-looking: her broad white forehead, black hair parted in the middle, and large gray eyes gave her a classical appearance which her rather large, full-lipped mouth could not spoil. Her voice was so gentle as to be often almost inaudible. She was half-a-dozen years younger than Lina, unmarried, and lived with her widowed mother in an extremely red, square little house on the top of a small hill, which she herself called The Doll's House.

Lina's early experiences in friendship had left her diffident. She was always a little surprised, and a little grateful too, when anyone seemed to like her. Janet had shown her preference from the first, and Lina had reciprocated it at once. Each of the two had recognized in the other the only person in the neighbourhood with whom she could become really intimate; and their intimacy had shot up in the extremely rapid growth which women are so often able to induce in a friendship between themselves.

And it had lasted.

A great deal of tea had been drunk, and an immense amount of talk poured out, in Lina's long, airy drawing room while Johnnie wrestled with his farm accounts twenty miles away.

On an afternoon in early November the two were sitting in front of the log fire, waiting for tea to be brought in. The conversation had been desultory, until Janet pulled it up with a jerk.

"Lina," she said, in her gentle, almost complaining voice, "why don't you have a baby?"

"You may well ask," Lina answered, with a little laugh. "I assure you, it isn't my fault."

"Johnnie's?"

"Nor Johnnie's. Nature's."

"Do you want one?"

"I suppose so." Lina was a little embarrassed. It was the first time she and Janet, in spite of their intimacy, had discussed such a personal matter. They prided themselves in differing in this respect from others of their sex, whose avid eagerness to pry into the secret lives of their friends, or, with a kind of psychological exhibitionism, reveal their own, disgusted both of them. "I suppose so. But Johnnie's such a child himself that perhaps I don't miss another as much as I might."

Janet leaned back in her chair, her broad, white hands clasped over one knee. "If ever I married, it would only be to have children."

"It's quite nice to have a husband in any case," Lina observed mildly.

"Yes?" said Janet.

Janet did not like Johnnie.

She was, so far as Lina knew, about the only woman who had never succumbed to Johnnie's charm. Of course, Janet never said she did not like Johnnie, and she obviously tried not to hint it; but it was quite evident. Janet never stayed more than a perfunctory few minutes if Johnnie came back before she had gone, and it needed quite a lot of persuasion to get her to dinner. Lina thought it all rather unnecessary, as Johnnie was always quite charming to Janet and did not return her dislike in the least; though he did mimic her quiet voice and deliberate movements rather funnily when she was not there.

It had never entered Lina's head that Janet might be jealous of Johnnie.

"And a house of one's own," she added now, thinking of Abbot Monckford. "I can quite understand a girl marrying a man she didn't care two pins about, just to get a home of her own."

"But you didn't?"

"Me? Oh, no. In fact, I was rather frightened of it. Before I was married the idea of housekeeping was a positive nightmare. I felt I couldn't *bear* it."

"And now I suppose you're about the most efficient housekeeper on this side of Dorsetshire," Janet said, as if stating a simple fact. "I'm quite sure I've never had better dinners in any private house than I've had here."

"It's an easy secret," Lina laughed. "I've told you hundreds of times. Keep a good cook—and know how to cook just a bit better yourself. That's all."

"Quite easy," Janet smiled, as the tea arrived. Janet could not cook at all and would not let Lina teach her.

They talked on trivial subjects while the maid was in the room.

When she had gone Janet sat for some minutes staring at a crumpet on the plate on her lap, before beginning to nibble it absently.

"What I couldn't stand about marriage," she said at last, "would be the intimacy. I should hate a man to see me half-dressed."

"One gets used to it. And when the man tells one that one looks quite nice . . . Janet, *are* you thinking of getting married?"

"Oh, heavens, no. It just interests me. It's funny we've never talked about the personal side of marriage before. —Does Johnnie tell you that?"

"Johnnie's the perfect husband: he always notices what I've got on. As a matter of fact, he's quite interested in women's clothes. And he's got very good taste."

"So long as it's only the clothes and not the women

inside them," Janet said drily. "Are you ever jealous of Johnnie, Lina?"

"No," Lina said simply. "I've never thought about it. And, in any case, I've no cause to be. I should know at once if I had. Johnnie's far too transparent to be able to hide anything like that."

"Never underrate your opponent, my dear."

"I suppose," Lina mused, "that I should be upset if Johnnie ever were unfaithful to me. I try to persuade myself that I'm modern, and unfaithfulness doesn't matter really, so long as it's only an incident and nothing serious; but . . . Yes, I should be upset. But I shouldn't go off the deep end. In any case, Johnnie would always come back to me."

"He'd be a fool if he didn't," said Janet with conviction.

"Mrs. Newsham," said the parlourmaid, opening the door.

"Damn!" said Janet, under her breath, with gentle inaudibility.

Lina echoed her sentiment silently. Janet had shown signs of getting most interesting.

"Well, I suppose I've got to get along to my guides. Thanks for tea, Lina," said Janet, who did not like Freda Newsham.

3

Lina's drawing room gave her a great deal of pleasure. It was a long, high, rather narrow room, with three tall windows that came down to broad sills within a foot of the floor and through which one could step straight out onto the lawn that ran up to the walls of the house.

Lina had furnished it sparsely. There was a polished

board floor, with a few good rugs, a piano (on which Lina did not play so much as she should), a couch, a few easy chairs, and a couple of occasional tables; the end opposite the fireplace was covered entirely by bookshelves. There were no unnecessary ornaments or fripperies; Lina's taste was severe to the pitch of strictness.

The only possibly inutilitarian objects in the room were four Hepplewhite chairs, which Lina's mother had given her from home and which were really too good to be sat in; but their painted backs had provided the keynote on which Lina had based her whole colour-scheme; just as she had built up that of the dining room from the tints of a big Pieter Snyders still life that hung over the mantelpiece.

She came back one afternoon in late January from a shopping expedition into distant Bournemouth, to find Johnnie unexpectedly consuming a late tea by the fire. Almost as she entered the room she was conscious vaguely of a feeling of something lacking, but the indefinite sensation was lost in her surprise at seeing Johnnie.

She came forward, pulling off her gloves, to give him the kiss without which he would never let her enter a room in which he was. "You're back early to-day, darling."

"Yes," said Johnnie. "Had a good day?"

"Fairly. I couldn't get quite what I wanted, but——"

"Hullo, you've got a new hat. I say, that's a peach, isn't it?"

"Do you like it?" said Lina, pleased.

"It's the prettiest you've had for years. Clever little monkeyface, aren't you?" He caught her hand and pulled her down on his knee.

"Darling, I want my tea," Lina protested with a laugh, and thought how wonderful it was that after more than three years of marriage Johnnie should still want to sit her on his knee.

"Have your tea here," pronounced Johnnie.

Lina manipulated the teapot, her back to the room. Johnnie held her quite tightly round the waist

"Darling, I must get up. I want to take my coat off."

This time Johnnie let her go. She rose, took off her coat, and laid it over the back of a chair. Again the curious sense of emptiness invaded her. She looked round the room.

"Johnnie! Where are the Hepplewhite chairs?"

Johnnie jumped up from his chair and put his arms round her, holding her against his chest. "Sweetheart, I've got an awfully good bit of news for you. Listen. You remember that American I told you about? Well, he——"

"What American? You never told me about any American." Lina was perturbed already. Johnnie looked oddly guilty, in spite of his smile. And the way he was holding her made her suspicious. Johnnie always embraced her when he had to admit to something he should not have done.

She looked up at him without returning his smile.

"Why, that American who came back with me a week or two ago, when you were out. The one who was so interested in those chairs. Didn't I tell you? I thought I had. I meant to. Well, he came over this afternoon, and——"

"Weren't you at Bradstowe this afternoon?"

"No, I came back after lunch; there was nothing to do. But listen, darling. This fellow, this American—you wouldn't believe how keen he was on those chairs. He offered me a deuce of a lot for them: more than they were valued at, for the insurance. Of course," said Johnnie virtuously, "I told him I couldn't think of sell-

ing them. So what did he do? Damn it, monkeyface, he
pretty nearly doubled his offer. It would have been madness not to take it."

"Johnnie—you *didn't* sell them?"

"Darling, I tell you: it would have been madness not
to, at the price he offered."

"Let me go. No, Johnnie, let me go." Lina pushed
with her hands against Johnnie's chest, so that he had to
release her.

"Look here, monkeyface, you're not cross, surely?
Honestly, darling, it would have been———"

"But you couldn't sell them. They weren't yours to
sell. They were mine."

"Oh, hang it all, sweetheart, I know that, technically,
they were yours. But—well, I mean———"

"They *are* mine," Lina said violently. "And I don't
want to sell them. I don't care what your American
offered. I won't sell them. Where are they?"

"Why, he took them away. In his car."

"Then you'll have to get them back."

"But, dearest, do be reasonable. I don't know where
he's gone. I don't know anything about him."

"I don't care," said Lina, breathing quickly. "You'll
have to find out, that's all. I won't sell those chairs, so
you've got to get them back."

Johnnie tried to take her in his arms again. "Darling!"

"No, I mean it. No, don't, Johnnie. I'm very angry
with you. You had no right to sell them without asking
me."

Johnnie looked extremely crestfallen. "I only thought
I was doing you a good turn."

"Yes, I know all about that. Don't do me any good
turns like that in future. Well, I suppose you'd better
give me the money. I'll keep it to give back to him when
you've got the chairs again."

"I haven't got it," Johnnie said quickly. "He's going to send the cheque on."

Lina stared at him. "What? You don't know where he's gone or anything about him, and yet you trusted him to send the cheque on?"

"Oh, he's all right. Absolutely all right. I mean, he's a friend of Melbeck's. And in any case, we could always get him through the American embassy. He just hadn't got his cheque book on him. Hang it, darling, one must trust people occasionally. He'll send it on all right."

"He'd better."

"Monkeyface!"

"Well?"

"Not really cross with me, are you?"

"Yes, Johnnie, I am. Really." But Johnnie was looking so penitent that Lina had to let her expression relax.

Johnnie was on to it at once, and caught her to him. "My darling, you're not. Not any more. I'm terribly sorry. I thought you'd be so pleased."

He looked so disappointed that Lina had to forgive him altogether.

"But mind you," she said, under his kisses, "I hold you responsible for getting them back, Johnnie."

"I'll get them back," Johnnie promised with fervour, "if I have to chase him over to America for them."

4

But Johnnie did not get them back.

The American, it seemed, had simply vanished. Nor did he send the cheque. Johnnie was most upset about it, but what could one do?

"Go to the police," said Lina, some three weeks later. "We ought to have gone before. I'll ring up the Dorchester police station to-day and report it."

"Oh, I shouldn't do that," Johnnie said.

"Why ever not?"

Johnnie's reasons were vague but emphatic. Lina gathered that somehow it would offend Captain Melbeck extremely, and perhaps even imperil Johnnie's job, if she rang up the Dorchester police.

"Nonsense!" she said briskly. "The man was obviously a thief. Captain Melbeck must have been taken in by him as well as you." But her mind did not contain quite so much decision as her words. The last thing she wanted to do was to imperil Johnnie's job.

Johnnie, however, did not know that. "Look here, Lina," he said slowly, and Lina knew that something important was coming from the use of her name, which he hardly ever employed. "Look here, you mustn't ring up the police."

"But I intend to. Why mustn't I?"

"Well, look here," Johnnie said, with a desperate air, "he did give me the cheque."

"He did? Then why did you tell me he didn't?"

"Because I'd spent it."

"You'd spent it? Well, really, Johnnie! What on?"

"I had to pay some debts," Johnnie said with reluctance.

"What debts? I didn't know you had any debts. What debts?"

"Oh, well, if you must know, racing debts. Look here, I know I oughtn't to have done it, but the truth is that I was in a pretty tight corner. And then that American's offer came like a godsend. I simply had to take it. I'm awfully sorry, monkeyface."

Lina knew that she ought to be angry, but Johnnie was looking so ashamed of himself that the wind was taken out of her sails.

"Have you done any racing since then?"

"No. Not a bet."

"If I forgive you, will you promise not to make any more bets?"

"Not a one. Once bitten, twice shy."

"Never again? It's a promise, Johnnie?"

"I swear it. Monkeyface," said Johnnie fervently, "you're the dearest, sweetest, most wonderful woman . . ."

Lina knew it was worth the cheque.

5

Just a fortnight later she was in Bournemouth again. Johnnie had not wanted her to go, but there were some things which could only be got there.

She passed Marshall's antique shop, in South Street. In the window was an undoubted Hepplewhite chair. Lina recognized the picture on it.

She stood for quite five minutes staring at it before she went inside the shop.

Mr. Marshall himself came forward and answered her questions.

"Oh, yes, madam, it's a Hepplewhite. Yes, I've got four of them. The other three are through here, if you'd care to see them."

Lina followed him and stared for a few moments at the other three, wondering how to get the information she wanted.

"You have their pedigree, I suppose?" she said slowly at last. "Yes, yes; no doubt they're quite genuine; but do you know where they came from?"

Mr. Marshall rubbed his white-stubbled chin. "I could give you the information of course, madam, if you bought them. I do know where they came from. In fact, I negotiated the sale myself from the owner in whose family they've been since they were made by Hepplewhite himself. I can assure you their pedigree's quite in order."

"I should like to know the name," Lina said tonelessly.

Mr. Marshall hesitated, and then gave way in an access of confidence. "Well, quite between ourselves, madam, it was a member of the Aysgarth family. You know the name, of course?"

"Yes," said Lina, "I know the name. Thank you. I'll let you know if I want them."

She walked out of the shop.

Lina never said a word to Johnnie about the incident. In any case, she had his promise.

6

Janet Caldwell stiffened. "Surely that isn't Johnnie already?"

Lina wondered: Why does she dislike him so? How absurd she is.

Undoubtedly it was Johnnie.

His voice, raised to its merriest tones, came flooding through the drawing-room door as he rallied the grenadier-like parlourmaid, Ella's less prepossessing and more permanent successor.

Involuntarily Lina's face lightened. Janet had been rather heavy this afternoon. Johnnie's arrival was like a warm wind, driving thin academic ghosts away through keyholes and window fastenings.

He came impetuously into the room.

"Hullo, monkeyface! Hullo, Janet! Hullo, Janet! Hullo, monkeyface! Two pretty women and one pretty man; so who the deuce cares who also ran? Hullo, monkeyface, my sweetheart." He kissed Lina. "Hullo, Janet, my precious." He dabbed a kiss on Janet's un-expecting cheek.

"Johnnie," said Lina, laughing, "what is the matter with you? And why are you home so early?"

"It's a red-letter day," said Johnnie, at the door again.

"Ethel! Ethel! Ethel, look here, I only see two cups, two plates, and hang it all, only two saucers on the tea tray. Now, why is that, Ethel? Here I am, thirsting for tea, and you simply deny it me. You don't even provide a saucer for me, in case I'd like to lap. Is that necessary, Ethel? Is it wise, Ethel? Is it even kind?"

The grenadier giggled. "I didn't expect you'd be back, sir."

"But I am back! Good heavens, didn't you recognize me in the hall? Here I am, simply asking you to get me a cup, and you stand there arguing. Run along, Ethel, and bring me that cup at once."

Still giggling, Ethel departed.

"Johnnie darling, have you gone quite mad?"

"Not quite, Mrs. Aysgarth, my love. It was just the shock of seeing Janet here. Janet, did I really and truly kiss you just now, or was it a dream?"

"You did kiss me," said Janet, with a polite smile. "I'm sure I don't know why."

Johnnie dropped on one knee and struck a theatrical attitude with outstretched arm. "Because I love you. Be-cause I adore you. Miss Caldwell, forgive my bold words, but the time has come when I can no longer conceal my respectful passion. For long have I nourished, like a viper in my bosom, the hope that one day I might—— I'll tell you the rest another day." Johnnie rose with dignity and dusted his knee as Ethel entered with his cup.

Ethel departed, among inadequately stifled noises.

"Johnnie, *will* you tell me what's the matter with you?"

Johnnie put his hand into his coat pocket, pulled out an object, and dropped it into Lina's lap. "Have a nice necklace, darling? Have a diamond ring? Have a brooch? No, I think we'll give that to Janet, to stop her getting jealous of you. There's a fur coat for you in the car. There are some other things as well, but I can't quite remember what; I bought anything they put in front of me; but I think hats figured. I thought you'd rather choose some frocks for yourself. You can send the hats back if you don't like them. I was still sober enough to remember to insist on that."

"Are you drunk, Johnnie?" Lina demanded, staring with incredulous eyes at the jewelry in her lap.

"Pretty well," Johnnie admitted. "Don't look at it in that distrustful way, my poppet. It's a real diamond. I called in at Bournemouth on my way back. It's guaranteed genuine by the mayor and corporation." Bradstowe was a good deal nearer to Bournemouth than Upcottery was.

"But . . . ?"

Johnnie beamed at her. "You didn't perhaps know that the Grand National was run to-day? Well, I just happen to have backed the winner. At forty to one, my little monkeyface. Forty to one! What do you think about that?"

"Johnnie!" Lina was scarcely less excited herself. "How much have you won?"

"Hold tight, and I'll tell you. Four thousand of the best—and not one penny less."

"Not—four thousand *pounds?*" It was eight years' housekeeping.

"Four thousand *pounds*," said Johnnie, with conscious pride. "Oh, if you prefer it in shillings, eighty thousand of them."

"My sacred aunt," muttered Janet, who dressed herself on forty-five pounds a year.

Lina's breath had almost disappeared. "Johnnie!" she gasped. "I—can't believe it." Her practicality approached the incredible thing, slid off it, and finally gripped it. "What shall we do with it?"

"Do with it?" Johnnie echoed in surprise. "Why, blue it, of course."

7

They were still discussing what to do with it.

Janet had gone, without the brooch, which she utterly refused to accept; there had been a couple of hours' excited talk in the drawing room; they had gone upstairs to dress quite fifteen minutes after Lina's usual time; and the discussion was being continued through the open door between Lina's bedroom and Johnnie's dressing room.

Johnnie wanted to blue his windfall: Lina did not think it ought to be blued.

Lina was hampered in the discussion by the lavishness of Johnnie's generosity, and her own warm realization of it. His first thought when he got the news must have been for her. He had got straight into the car, it appeared, and driven madly into Bournemouth to buy her anything that came into his mind. The diamond in her ring was a magnificent one; Lina thought it must have cost two hundred pounds at least. The necklace had an emerald pendant; the brooch contained a fine pearl; the fur coat had proved to be mink; the car had been stuffed with hats and clothes for her to choose from. Lina was appalled, and at the same time intoxicated, by such recklessness on her behalf.

"But you haven't paid for all these things?" she had asked, bemused.

"Every single one of them," Johnnie had assured her.

"But where did you get the money? You said you wouldn't get the cheque till next Monday."

"Oh, I got the money all right."

Lina had been too muddled with happiness and dismay to find out how Johnnie had got the money.

It was surprising too for her to realize, as she had not done for quite a long time, how completely she had overlooked the fact that Johnnie had broken his promise. But there is such a difference between winning and losing bets that even when she did remember that fact, her reproaches had been only perfunctory.

"Johnnie, you promised me you'd never bet again."

"Oh, come, darling, you know you didn't really mean that."

"But I did. Of course I did."

"Would you rather I hadn't won this little packet?" Johnnie had grinned mischievously.

"I should have been very annoyed with you if you'd lost. What did you bet? At forty to one it must have . . . Johnnie, you betted a hundred pounds. Johnnie—a hundred pounds!"

"It was an absolute certainty," Johnnie pleaded. "I had it from the man who owns the animal. There wasn't any possibility of losing. It wasn't a bet at all; it was just dipping my hand into the bookie's pocket."

"Hum!" said Lina, trying hard to be severe.

"Besides," Johnnie had added inconsequently, "you can't count the Grand National. Everyone has a bit of a flutter on the National."

"But, Johnnie, you do promise me you'll never do anything like this again?"

"Of course, sweetheart," Johnnie had said easily. "This really was a special occasion. And what an occasion!"

Lina had been quite content to leave it at that.

And now, what was to be done with the money?

In any case, there were no longer four thousand pounds.

Johnnie now divulged that he had debts.

Not racing debts: just debts. He could now get them all cleared off. What debts? Oh, just debts. Some of them quite old ones, that Lina did not know anything about; yes, dating right from before their marriage. What did they amount to? Oh, well, a couple of thousand would cover the lot easily.

"Two thousand?" Lina said, taken aback. "You owed two thousand pounds that I never knew about?"

"What the mind doesn't know, the eyes don't cry over," Johnnie said gaily.

Lina had to laugh. "Johnnie, you're incorrigible."

In the end it appeared that, what with this and that, there would not be much more than eight hundred pounds to blue or not to blue.

"But you didn't spend twelve hundred on *me*," Lina called out, after a hurried mathematical exercise while she fastened her suspenders.

"No, but there's this." Johnnie strolled into the room doing up his braces. In his hand was a cheque.

"What's this, darling?"

"For those chairs. You remember?"

Lina looked at the cheque. It was for a sum exactly double that at which the chairs had been valued.

"Oh, Johnnie!"

She hugged him in a tempest of adoration. Johnnie did know how to make amends. Everything was wiped out now.

"There's the gong," said Johnnie. "Hurry up with your

frock, monkeyface; I hate cold soup. What are you going to put on?"

"My blue georgette? I was going to."

"Put on your black velvet. You look more adorable in that than anything."

"Do I, darling?"

Lina sang with happiness as she put on her black velvet.

8

Three days later they split the difference. Four hundred pounds was handed over to Lina, to do precisely what she liked with; and four hundred pounds was left for Johnnie to blue.

They went to the south of France on it, to Antibes.

Under Lina's guidance, a hundred pounds took and kept them there for three whole blissful weeks. Then Johnnie escaped from her, went over to Monte Carlo, and lost the rest in three hours.

"My poor idiot boy," Lina said comfortably as she shepherded a rueful Johnnie into the Paris train. "I only hope it will teach you not to gamble any more, that's all. If it does, I dare say it'll be cheap at the price." For, after all, it was Johnnie's money, for him to spend as he liked; and the three weeks had been utter bliss, with Johnnie sweeter to her than even he had ever been before; and it is tempting fate to draw out bliss too long.

"No more Monte Carlo for me," Johnnie replied with conviction.

Lina went back to England invigorated, expectant, and more in love with Johnnie than ever.

CHAPTER VI

MRS. NEWSHAM was a small, eager woman of Lina's own age, with a vivacity which she mistook for wit, just as she mistook her commonplace prettiness for beauty. As Janet, who did not like her, had once said, Freda Newsham never made the fatal mistake of underrating herself.

Lina did not like her very much either, but she was compelled to a grudging admiration. Freda Newsham had all the qualities which she herself would have liked to possess and knew she did not; though it is true that their possession did not seem to make Freda a really nice person. She was intensely sure of herself, she had unlimited aplomb, and she dominated her magnificent husband as the jockey dominates a race horse. Lina, however, would never have liked that.

The Newshams had arrived in Upcottery just a few months before the Aysgarths. As two newcomers, Lina and Freda had naturally gravitated together four years ago; and though, since Lina became really intimate with Janet, she had not seen so much of Freda, who also had other fish to fry, they dined in each other's houses three or four times in the half year.

The Aysgarths were dining with the Newshams one evening in the October that followed Lina's and Johnnie's truncated visit to the Riviera.

And Harry Newsham had boiled the port.

And Johnnie laughed.

And Freda, who could not bear to be laughed at, even vicariously through her husband, lost her temper.

"You idiot, Harry! Anyone would think we'd never had port before. What on earth did you want to put it in front of the fire at all for?"

"Take the chill off, you know," mumbled Harry Newsham, feeling his cavalry moustache as he looked unhappily at the steaming contents of the glasses. "Right thing to do with port, isn't it, Johnnie?"

"Absolutely," said Johnnie, with a far too obvious wink across the table at Lina. "Never ice the port."

"It'll be quite all right in a few minutes," Lina suggested, deprecating the wink but deprecating far more Freda's anger.

"Nonsense!" Freda snapped. "Get another bottle up, Harry. Thank goodness there are plenty in the cellar."

"All right, dear."

"And after Lina and I have left you," added Freda nastily, "you'd better get Johnnie to give you a few hints on how to deal with wines."

Harry edged apologetically out of the room.

He was a tall, well made man, who looked exactly like a cavalry officer. Actually he had inherited a cotton mill in Lancashire, sold out in the boom period after the war, and settled down on the proceeds (on the instructions of his wife) as a country gentleman. Having failed in this respect in the Midlands, he had caused himself (on the instructions of his wife) to be adopted as Liberal candidate for the constituency in which Upcottery was situated and had settled down there to try again (on the now somewhat acrimonious instructions of his wife).

The fresh bottle of port was opened and consumed, and Harry, with accentuated magnanimity, forgiven.

Lina and her hostess retired conventionally to the drawing room. Neither of them wanted in the least to go, but to go was the right thing; and in Freda's house the right thing was invariably done—by Freda, if not, it would appear, by Harry. Freda in her tweeds following hounds on foot was more absolutely right than any ladies' tailor-and-outfitter could have conceived.

Lina did not, however, think they would be alone long. It was Harry Newsham's habit to entertain his male guests, and indeed anyone else whom he could lure at any time into any secluded place, with a discourse upon Free Trade and, as a corollary, the dishonest iniquities of Tariff Reform: a subject in which he was distressingly interested. Harry really took politics seriously.

In her just overfurnished, or, as she herself called it, cosy, drawing room, Freda settled herself down on the big settee and lifted her feet onto the seat.

"Now, my dear," she said to Lina, in an easy chair on the other side of the fireplace. "Now we can have a really good gossip." Freda was very fond of the phrase. Her really good gossips consisted in talking as hard and as fast about nothing at all as she could possibly manage, while her presumed fellow gossiper put in a bare affirmative or negative in any vacant space she could find.

"Yes," said Lina, who did not like really good gossips but knew from experience that she was a good listener.

In deference to Lina's notorious tastes Freda at once began to talk brightly, and with an effect of inside knowledge, about books.

Freda, on her own statement, read simply everything. Naturally, therefore, she considered herself well read. She was most devastating about any author who came above her standards.

Lina listened, and agreed. It was always less trouble to agree with Freda than not.

Lina went on listening.

Often and often there fell from her hostess's lips some

emphatic statement with which, had it been Janet who had made it, Lina would have at once joined argument. But of course one could not argue with Freda. Freda was one of those women to whom the word "argument" is exactly synonymous with the word "quarrel." "Oh, well, my dear, don't let's *argue* about it, for heaven's sake," Freda would say; and Lina would long to box her ears.

She agreed now that neither of their husbands could be credited with any really fine literary perceptions.

"Though of course," said Freda, "I make Harry read anything I get from the library that's *really* good. The first-rate novelists, I mean: Wells, and Warwick Deeping, and so on. But I'm afraid they're rather lost on him, poor dear."

"Johnnie reads nothing but detective stories," said Lina.

"I know. Of course *I* never read detective stories."

"Oh, don't you?" It was not the first time Lina had heard this inept remark. She wondered why people who never read detective stories are so proud of the fact. "I love a good detective story."

"Oh, yes, my dear. I know you say that." Freda gave her a knowing smile. "How is your brother-in-law getting on with his new novel? Oh, my dear, I must tell you. I was talking to some people at the meet the other day— the Longthwaites; do you know them? Lady Longthwaite, it was, as a matter of fact—and of course she didn't know I knew your brother-in-law." Freda detailed at considerable length the incident and left Lady Longthwaite wallowing in her literary inferiority.

"Ha, ha," said Lina dutifully.

"By the way, talking of meets, how did Johnnie get on at Merchester last Tuesday?"

"Merchester?" Lina echoed stupidly.

"Yes, the races. We saw him there, but we didn't speak to him. I waved, but he was looking far too busy to wave back. I don't know whether he even saw us. Didn't he tell you? Then I suppose he didn't see us. My dear, we had a terrible day: lost simply *pounds*. I hope Johnnie came out of it better?"

Lina kept her head. "Oh," she said lightly, "I don't think he did so badly."

"Janet must have brought him luck." Freda could not keep a slightly malicious note out of her voice.

"Janet?" Just as Lina had never suspected that Janet might be jealous of Johnnie, so it had never occurred to her that Freda might be jealous of Janet. All she knew was that the two disliked each other, and rather more intensely than the difference between their temperaments seemed quite to warrant. "Janet? Oh, yes, I believe he did say she had."

Johnnie's indifference to Free Trade saved her. On a hint too open to be disregarded Harry had been forced to bring it with him to the drawing room.

"If we could only get the Tories to understand that simple fact," he was saying, as he opened the drawing-room door, "we might be able to——"

"Rather!" said Johnnie with enthusiasm. "I expect you're absolutely right, Harry. Anything on the wireless, Freda? My goodness, I envy you your set. We can't get anything but Daventry on our rotten little portable."

The wireless put an effective stop to Free Trade.

But not to Harry.

He got out his one-stringed fiddle and accompanied Jack Payne a grim half-bar behind the tune for the next two hours.

"Why," thought Lina despairingly, "do we put up with this sort of thing in the name of social intercourse?"

2

She tackled Johnnie in the car going home.

"Johnnie, have you been racing again?"

"Racing?" Johnnie repeated, with virtuous indignation. "Of course I haven't. Why?"

"Then what were you doing last Tuesday afternoon?"

"Last Tuesday afternoon?"

"That's what I said."

"Working, I suppose. What else should I have been doing?"

"Oh, Johnnie," Lina said impatiently, "don't bother to lie to me. You were at Merchester races last Tuesday. The Newshams saw you there. Don't go on pretending you weren't. You were with Janet, and I've only got to ask her."

"Oh!" said Johnnie, in a tone of understanding. "I couldn't think what you were getting at. Yes, of course I was there last Tuesday. I'd forgotten for the moment. I had to go over to Merchester on business, and just popped into the course to see the big race, and ran into Janet there. Of course."

"Johnnie!"

"What, darling?"

"Is that true?"

"Well, really, monkeyface . . ."

"That's all it was, and you haven't been betting again?"

"Good Lord, no. No more of that. I should think not. I didn't even have a bet last Tuesday. You sounded," said Johnnie in an injured voice, "as if you thought I'd broken my promise."

"Darling," said Lina penitently, "I did think so."

"I promised not to bet. I didn't promise never to go inside a race course again."

"No, of course not, darling."

"You really must trust me a bit more than that, mon-keyface."

"Yes, darling. I'm sorry."

"Oh, that's all right," said Johnnie magnanimously.

3

But just to be on the safe side Lina had a word with Janet.

Oddly enough, it was Janet herself who gave her the opportunity.

Janet had called for her to go for a walk, as she did quite often. They had not gone more than a few hundred yards before Janet said casually:

"I ran into Johnnie last week at Merchester races. Did he tell you?"

"Yes, I heard. Don't tell me you've taken to racing, Janet."

"Oh, no. Some friends of mine were going and offered me a lift in their car, so I thought I might as well, as they practically passed our door on their way. I'd never been to a race meeting before. It was quite amusing."

"Merchester's a long way from here. It's quite close to my home."

"Yes, it is a long way, I suppose," Janet agreed vaguely.

Lina thought: No, I won't ask her if Johnnie had a bet while he was with her. I believe him. He didn't.

She said:

"And how did you get on with Johnnie?"

"Perfectly well," Janet answered, with a little laugh. "I always do, don't I? In any case, I don't suppose I saw him for more than five minutes."

"Well, don't get bitten with the racing fever, Janet."

"I promise you I shan't do that. Why?"

"Oh, people do," Lina said slowly. "Johnnie was once."

"Was he? You never told me."

"No. He's got over it now of course, but . . ."

"What?"

"Well, if you ever do see him at a race meeting again," Lina said, rather desperately, "it would be the act of a friend to tell me. That's all."

Janet nodded. "I see. Serious, was it?"

"It might have been."

"All right, I will. In fact I can't think why I didn't say anything last time I saw you. I'd quite forgotten I ever saw him there—or for that matter, that I'd been myself. But of course I didn't know, then."

"No, of course not."

There was no need to say any more.

Lina was thankful for Janet's understanding, and her tac̣

She gave her arm a little grateful nip with her fingers and Janet smiled her comprehension of it.

Lina smiled back. She felt it was a wonderful thing to have a friend so completely in tune that everything really important could be said without words.

4

It was less than a week later that Lina missed her diamond ring: the ring Johnnie had given her when he had won his big bet that same spring.

Almost the same scenes were enacted as two years ago. Lina's room was turned out, the house ransacked, the servants questioned and cross-questioned, without result.

And now there was no Ella to suspect. The grenadier was far too stupid to be dishonest.

Lina was extremely upset.

The ring had been much more than a valuable diamond to her. It had been a constant symbol of Johnnie's generosity and thought for her. It had reminded her always, whenever she had allowed herself to get irritated with him, that on that great occasion it was she who had been in the front of his mind, and that his first impulsive way of giving expression to his exuberance had been to overwhelm her with presents. It had symbolized Johnnie's love for her.

And it had gone.

Johnnie, of course, was most sympathetic. He reminded her, as he had done before, that at any rate the ring was insured for its full value, so that it could be replaced identically. Lina agreed, and wept secretly, since for all her practicality she was a whole-hearted sentimentalist; and no substitute ring could mean the same to her as the very one that Johnnie himself had chosen and bought and handled and dropped, like a bit of crystallized love, into her lap. She almost wished, insanely, that it had never been insured at all, so that it could never be replaced.

The cook, under Lina's evident suspicion, gave notice and walked out of the house.

And then Lina made another startling discovery. Her ring was not the only thing that was missing.

When at last she was alert to the fact it was astonishing that she should never have noticed the absence of so many objects. The rooms now appeared almost denuded. Two Wedgwood figures from the drawing room, a pair of old brass candlesticks from the dining-room mantelpiece, a whole Sèvres dessert service from the store cupboard, a dozen other small things of value from various places: all had vanished. It was clear that there had been a thief in the house.

Johnnie was no less taken aback than Lina. He did not, however, think there could have been a thief in the house. It was his theory that someone must have got in from outside, someone who knew the value of such things, and taken what he wanted. Johnnie was most indignant at the idea. He was sure that the defaulting cook was somehow to blame: probably she had left the house empty one afternoon and the back door open.

He was, however, quite opposed to Lina's intention of calling in the police. Strongly opposed to it.

He explained that it was impossible to say when the articles had been taken, it was not even possible to furnish a full list of them, there would be endless trouble, and the police would do nothing. Why bother?

He insisted so strongly that it would be only a waste of everyone's time to call in the police that a horrid fear at last began to form in Lina's mind.

She paid a visit to Bournemouth, and to Mr. Marshall's curiosity shop.

To Mr. Marshall himself, by whom she asked to be served, she said: "I was wondering whether you have a nice old dessert service at a reasonable figure."

Mr. Marshall beamed. "Why, just as it happens, madam, I have. It only came in a matter of three weeks ago. Sèvres—a real beauty. Shall I show it you?"

"Please," said Lina.

Two minutes later she was looking at her own dessert service.

But the price was not reasonable. It was staggering. Mr. Marshall assured her, however, that even at that figure the service was a bargain. "And that doesn't give me any too much profit on what I had to pay for it, madam," he added.

Lina bought instead a pair of old brass candlesticks.

5

She put them on the dinner table that night in addition to the silver ones: one in front of herself and one in front of Johnnie.

When they had reached the dessert Johnnie smiled across the table at her. "Still feeling hipped about the ring, monkeyface? Poor old thing. Never mind: we'll get you a better one some day, when our ship comes home."

"Johnnie," Lina said abruptly, "have you noticed these candlesticks? I bought them to-day at Marshall's curiosity shop, in Bournemouth. Do you like them?"

Johnnie looked from her to the candlesticks and back again. He did not answer. The smile faded from his face, and he watched her.

"Mr. Marshall showed me a Sèvres dessert service too," Lina said slowly, dropping her words out one by one as if timing them between the thuds of her heart. "But it was too expensive."

Still Johnnie did not answer.

"Johnnie, how much did you get for my ring?"

Johnnie began to fiddle with a crumb of bread on the table.

He looked up at her. "It wasn't exactly your ring, darling, was it? I mean, not exactly."

"Wasn't it? I thought you gave it me."

"Yes, I know. But . . ." Johnnie jumped up suddenly, went round the table, and put his arms round Lina where she sat. "Monkeyface, I've had a hell of a time just lately."

Lina sat rigid in his embrace. "You've been betting again?"

Johnnie, his cheek against her hair, nodded his head.

"And lost?"

"Yes, a bit. During the last few weeks. But——"

"And had to steal things out of the house to pay up?"

"Oh, draw it mild, darling. One can't steal one's own things."

"They weren't yours. They were mine."

"Yes, but what's yours is mine, and what's mine's yours. You can't say they were more than half yours. Darling, I simply love the scent of your hair. It's——"

"Oh, damn the scent of my hair!" Lina suddenly threw off Johnnie's encircling arms and jumped up. "You needn't think you're going to get away with it like that, my lad. You've stolen a lot of things of mine, and I want to know what you're going to do about it."

Johnnie thrust his hands in his pockets and glowered at her. "Damn it, you'll be calling me a thief soon," he said sullenly.

"I do call you a thief!"

They held each other's angry eyes for a moment.

"And I," said Johnnie loudly, "call you a damned hard, stingy bitch—in bed or at board about as much use to a man as a cold in the head."

A torrent of rage obliterated all Lina's dignity. She snatched a book out of the bookcase and threw it with all her strength at Johnnie's head. But even as she had snatched it, she had instinctively chosen something that would not really hurt if it hit him.

It went at least two feet wide.

Johnnie caught it rather cleverly and stared at her. Then he burst into a shout of laughter, and handed the book back to her.

"Of all the rotten shots! Try again."

Lina ran out of the room, up the stairs, and into her bedroom. She locked the door, threw herself on the bed, and burst into tears.

Whatever Johnnie had done, whatever Johnnie ever might do, when she threw books at him she did not want them handed back to her.

She wanted to be shaken till the teeth rattled in her head.

6

"But, darling, I tell you it's the goods. There's a fortune in it. This has only been a run of bad luck. It *can't* fail in the end."

Johnnie was explaining his racing system to Lina. She had never seen him so excited over anything before.

"Surely you can see it must win in the end," he pleaded.

"You've been tyring this system how long?" Lina asked wearily.

"About six months. Look here, monkeyface, you must realize——"

"Ever since we came back from France?"

"Pretty well. It came out trumps at first, but——"

"Although you'd promised me you wouldn't bet any more?"

"Oh, well." Johnnie smiled away the seriousness of such a promise.

"And although you've always said since, whenever I asked you, that you weren't betting?"

"Look here, do you know why most wives deceive their husbands? Because their husbands try to ride 'em on too tight a rein. And then all the little wives say: 'Well, my dear, he did ask for it, didn't he?'" Johnnie's squeaky imitation of the erring but impenitent wife was most amusing. "Haven't you rather asked for it too, monkeyface?"

Lina did not smile. "But you're simply not fit to be trusted."

"That's what all the husbands say."

"When I make a promise I keep it," Lina said impatiently, "and I expect other people to keep theirs."

"Have another spot of whisky," said Johnnie.

He refilled her glass.

Lina sighed.

They had been over all this ground before. Johnnie seemed really to think that he had been quite justified in breaking his promises to her. He quite sincerely believed too that the untruths he had told her were not lies at all. "I'm not a liar," Johnnie had said indignantly; as if the fact of it being Johnnie who uttered the lie made it not a lie at all. In the same way Lina had been quite unable to make him understand that his filching of her belongings had been nothing more nor less than plain thieving. Johnnie was not a thief, therefore Johnnie could not thieve. It had perhaps, Johnnie admitted virtuously, been not quite playing the game; but thieving. . . . The idea just amused him. Johnnie was not a thief.

Jumping into the gap in the conversation, Johnnie began once more to expatiate on his system.

Lina did not listen. She was wondering what to do. If Johnnie were not cured of this fever he would leave them sooner or later, and probably sooner, without a possession to their names.

"So you see, one must have a certain amount of capital. That's been my trouble. You can't double up like that without something to fall back on; but if you do, you're absolutely bound to come out on top before long.

So you see what a pity it would be to have to chuck it now. Look here, monkeyface, what about your father? Couldn't you touch him for a spot, just so that I shan't have to spoil everything when my luck's beginning to turn?"

"No, I couldn't."

"I don't see why not. We never have touched him yet. Why not?"

"What? Oh, because I won't."

"It's devilish short-sighted of you," Johnnie grumbled. "I might win a packet any day now. Like I did before. It's a damned nuisance to be held up just for a spot of cash for the next day or two. Oh, well, I suppose it can't last forever. How old is he?"

"Father?" said Lina absently. "I don't know. About sixty-five, I suppose."

"Damn well time he popped it, then," said Johnnie, but under his breath. He added aloud: "Seriously, monkeyface, I wish you would touch him for a hundred or two. He could afford it easily enough."

"Doesn't all this betting take up a great deal of your time?" Lina asked abruptly. "You can't be doing much work nowadays."

"Doesn't interfere with that," Johnnie said easily. "Just one wire a day, that's all. Look here, darling, do listen. I don't believe you've got the hang of this system at all. You don't realize how absolutely safe it is, in the long run." He began to explain it all over again.

Lina had to forgive him before they went to bed. He was so much in earnest, and so gullible, and so young.

There was their usual grand reconciliation scene, with Johnnie alternating between pouring out more whisky and kissing her, and Lina crying and laughing at the same time. But she did not try to get another promise out of

Johnnie. She knew he would give it, glibly; and it would mean just nothing at all. She had got to find some more effective means of stopping Johnnie in his lunacy.

She decided, after she had lain awake three hours with Johnnie sleeping beside her, to speak to Captain Melbeck.

7

Although she had adopted it, because she had no choice, Lina heartily resented the responsibility which Johnnie, by his infantility, had passed over to her. She did not want to be responsible, for anything or anyone; she did not want to be responsible even for herself. She hated responsibility with its nagging unrest.

It was not at all fair.

A husband should be responsible for a wife. When she married, Lina had taken it for granted that she would be led, and she had been very ready to follow. Now she had to do the leading herself; and not merely leading, but driving. It was the impulse to shift at any rate some of the responsibility onto male shoulders, which after all should naturally bear it, that determined her to consult Captain Melbeck about Johnnie. In any case, he was some kind of a connection, so that there should be a family as well as an employer's interest.

She rang Captain Melbeck up the next day and asked him to lunch.

Captain Melbeck seemed oddly reluctant to come to lunch. He stammered excuses for every day that Lina suggested. But Lina, who could be as determined as anyone when she had bolstered herself up to the necessary pitch, broke through his defenses.

"It's very important," she said desperately. "I want to talk to you about Johnnie. If you won't come to lunch,

I suppose I shall have to come over to you, but it's awkward, because I haven't the car and I don't want Johnnie to know. Can't you possibly put off your engagement tomorrow and come to lunch? Or tea?"

"Johnnie won't be there?" Captain Melbeck said cautiously.

"No, no. I said he wouldn't. I want to talk about him to you."

Captain Melbeck promised to come to lunch the next day.

He came, a big, burly man with a cropped moustache, and eyed Lina with apprehension over his cocktail. Lina wondered, with some annoyance, why people were so often nervous of her, and what they would think if they knew just how nervous she was of them.

"It's very good of you to come," she said, with the forced brightness which still imposed itself on her when she was not at ease. "I'm so worried about what's going to happen to Johnnie."

"Oh, well," mumbled Captain Melbeck, "I told him I wouldn't prosecute, of course."

"What?" said Lina, startled.

"I told him I wouldn't prosecute," Captain Melbeck repeated uncomfortably. "He's paid some of it back already, too."

"What on earth are you talking about?" Lina asked sharply.

"Why about—don't you *know?*"

"Don't I know what?"

"Oh, hell," groaned Captain Melbeck. "I seem to have put my foot in it."

He did his best to leave things at that, but of course Lina got them out of him during lunch.

The long and short of it was that an unexpected audit

of the estate accounts had revealed that Johnnie had been helping himself during the last few months to cash amounting to nearly two thousand pounds. Captain Melbeck had had to discharge him more than six weeks ago.

"Six weeks!" echoed Lina, aghast. "But he's never said a word to me. He pretended he was still with you."

"Rotten business altogether," muttered her guest, and gloomily swallowed some hock the wrong way.

After he had gone Lina sat for two hours in her drawing room, too numbed even to weep, trying to face at last the fact that her husband was a liar, a thief, and an embezzler, and completely lacking in any sense of right or wrong.

8

Johnnie had lost his job, and Lina was too dispirited to try to find him another. With what Captain Melbeck knew, and with what Captain Melbeck would almost certainly hint to any other possible employer, the task in any case looked almost hopeless. They were reduced to Lina's own five hundred a year.

However, this state of affairs did not last for more than a few weeks.

Timing the event with singular neatness so far as his elder daughter and her husband were concerned, General McLaidlaw died that same Christmas, while Johnnie and Lina were staying in the house, rather suddenly, of arterio-sclerosis, and Lina came into an income of two thousand five hundred a year.

CHAPTER VII

Sitting in her kimono in front of her dressing table, Lina was doing her face. In the daytime she used nothing but a little powder on her nose, but for the evening lip stick, and sometimes the rouge pad too, were called in.

The door between the bedroom and Johnnie's dressing room was open.

"Is that you, darling?" Sounds had reached her alert ears of someone coming upstairs.

"Who else do you expect in your husband's dressing room?" Johnnie's voice answered cheerily. "Young Caddis-worm?"

"You'll have to hurry."

"Plenty of time. I wanted to go over the vines again."

There was not really plenty of time, but though Johnnie always came up late to dress, he was never late down.

Lina took off her wrapper and walked over to the doorway in her step-ins. It was what she had been waiting for.

There was no need for her to do so now, but Lina still made all her own underclothes. She enjoyed fine sewing. She had put on this evening for the first time a new set that had just been finished, and which Lina privately thought was rather successful.

She leaned in the doorway, a hand on either jamb. "Did Ethel put out a shirt for you?"

"Yes." Johnnie, fitting studs into the shirt, looked up at her with a smile. "Hullo! Those the new knick-knacks? I say!"

"Nice?" said Lina, spreading out the little peach skirt.

"The best ever," said Johnnie, with complete conviction. "Turn round and let's see them properly. Yes, you've hit the mark this time, and no mistake. You look as wicked as a French farce. Clever little devil, aren't you? Come and be kissed in 'em."

"Do I really look wicked?" Lina asked happily, under Johnnie's kiss.

"As wicked as they make 'em," Johnnie assured her.

She went back to her bedroom in a glow of satisfaction. How many husbands, she wondered, still take an interest in their wives' undress after six years of marriage?

But Johnnie never failed her in that way. Dress or undress, he was still as interested in her appearance as on their honeymoon: and still as enthusiastic when she looked nice. And he still told her how pretty she was. Lina knew, better than ever, that she was not pretty (though she did not consider she looked anything like her thirty-five years), but she adored Johnnie to tell her so. And Johnnie did.

Whatever Johnnie had done, or been once, Lina knew, as well as she knew the alphabet, that he had never once since their wedding looked beyond her at any other woman. She had that, at any rate, to be thankful for.

She had other things now, too.

Since that terrible time, two years ago, when Johnnie had lost his job at Bradstowe for what had been nothing less than sheer dishonesty, explain it as he might, and had, Johnnie had given her no more worry. He had had a fright, a real fright; and it had done him all the good in the world. He might still be a little hazier than most people upon the moral side of *meum* and *tuum,* but he realized at any rate what other people thought about it:

and what they might do if his practice differed from their precept.

Since that day the contents of Dellfield had remained undiminished.

Of course Johnnie did no work nowadays, but that no longer mattered. The money was not needed, and technical idleness had not seemed to hurt him. Not that Johnnie ever was really idle. He had taken to gardening, and a few of the fields surrounding Dellfield had been bought, which Lina had stocked and Johnnie did his best to farm; he was most interested in a line of pedigree cattle with which he was experimenting, and which were to pay better than any other line of cattle. Johnnie's cattle kept him busy, and the losses on them did not cost Lina more than a hundred or two a year at most.

Besides, Johnnie could not afford to take any more risks.

He was a most important man nowadays: a member of the county council, a J. P., and all sorts of other things that a country gentleman ought to be. Captain Melbeck had been more than fair. He had breathed no word to anyone else of Johnnie's peculations; the money had been repaid; the affair was forgotten. And he had most conveniently been in Africa when Johnnie had been made a county councillor and a J. P., so that no opportunity was afforded to his conscience of becoming difficult.

Johnnie the county councillor, Johnnie the J. P., had nothing more to fear from that old, now almost incredible spectre of Johnnie, the dishonest steward.

But for all that Lina kept a controlling hand on the purse strings.

She would probably have done so in any case, for she was exceedingly jealous of her own possessions; but she had been too badly frightened to take the smallest risk.

Johnnie, of course, had wanted to look after her capital for her. He had promised investments, just as safe as the government securities in which it lay, that would bring in a certain ten per cent. He had begged hard for just a couple of thousands with which to speculate on his own account. ("Don't you see, the loss of it couldn't hurt us in any case, monkeyface, and I might make a fortune.")

But Lina had been firm. She made Johnnie what she considered a more than generous personal allowance, of five hundred a year; over the rest, and over the capital, she kept complete control. Johnnie had sulked about it for weeks, at the beginning, but Lina had shown surprising firmness.

In the end Johnnie had accepted it.

Lina wished sometimes that he had not. It went against all her canons that a husband should be content to live, in apparent idleness, on his wife's income. This point of view apparently never occurred to Johnnie. He took it for granted that he should do just that. Lina had never suggested that he should try to earn enough money of his own at any rate to keep him in cigarettes, because it was up to Johnnie to make the suggestion himself; but she was sure that if she had, Johnnie would have been quite genuinely surprised; he would have pointed out that they did not need the money in the least. And yet no one could have called Johnnie spineless.

He was still the most popular man in the county.

As Janet once said to her, Lina was as proud of him as if he had ever done anything to deserve it.

She patted and pulled her frock into place, and glanced at the watch on her wrist. There were five minutes before the first arrival might be expected.

"I'm going down, Johnnie."

"Right-ho! Who did you say were coming?"

"The Newshams, Janet, and Martin."

"Good. Young Caddis will argue with Harry, and I shan't have to pretend to be listening."

Lina sped downstairs and into the kitchen.

"Everything all right, Lily?"

"Yes,'m, quite all right." Lily beamed through her glasses. She had a right to beam complacently. She was a very good cook, and she knew it. Lina had always got on very well with her during the two years of their acquaintance. They taught each other new and exciting dishes, and experimented in making them. Lily would always ask, after Lina had been out to dinner, whether anything unexpected had been in the menu, and if so how Lina thought it had been made. Lily really enjoyed cooking.

Lina lifted the lid of the saucepan containing the soup and sniffed at it. Lily handed her a spoon. "Just a touch more salt, I think, Lily." There was no need to look at the birds inside the oven; Lily never omitted to baste them enough.

Everything seemed quite satisfactory.

"Remember, Alice," Lina said to the parlourmaid, who was young and not yet completely trained (the grenadier had left to be married six months ago), "don't bring round the tray for the soup cups until everyone's emptied them. It looks so bad for you to stand and wait at somebody's elbow."

"Yes, madam," said Alice seriously. She contracted her eyebrows in an effort to remember never to wait at a diner's elbow for his soup cup. Alice was very willing not merely to learn, but to please her mistress. Lina never seemed to have the trouble with her servants that some of her friends in Upcottery had. She put it down to the fact that she paid them more.

She hurried along to the dining room and gave the table a long, critical look.

Everything here seemed quite satisfactory too. She gave the flowers in the centre of the table a little perking up and moved a dish of salted almonds out of the exact symmetry with its counterpart in which Alice had carefully put it.

In the drawing room everything was not so satisfactory. There were no cocktails standing on the Queen Anne bureau. Johnnie had come in too late to mix them.

With a cluck of annoyance, Lina hurried back to the dining room.

"Details, details, details!" she thought, as she hastily poured together orange juice, gin, and the vermouths. "That's what women's lives are made up of. Nothing but silly little details. Shirts, soup, flowers, powdering noses, mixing cocktails, telling Alice things, talking to people one doesn't want to talk to, about things one doesn't want to talk about—nothing but details; nothing lasting. That's why we never get anywhere."

She sipped her mixture, and her expression grew more serious.

"I wonder if I've put enough gin in this."

2

> "*Monna Lisa, oh, Monna Lisa,*
> *There's such temptation,*
> *And aggravation, and guile,*
> *In your little smile,*"

sang Johnnie, as he put the record on the gramophone. "Yes, I saw it in Murdoch's, and I got it at once, for you, Janet."

Janet smiled painstakingly.

Martin Caddis uttered a loud laugh. He had had just a little too much of Johnnie's impeccable port. "You call her 'Monna Lisa,' Aysgarth?"

"Yes. It's her smile. It's very disturbing. I never know whether she's laughing with me or at me." He set the needle on the record.

"How absurd you are, Johnnie," Lina laughed.

Janet continued to smile painstakingly.

"Dance with me, Janet." Johnnie's twinkling eyes taunted her.

"No, thank you, Johnnie. I never dance so soon after dinner."

"Not even with me?"

"Not even with you."

Lina made a note to tell Johnnie that he really must not tease Janet in public. He had been doing it all the evening. Janet did not understand teasing.

She went to Janet's rescue. "Janet, have you heard about Martin's novel? He's found a publisher for it."

"Have you really, Martin?"

Johnnie turned to the Newshams, who were sitting together a little aloofly, on the couch. "Bring your one-stringer, Harry?"

"Yes," Harry Newsham said, not without eagerness. "It's in the hall."

"Good!" said Johnnie, very heartily. "We must have it in soon."

"He would bring it," Freda Newsham interjected. "I told him nobody would want to be bored with it, but he insisted."

"I should hope so," Johnnie replied perfunctorily. "What did you think of the run last Tuesday, Harry? A corker, wasn't it?" Johnnie was able to hunt now.

Freda Newsham somewhat elaborately turned her shoulder towards him and yawned.

By the open window Lina, Janet, and Martin were discussing Martin's novel. Martin himself, a short young man with lots of fair hair, always untidy, and a very large head, who stammered when he was excited, was rapidly approaching the stammering stage. His own novel always excited Martin tremendously.

He had first told Lina the story of it five years ago. On hearing that she was the sister-in-law of Cecil he had told it to her again. He continued to tell it to her at intervals, until he began to write it. Then he brought it to her, chapter by chapter. Lina had found it far too long-winded and very dull. She had not told Martin so.

Martin, thus established as Lina's literary protégé, came to Dellfield a great deal. Lina had encouraged him, at first. It flattered her to have a young man hanging on her criticisms, and accepting her judgment as final, to say nothing of acting as Mæcenas to the young white hope. Martin would argue fiercely with Janet when, as not seldom happened, she disagreed with Lina. Johnnie, whom Martin frankly bored, laughed at her, called Martin "the Caddis-worm," and made no objections on finding him so often deep in earnest discussion with Lina on Higher Things when he came back from work.

A year or more ago, through Lina's intercession with Cecil, Martin had been offered quite a good post on one of the more serious weeklies, and since then Lina had not seen so much of him. She had not been unthankful.

Stammering with excitement, Martin explained to Janet the alterations he had made since she last read the manuscript. Lina of course had been kept informed of them by letter. Her attention wandering, she turned, to find that Freda had joined them. On the couch Johnnie and Harry were still talking hunting shop.

Freda listened for a few moments with an expression of intelligent corcentration. Then, finding that the young author continued to confine himself to Janet, let the expression slip and turned to Lina.

"Let's walk round the garden, shall we? It's quite warm, for September. I don't seem to have seen you for ages. I've been longing for a real gossip again."

They edged past the other two out through the window.

Freda linked her arm through Lina's and exclaimed loudly at the gladioli, still obstinately resisting autumn and dimly to be seen, standing at attention like a particoloured platoon, in the darkening twilight. But Freda's gladioli, it immediately transpired, were taller, stronger, and less ready to fade.

"Are they really?" said Lina.

The two women paced, gleaming wraiths to Janet and Martin, round the neat gravel paths.

"What on earth," said Freda abruptly, "is the matter with Johnnie this evening?"

"Johnnie?" Lina echoed, surprised. "Nothing, so far as I know. Why?"

"He's been positively rude to me all the evening."

"Has he? I'm awfully sorry, Freda. Are you sure? I never noticed . . ."

"No, my dear. You wouldn't." There was a really vicious edge to Freda's voice.

Lina wondered what on earth was the matter with her, not with Johnnie. Johnnie had not been rude to her in the least. He had not taken very much notice of her. Perhaps that was the trouble. It was Freda's enormous vanity.

"I'm getting sick of this place. Thank goodness I'm going up to town the day after to-morrow, for a week."

"Are you?" Lina said enviously. There was no reason why Lina should not go up to town for a week too, if she wanted; but somehow she never did. At the back of her mind, though she refused to recognize it, was the feeling of wardership. Johnnie was quite all right now, of course; but still—better not leave him.

"Yes. Charlie Bowes—I've told you about him, haven't I?—is going to be up, and wanted me to join him."

"Oh, yes." Lina accepted this surprising statement quite calmly. Freda had half-a-dozen men friends whom she favoured with her society in London, in return for theatres, dinners, dances, and attention. She stayed at one hotel, and her escort of the period at another. Freda was very insistent that everything was quite all right. Besides, Harry knew all about it and didn't mind in the least. Lina, who considered the arrangement extremely undignified, to put it at its mildest, thought that probably Harry had no option.

"I'm looking forward to it. I like Charlie. He's tremendously fond of me, of course. Yes, it'll be quite nice to get a little attention, for a change."

"Freda, how absurd you are. Nobody could be more attentive than Harry. He's positively maudlin, for a husband."

"I wasn't thinking of Harry."

Good heavens, Lina thought, was she thinking of Johnnie? Surely she can't be falling in love with Johnnie after all this time. If so, she's got a poor chance.

She smiled into the growing darkness. A very poor chance! Johnnie had always said that he never saw Freda without wanting to smack her, hard. He had even implored Harry, in Freda's presence, to smack his wife, hard and often. Johnnie did not like Freda.

That was a funny thing about the country, Lina reflected idly. Joyce, in London, only had for friends people she liked. In the country one does not necessarily like one's friends at all. They are one's friends because they are there; and though, of course, one does not detest them, one rarely likes them. However, this arrangement does provide something to talk about; and heaven knows, in the country that is needed badly enough.

Out of this evening's gathering, for instance, only she and Janet, and perhaps she and Martin Caddis, really liked one another. The rest were either indifferent, or friendly on the surface and never missing a chance of saying something nasty in the others' absence, like Freda and Janet. And yet one asked them all to dinner, as a matter of course.

Freda and Janet . . .

And now, it seemed, Freda and Johnnie.

How absurd!

"How absurd!" said Lina.

"What's absurd now?"

"Why, your saying that Johnnie had been rude to you this evening." Lina realized that, unthinkingly, she had spoken a rather tactless thought aloud; but, committed, still more tactlessly amplified it.

"I assure you, it wasn't absurd in the least." Freda was beginning to breathe quickly.

She's really annoyed! thought Lina.

"Johnnie's never rude to anyone. Except intentionally."

"Thank you. Then it was intentional."

"But, my dear Freda, there wasn't any rudeness." Lina was getting irritated herself. The woman really was a fool.

"No?" Freda was silent for a moment. "Then I suppose if he wasn't rude to me, he was rude to Janet?"

"What do you mean? I simply don't understand you."

"No, I can quite believe that. Well, all I'll say is that I was under the impression that Janet and Johnnie didn't like each other any too much."

"Nor they do. At least, Janet doesn't like Johnnie. I'm sure I can't imagine why."

"And yet Johnnie calls her Monna Lisa and buys gramophone records for her?"

Lina paused for a moment, to control her temper. "Freda," she said coldly, "don't you think you're making rather an idiot of yourself?"

"Thank you," Freda returned angrily. "That comes pretty well from *you*."

"What do you mean?"

"Oh, nothing."

They walked a dozen yards in silence.

"I saw your maid Ella, the other day," Freda said, more calmly. "You remember her? The one you had here first."

"Oh, yes. Did you?" Lina recognized the olive branch, and accepted it instantly. Her tempers were often matters of seconds only. "How's she getting on?"

"She's married. I believe she married soon after leaving you. Why don't you go over and see her? She lives at Pensworthy. Her husband's got a grocer's shop there." Pensworthy was a small town, perhaps twenty miles away.

"I might call in one day, when we're going through in the car," Lina said, without enthusiasm. Ella was connected in her mind with an unpleasant period. She had no wish to see her again.

"She was a pretty girl, wasn't she?"

"Yes, quite."

"She's got a little boy now. About five years old."

"Has she?" Lina wondered why Freda should be apparently so interested in the almost forgotten Ella and her new appurtenances.

"If I were you," said Freda quite passionately, "I should go over and see her, Lina."

3

The Aysgarths spent Christmas that year, as usual, at Lina's old home. Joyce and Cecil were there too, with the children. Mrs. McLaidlaw was getting rather feeble now, and everyone was as kind to her as possible. She still lived at Abbot Monckford, but since the General's death and the inheritance which had passed to his daughters there was barely enough money to keep the place up, and half the house was closed. Mrs. McLaidlaw had a little money of her own, strictly tied up, of course, as women's money was, when she had married, which would pass to her own side of the family when she died.

It would have been rather a melancholy little gathering but for Johnnie. He kept everyone's spirits up. Joyce's children, Robert and Armorel, adored him, and he seemed scarcely less fond of them. They never left his side except when forced, and then they had to be prised away.

While they were there Johnnie asked Lina, in his insinuating way, to raise his allowance.

"But why, darling?" Lina asked. "It isn't as if you'd got any expenses. You spend it all on yourself. Why do you want more?" It was Christmas night, and they were in bed, comfortably full of turkey and plum pudding and good-will.

"I have got expenses, monkeyface," Johnnie said, stroking her hand. "I keep the car up, and all that. Silly little tiny soft hand you've got, haven't you? I wonder you can ever do anything with it at all, it's so small."

"What does the car cost you?"

"To run? Oh, I suppose about three hundred a year, with everything."

"Three hundred?" Lina repeated, astonished.

"Quite that. Probably a bit more."

"But that's all it cost new."

"Cars are devilish expensive things," opined Johnnie. "And I've got lots of other expenses, of course."

"What?"

"Well, it costs me a good bit, being on the county council. I could chuck that, though, if we're hard up."

"No, of course you mustn't, darling. You know I like you to be on the county council. But still—five hundred, just for yourself."

Johnnie rubbed his nose against her ear. "It costs me half that to hunt. Don't be a mean little monkeyface. You can afford it."

"Darling!" Lina turned her head and kissed him. "But I'm not so sure that I can. How much do you want?"

"I can't do on much less than a thousand," said Johnnie cheerfully.

"Johnnie!" Lina withdrew from him sharply. "You're mad."

"Too much?" said Johnnie, in a resigned voice.

"I should think it is too much. You don't understand what that house costs, my lad."

"Well, make it seven-fifty. I can always chuck hunting, if you're so keen for me to stop on the council."

"But darling, I don't want you to chuck hunting." Lina softened at once before Johnnie's disappointment.

"Must. You don't understand what hunting costs, my girl." Johnnie, who disliked being called "my lad," always retorted with "my girl." Then Lina would remember he disliked it and feel penitent.

"Well, we can't decide now. We'll go into the figures when we get home, and I'll see what can be done." Lina hated going into figures, but she could not quite believe that running a car, being on the county council, and hunting, could cost a thousand a year and leave nothing over for cigarettes.

In the end Lina took over the car, which cost her just forty pounds a year, and Johnnie got six hundred.

After all, she could afford it. She spent very little on herself, and she wanted Johnnie to be happy.

4

Lina stared at the cheque. Then she put it down on her breakfast tray and read the letter again.

The Southern Counties Bank, Ltd.,
Culhampton,
Dorset.

Mrs. J. H. C. Aysgarth,
Dellfield,
Upcottery.

Dear Madam:
We enclose the cheque which was presented yesterday for payment by Mr. J. H. C. Aysgarth for verification of your signature, which appears to us to differ from your normal signature.

We would also call your attention to the fact that there are not sufficient funds in your current account at the moment to meet so large a sum.

Yours faithfully,
The Southern Counties Bank, Ltd.

The cheque was for £500.

Johnnie had taken to forgery.

5

Lina did not see him all day.

She realized that he would have known that the bank would communicate with her, and he had been afraid to face her. He had probably tried to intercept the letter by the first post, not expecting that the bank would send it over by a special messenger; when there was no letter, he must have thought they would telephone. He had run away.

The special messenger meant that the bank knew. The bank knew that Johnnie was a forger.

Lina had done her best. She had written to the bank that the signature was quite in order, the difference being due to the fact that she had sprained her thumb, but that as there were not sufficient funds to meet the cheque she was cancelling it.

All day long she repeated to herself:

"He goes down to two hundred a year for this."

He could give up hunting, he was not fit to remain on the county council, she did not care about the car. She felt she did not really care about anything, now.

But Johnnie should pay for it. Johnnie should be cut down to two hundred a year. That was settled.

She spent the day between tears and rage.

Johnnie did not come back till after she was in bed.

All day, while she repeated to herself Johnnie's punishment, she had visualized the scene. This time she would stand no nonsense. This time she would be absolutely firm. Not angry: it was simply no use being angry with Johnnie: it was no more good being angry with

Johnnie than with a puppy that steals a chop off the kitchen table. But puppies have to be trained, and Johnnie had got to be trained too. And when puppies grow up into dogs and have lapses, they have to be punished, for their own good.

Lina, weeping with disappointment that Johnnie had not been trained after all, realized that the only hope for him lay in her own firmness.

She would not be harsh with him. She would try hard to be kind, and sympathetic, and understanding. She would not let her bitterness come to the surface. But Johnnie must be taught that dishonesty simply does not pay.

It seemed very hard to Lina that she, of all the world, must teach him.

She made up the speeches she would say, going through them over and over again until she had them completely by heart. She knew the expressions she would wear, she saw exactly the expressions on Johnnie's face. Johnnie would not say much. He would be penitent, as usual, and probably try to blarney her. She heard him blarneying, with the exact words that he would use. But she would not be blarneyed. Gently, but very firmly, she would make him understand that he must be punished; and she would cut him down to two hundred a year.

Over and over again she rehearsed what she would say.

When at last she heard Johnnie come into his dressing room she felt quite sick with nervousness.

Her heart thumping unbearably, she lay and listened to him moving about. He seemed neither hurried nor dawdling, just normal.

Then he came into the bedroom, in his pajamas.

He smiled at her, mischievously, quite impenitently.

"Well, monkeyface? Heard the grim news?"

She sat up in bed, looked at him for a moment, her mouth trembling, and then burst into tears. "Oh, *Johnnie!*"

Johnnie took her in his arms, and she clung to him. He kissed her repeatedly.

"Poor old thing. I'm a rotter, aren't I? It's tough luck on you, monkeyface. But I really was in a hell of a hole."

"Oh, Johnnie, how could you?"

Lina knew that she would never utter a single one of her careful speeches, never cut Johnnie down to two hundred a year, never punish him at all.

6

Johnnie was in a hell of a hole.

Lina gave him four of the five hundred pounds he wanted.

Johnnie volunteered a passionate promise never to get in a hell of a hole again.

CHAPTER VIII

LINA had been extremely disappointed that she and
Johnnie had no children. She had wanted a child, badly.
Now she began to think that perhaps it was not a bad
thing that there were none. It would be terrible if Johnnie's children turned out like Johnnie.

General McLaidlaw had been right. The Aysgarth
stock was rotten. It was a pity that its rottenness had not
come out in Johnnie physically, instead of providing a
warped mind for his sound body.

Johnnie of course was very quiet for a week or two
after the episode of the cheque, grateful for his four
hundred pounds and most attentive to Lina. Then gradually (Lina could see it happening) the money became a
right instead of a favour, and Johnnie rapidly began to
forget that he had ever made an attempt, and a very
childish attempt, at forgery. Lina wondered desperately
whether she had marred forever when she might have
made him, or whether her weakness had really been wis-
dom in disguise.

It was the childishness of Johnnie's crimes that seemed
to her so pathetic.

If they had not been so very amateurish, she might
have found the strength to be sterner with him. To the
trained eye of a bank cashier, his effort at forgery must
have been ludicrous; the theft of her chairs was bound
to come out almost at once, for the feeble story about
the American would have been torn to shreds the moment the police were called in; if he had thought for a

moment, he could not have hoped to conceal his dismissal from Bradstowe for more than another week or two at the most. Johnnie had seemed to commit his misdemeanours in the same spirit of light-hearted irresponsibility as that in which he teased Janet over a dinner table.

Lina could only hope, intensely, that the tale of them was now at last at an end.

In any case, Johnnie, who had appeared at first really to understand this time the enormity of his offense, had quite got over it by the time Freda Newsham came back from London.

Freda had been up in town for a fortnight or more.

Charlie Bowes had still been there; and then, when Charlie himself had to go, Archie had come up, on purpose to see her, and of course, her dear, she couldn't let Archie down, could she? She meant, not when Archie was as devoted to her as he notoriously was.

"Of course not," said Lina.

So Freda had come over in her car, on a nice March morning, to have a really good gossip about it all.

Having talked about herself for an hour by the clock, she asked after Johnnie.

"He's all right," said Lina. "He's taken the car over to Bournemouth to have something done to it."

"What?"

"Good heavens, I don't know. Don't ask me anything about cars' insides. I can't bear them."

"I can do any running repairs myself. My dear, I don't think anyone should drive a car at all who can't."

"Well, I don't drive a car," Lina said brightly. "What about a cocktail?"

"My dear, I should simply love one. You make the best cocktails I know. I wish you'd teach Harry one day, he's so stupid about drinks."

"Nobody should drink a cocktail who can't mix one," said Lina, and went off to give orders that there would be two to lunch after all.

Freda would talk about Johnnie at lunch. Lina did not want to discuss Johnnie with Freda in the least, but Freda continually brought the conversation back to him.

Lina got a little irritated, and, as always, showed it. It seemed to her that Freda spoke of Johnnie in a positively proprietary way. Her jealousy of Janet, whom she was now pleased to assume to be a really close friend of Johnnie's, was quite plain.

She resented Lina's irritation, and responded to it with exasperation of her own. Lina, never slow to take up the tone of anyone with whom she was talking, grew exasperated too. By the end of lunch the two were openly snapping at each other.

How absurd we are, Lina thought as she poured out coffee in the drawing room. I don't like Freda, and I'm sure she doesn't like me; but why need we show it? I shouldn't take her ridiculous remarks about Johnnie seriously.

She began to talk, a little too brightly, on impersonal subjects; but Freda still remained curt.

Then Freda glanced at her wrist watch, and said:

"My dear, I was quite forgetting. I've simply got to run over to Pensworthy this afternoon. Why don't you come with me?"

"Pensworthy?" said Lina. It seemed an odd place for an errand.

"Yes. I promised I'd go this afternoon. You've got nothing to do."

"If you're going to call on people . . ."

"No, no. It's only to a shop. Something Harry wanted, and he says he can only get it there."

"I should have thought that anything one could get in Pensworthy one could get better in Bournemouth."

"It's a particular man," Freda said vaguely. "Anyhow, I've got to go. Come with me."

"Well, I don't know," Lina said weakly. There were plenty of things she would rather do than go over to Pensworthy with Freda. There was a new book from the library for instance . . .

But Freda was determined that she should go, so Lina took the easiest line and went.

Freda seemed preoccupied on the journey.

When they reached Pensworthy she parked the car on one side of the little town's broad street and jumped out. Lina followed.

"I shan't be a minute," Freda said. "Oh, look: we've stopped right outside Ella's shop. You'd like to have a word with her, wouldn't you? I'll pick you up there when I'm ready." Before Lina could answer she had hurried off down the street.

As it seemed determined for her that she should call on Ella, Lina walked to the shop which Freda had indicated. It was a shabby little affair, with a board above the small window which announced that J. Banks, provision merchant, was licensed to sell also cigarettes and tobacco. Lina opened the door, which caused a bell above it to utter a sharp ping! and passed into the rather dim interior.

In answer to the ping! a young woman came leisurely out from the room behind the shop.

"How are you, Ella?" said Lina graciously. "You remember me, I expect? I heard you were living here, and——"

"Lawks!" said Ella, and rubbed her hands nervously on her dress. "It's Mrs. Aysgarth."

"Yes." There seemed very little to say. Lina looked hurriedly round the shop for something to buy instead. "Yes, so you're married now, Ella?"

"Yes, Mrs. Aysgarth."

"I hope you're getting on well here?" Lina's eyes roamed vaguely over a stack of tinned fruit to a string of onions hanging from a nail.

"Yes, thank you, Mrs. Aysgarth. It's—it's a bit of a struggle, of course, in these times; but everyone's the same, nowadays, aren't they?"

"Yes, things are certainly in a very bad way everywhere." Lina wondered why Ella should be so extremely nervous. She used not to be of the nervous type.

"And—is Mr. Aysgarth quite well?" Ella asked in a rush.

"Quite, thank you." Lina, unable to decide whether it would be tactless to buy something at once and put an end to this inane conversation, racked her mind for something to say. "I hear you've got a little boy now, Ella?"

Ella went positively pale. "Wh-who told you that?" she stammered.

"Why, Mrs. Newsham. You remember her? Is your little boy here? I should so much like to see him."

"He's out." Ella discharged the words quite breathlessly.

Lina received a definite impression that Ella did not wish her to see the child. "Oh, what a pity," she said, a little puzzled but indifferent. "Well, Ella, there are one or two things I want for the house, and I should like to get them here."

She bought a pound's worth of assorted groceries.

Ella, who seemed to have got over her nervousness, was grateful, but not unduly.

Lina noticed that she kept glancing a little apprehensively towards the door. There's something wrong here, she thought: it looks as if the husband was a bad lot; anyhow, it's none of my business.

While Ella was doing up the package, the shop door opened and a small boy came in. He marched up to the counter behind which Ella was standing.

"I bin up to Willie Brooks's, mum," he announced. "They'm got a new calf."

A ray of sunlight, coming through the dusty window, fell directly on his face.

In one glance Lina understood everything—Freda's hints, Ella's nervousness, everything.

She got out of the shop somehow.

2

When fate is ready for something, she piles up her effects as lavishly as ever Mr. C. B. Cochran did.

Lina had left word at home that she would not be in to tea, as she would be going on to Mrs. Newsham's. Instead she had asked Freda, quite calmly, to excuse her as she had a headache. Freda, looking a little worried now, took her back to the front gates of Dellfield. They spoke very little on the hour's journey, and neither of them referred to the subject which was bursting both their minds.

Lina let herself into the house very quietly. She wanted no one to know that she had come back. She intended to go up to her room and think and think. Till now she had been unable to do that.

To reach the stairs she had to pass the drawing-room door. It was just open, and from inside came the sound of voices. Lina paused instinctively to learn who was there.

There was Johnnie's voice, and then there was Janet's. At first Lina did not take in what they were saying.

"Darling, of course you can stop to tea. You didn't know she was going to be out."

"But it looks so bad. She's sure to hear about it."

"Well, what does that matter, my little Janey? Surely I know you well enough to be able to ask you to pour out my tea."

"But I'm supposed not to like you. Oh, Johnnie, it's been difficult to keep that up these last months."

"My precious!"

There was the sound of a kiss. Of kisses.

Then Johnnie said:

"It's all right about next Wednesday?"

"Yes. But . . ."

"But what, my Janeykins?"

"I'm so afraid we shall be caught one day. I know so many people in Bournemouth. And so do you."

"Sweetest, it's all right so long as we don't go to the flat together. Nobody ever gets a chance of seeing us together. Honestly, it's as safe as houses. Besides—you want to come, don't you?"

"Johnnie! Need you ask that?"

"I want to hear you say it."

Lina crept upstairs.

3

That evening it all came out.

By an effort of which she would not have believed herself capable, Lina sat through dinner. She could not eat more than a mouthful. To Johnnie's inquiries she said that she had a bad headache. It almost made her begin to cry again to hear him asking with such solicitude, as if he was really fond of her.

She felt utterly crushed.

There was no anger against Johnnie or against Janet. Things were too serious for anger. All she knew was that the bottom had dropped out of life. It was the end of everything.

After dinner she went up to her room again and sat for what seemed hours in the chair by the window. She could not think, she could not plan. Her mind was numbed with misery. It was simply the end. All she had worked for, all her forbearance, all her struggles against Johnnie's worse nature, had gone for just nothing.

She sat on, in the dark.

Johnnie came up and turned on the light.

"Poor old monkeyface. Still feeling rotten? Why don't you go to bed? Shall I bring you up a spot of whisky or something? Might do you good." He came to her chair and made as if to embrace her.

Lina shuddered away from him. "Will you sleep in your dressing room to-night, please?" she said dully. By to-morrow she might be able to think: to decide what must be done.

"Really want me to?" Johnnie hated sleeping away from her. Or pretended to hate it.

"Yes, please."

"All right," Johnnie said magnanimously.

Lina began to cry.

"Poor old thing. Bad as all that, is it? Go to bed, sweetheart. I'll help you, shall I?"

"Go away," Lina said brokenly. "Go *away*."

"Don't you want me with you?" Johnnie put his hand on her shoulder.

"Don't *touch* me!" Lina sobbed hysterically.

Johnnie drew back. "What on earth's the matter with you?"

Lina did not answer that. She felt for her handkerchief, could not find it, and held her hands over her eyes. The tears trickled between her fingers.

"What's the matter with you?" Johnnie repeated, more suspiciously and more coldly.

Lina shook her head.

Johnnie gripped her shoulder. "What's the *matter?*"

"Oh, leave me alone."

"No. There's something up. Come on—what is it?"

"Something I've found out. I don't want to talk about it. Please leave me alone."

"No, I won't. What have you found out?" Johnnie went on persisting.

"Oh, about you and Janet," Lina sobbed out at last.

"Me and Janet? What on earth do you mean?" Above her head, Lina knew, an expression of preternatural innocence was only admitting Johnnie's guilt more plainly.

"You and Janet—and the flat in Bournemouth—and everything. Go away, for heaven's sake. Go *away.*"

"I simply don't understand what you're talking about."

It was Lina's own phrase, thrown back at her.

"Oh, don't go on lying," Lina moaned.

There was a long pause.

"And how do you imagine you know all this?" Johnnie's voice was a little uneven too.

"I heard you; in the drawing room; when I came in this afternoon."

"Eavesdropping, eh?" Johnnie sneered.

"Oh, what do *words* matter? I heard you. I know."

"Oh, you do, do you?"

Johnnie's tone filed across Lina's raw nerves. For the first time she faced him directly.

"Johnnie, don't you understand things are serious? I've stood your thieving, and embezzling, and trying to forge my name, and all the rest, but this is too much. My —my closest friend. I didn't want to talk about it to-night, but if you make me . . . How long has it been going on?"

Johnnie seemed to have recovered his grip. "You really want to know?" he said lightly.

"Yes."

"All right, then; don't blame me if you find afterwards that ignorance would have been bliss. Nearly a year."

"Do you love her?"

"Not in the least. She's beginning to bore me stiff." There were two spots of colour on Johnnie's cheekbones which, if she had understood them, might have warned Lina not to take everything he might say now at quite its face value. There is an impulse, when we are upbraided for something we really have done, to make ourselves out even worse than that.

Lina looked at Johnnie in horror. "You—you *cad!*"

"What do words matter? Anyhow, my dear, what do you think you're going to do about it?"

"Do?" Lina echoed dully. This was a Johnnie she had never seen before and never suspected. But it was all on a par. "What do you expect me to 'do' about it? Divorce you, of course."

"Oh, yes?" Johnnie sneered. "And where's your evidence?"

"In Bournemouth."

"Going to make a personal tour of all the flats in Bournemouth? You'll have a job, you know. I'm not a complete fool. We've covered our tracks pretty well. The house agent never even saw me." Johnnie actually laughed, with a kind of horrid triumph. "You'll have a hell of a job, my dear."

"Don't call *me* your dear."

"Purely conventional."

Lina began to tremble again.

Rage snatched her back from the edge of tears.

The Janet affair she might possibly have forgiven, had her forgiveness been implored; but that other one never. That supreme humiliation . . .

She jumped to her feet, breathing so hard that she could hardly speak. "I saw Ella's little boy to-day, too. My own servant—in my own house—the very first year . . ."

"Oh," said Johnnie calmly, "so you know about that too?"

"I didn't think even you could be so—horrible. I feel absolutely—filthy myself, ever having had anything to do with——"

"Well," Johnnie said slowly, "if we're going to exchange compliments, you're not really so clean in any case, are you?"

"What do you mean?"

Johnnie laughed. "Do you think I didn't realize what was going on between you and that tow-headed young would-be author? Not that I minded, in the least. But fair's fair, so don't be a hypocrite, my dear."

Lina gasped. "Johnnie—you cad . . ."

"Oh, deny it if you like." Johnnie shrugged his shoulders. "But do you think I don't know how any woman of thirty-five will fall for any young man who tells her she doesn't look as old as she does? It used to make me laugh, to hear him laying on the butter. But as I say, *I* didn't mind. Good luck to both of us, I thought."

Lina was beside herself with rage. "No," she said shrilly, "even if it had been true, I don't suppose you would have minded—so long as you could go on getting money out of me."

"Of course," Johnnie said evenly; though the spots of colour on his cheeks deepened and spread a little. "Of course. What do you think I married you for?"

"Oh! So it's come to that, has it?"

Johnnie pushed his hands a little deeper into his pockets and grinned at her cruelly. "Yes, I think it's about time you had a few home truths too, as we're going in for home truths this evening apparently. And after all, I'm getting a bit sick of smarming to you for your damned money that you're so mean with.

"I'm afraid, my dear, I never really cared two straws about you. After all, I do like my women to be pretty. But I took you in all right, didn't I? Good Lord, your people knew well enough what I was after. But you were so conceited, you never guessed.

"Really, my dear girl, what use do you think a woman like you would have been to a man like me, without your money? I believe you're under the impression that you've been what they call 'a good wife' to me? Well, all I can say is I'd sooner have a wet fish in my bed. Look what you were like on our honeymoon! Spoilt the whole thing. If you can forget all that, I can't. I promise you, if I've played about a bit, you've driven me to it.

"Yes, it's about time you did know the truth. And if you know so much, it won't do any harm for you to know a bit more. Did you know, for instance, that Freda Newsham and I——"

"You *devil!* Get out of my room. I won't listen—I won't listen." Lina threw herself face downwards on the bed and stopped her ears with her fists.

But Johnnie, standing over her, went on with his recital, and she did listen. Johnnie was pulling the wings off the fly at last.

He flayed her with names, sacrificing his mistresses to make a knout for his wife.

Lina heard them through a fog of horror—Mary Barnard, Olive Redmire, Edith Brough, girls from the village, any pretty woman Johnnie took a fancy to—even Clara Fortnum herself.

"And now," concluded Johnnie loudly, "you can do what you damn well like about it. And to hell with you and your blasted money!"

He flung out of the room.

PART TWO

CHAPTER IX

"My dear girl," Joyce repeated patiently, "take a lover." She said it as one might say: "Take a dose of castor oil."

"But I don't want a lover," said Lina, for the tenth time.

"Then divorce Johnnie."

"He said I couldn't. I haven't got any evidence."

"You haven't tried to get any. A good private detective could get it for you in no time."

"I hate the idea of a detective nosing into my affairs. I don't think I could bear it."

"Do you want to divorce Johnnie, or do you not?"

"Oh, I suppose so. I could never live with him again, of course. Never! Besides, he doesn't want me."

"He'll want you quick enough, when funds begin to run low."

"Oh, Joyce," said Lina weakly, and began to cry once more.

Joyce regarded her tears for a moment with a sisterly eye. Then she repeated her panacea.

"My dear Lina, what you need is a lover."

They were sitting in the drawing room of Joyce's house in Hamilton Terrace. Lina had not seen Johnnie since he had flung himself out of her bedroom, and out of the house, on that terrible evening a week ago, after saying things that could never be forgotten or forgiven. She had left for London the next morning, after a frenzied telegram to Joyce: left Johnnie forever, left Dellfield, left Upcottery with its treacherous Janet and its treacherous, malice-driven Freda, never to see any of them again—just thrown a few things into a small case and scuttled.

It had been a miserable week.

No word had come from Johnnie.

"He's biding his time," said Joyce.

Joyce was very outspoken about Johnnie. Not bitter, just practical. Lina had been more loyal than she need have been. She had not uttered a word about Johnnie's dishonesty, only about his unfaithfulness. But there was plenty for Joyce to be outspoken about without that.

"What you don't allow for, Lina, is that Johnnie knows women. It's about all he does know, but for women and horses he's got to have full marks. He's led you all this time by the nose. He always knew what you were going to do, and you always did it; he knew how to get anything he wanted out of you, and he always got it. He's always been one move ahead of you, and you've always worked to plan—his plan. Now it's up to you."

"How?"

"By not doing what he counts on your doing. My dear girl, you've got to face the fact that Johnnie's a complete rotter. No man who was worth a damn would be content to be kept by his wife as you've kept Johnnie; no man who wasn't a complete rotter would keep mistresses on his wife's money. It's easy enough to see what's in Johnnie's mind. He knows you're weak. He's giving you a month or two, and then he expects you to come crawling back to his feet saying he can keep as many mistresses as he likes on your money, if only he'll keep you too."

"I wouldn't say anything of the kind."

"Not so bluntly. But he expects that you'll turn a blind eye. I'm certain he does. If Johnnie knows women, I know Johnnie. He thinks he's got you just there."

"He'll soon find out he hasn't got anything of the sort."

"Then for heaven's sake let him! It's simple madness of you to keep on his allowance, and keep Dellfield going for his benefit. Shut the place up, cut him down to nothing, and file your petition *at once*. Do show a little backbone, Lina. It's now or never. Johnnie's not the faintest use to you, and you'll soon get over the loss of him. If you're weak now, he'll be a plague to you for the rest of your life. You'll never be happy, tied to that rotter. For goodness sake, don't be so spineless."

Joyce was very convincing.

"Perhaps I'm not so spineless as you think," Lina would retort.

She knew Joyce was right. There was no hesitation about divorcing Johnnie. Lina had been determined on that from the first. But she pretended to Joyce to be not so determined as she really was, because she wanted her conviction strengthened. She had spent a great part of the first week in tears, but they had been tears of anger and bruised vanity rather than tears of weakness; though she had not let Joyce altogether realize that. She liked Joyce to think her weaker than she was, because she wanted to depend on Joyce; and Joyce was so extremely dependable. Also she wanted to be comforted, and cosseted, and bullied into doing what she had already made up her mind must be done.

No, there never had been any question about not divorcing Johnnie. The only trouble was the first step. Lina always had hated first steps.

So, by playing up her weakness, she got Joyce to take the first steps for her.

It was Joyce who wrote dismissing the Dellfield servants with a month's wages. It was Joyce who went down and shut the house up. She did not see Johnnie. Johnnie, she learned, had left Dellfield too and gone to live in Bournemouth. She obtained his address and came back with it.

It was Joyce who sent a private detective to Bournemouth to obtain the necessary evidence.

Only one thing Lina would not do, and that was to stop Johnnie's allowance. On that point she was quite obstinate.

"Don't you see," she said to Joyce, "if it were the other way round and Johnnie was divorcing me, he'd have to maintain me till the decree was made absolute. I'd be his wife till then. Well, Johnnie's my husband till then. He can have his alimony."

Joyce could not but applaud the cynicism, while deploring the wasted money it would cost.

Cecil was very kind to Lina, in his gentle way.

He took her to a strange play produced by the Stage Society of which Lina could not make head or tail and which bored her exceedingly, though she told Cecil it was extremely clever. He took her, and Joyce, to a cocktail party given by an extremely famous novelist, mostly to other extremely famous novelists, who frightened Lina very much before she got there and disappointed her still more when she did. Everyone asked Lina what she did, and she had to confess to the humiliation of being the only person in the room who did nothing. Then they told her what they did.

"But how quite too marvellous," said a willowy young man, all spots and spats, and lifted his head to waft a yawn over hers. Then he caught sight of a friend, and his glazing eye brightened.

"What, you here, Frank? How too utterly marvellous. You know Mrs. Er-er-h'm, don't you?"

The willowy young man escaped, and Lina found herself being addressed by a short, stocky, prematurely bald young man, who dipped his head before speaking like a chicken about to drink.

"Chp chp chp chp chp chp chp chp chp chp chp," he observed, or as near to that as Lina could gather, in the gentlest possible voice. "Don't you think so?" he added, suddenly and clearly, on a rising inflection.

"Oh," said Lina, "I *do*."

As usual when nervous, she had thrown too much enthusiasm into her voice. The stocky young man, who thought he had only remarked that it was getting a little hot in here, looked at her in mild alarm.

"Chp chp chp chp chp," he said, with a dart of his head towards the other side of the room, and edged away with an uncertain smile.

Lina, feeling utterly provincial, followed his progress towards a strange young woman in crimson silk, with a black pork-pie hat and a white satin muff. The stocky young man seemed far more at home with her than with Lina.

Why do people find me alarming, she thought despairingly, when I'm simply terrified to death of them myself?

Cecil also took her, on her own request, to the National Gallery. Translating into ideas about painting the bias which made him approve of the dull expressionistic nonsense beloved of the Stage Society, he explained to her quite vehemently why none of the pictures should be there at all. Lina was surprised to find that her brother-in-law should hold such strong opinions about anything. That they should be so mistaken did not surprise her in the least.

But Joyce took her for a day's outrageously extravagant shopping, and after it to dinner at the Ivy and to

Bow Bells; and Lina laughed for the first time since she left home.

The first fortnight she spent in Hamilton Terrace was the most wretched time that Lina had ever experienced. She felt that life had been exploded for her like a toy balloon, and there was simply nothing left. At times she thought, quite seriously, of suicide, as the simplest way out—simpler, somehow, than divorce. Luckily, however, *Bow Bells,* and her new frocks, saved her from that.

Joyce plainly mistrusted her.

She was too sensible to overstate her case against Johnnie, but she continued to sound Lina subtly in order to make sure that she was not weakening.

Lina did not weaken.

"Oh, yes. I know it's impossible. That sort of thing can't go on. I mean to divorce him."

Joyce nodded sympathetically, satisfied.

"But the awful thing is that I still love him," Lina added mournfully. "He's my child."

Joyce snorted. "Lina! Don't be so *flatulent.*"

2

Lina met Ronald Kirby at a studio party in Kensington.

It was not the sort of party that Joyce would have dreamed of going to on her own account. Since Cecil had made his name, Joyce had become very particular about the parties she let him attend. A mixed gathering of artists and second-rate writers would not have been considered for a moment.

Lina had not at all wanted to go.

It was to be a silly party, with all the guests dressed as children; and Lina thought that, in her circumstances, it would be too dreadful. But Joyce had insisted. It would be good for her. It would take her out of herself. Besides, it might even be amusing. So Lina, too dispirited to resist, had allowed herself to be persuaded into an abbreviated red-and-white check frock and tied a large bow in her hair and felt rather ridiculous. Even the sight of Cecil, melancholy in black velvet knickers and a Lord Fauntleroy collar, but prepared to suffer so much for her sake, failed to cheer her. Joyce of course looked quite charming and about nineteen in rose-pink taffeta.

There was a great deal to drink, and it was not long before Lina began to feel guiltily glad that they had come.

She recognized, with surprise, that though they ought to be doing nothing of the sort, her spirits were beginning to rise. She began to forget, for quite long intervals, that she was a betrayed wife and a bruised soul, and remembered only that this impossible party actually was rather amusing. She knew she was drinking too much, but that was deliberate: a gesture of contempt and defiance towards the profligate Johnnie. She toyed with the idea of getting quite drunk and being disgraced.

As Joyce had said, the party comprised a mixed lot. Mixed parties are not usually successful, but this one was. They all seemed to know each other, and everyone was cheerful. Except for Cecil, no one was in the first class and so had no dignity to keep up. The host designed posters, and his wife wrote serials for the newspapers. Lina felt proud of being the sister-in-law of the most distinguished man in the room.

First they stood about in groups and talked, then there was dancing, and after that they played nursery games. It really was rather fun. Somewhat jovial versions of Hunt the Slipper, Oranges and Lemons, and Blind Man's

Buff were performed, and then someone suggested Hide-and-Seek in the dark. The suggestion appeared popular. The host shepherded the men into another room, and all the women put one of their shoes in the middle of the floor. Then each man appeared in turn and chose a slipper, whose owner was to be his partner for hiding. Lina felt quite excited as she watched a tall, dark man who had not yet been introduced to her pick out her slipper.

"That's mine," she whispered to Joyce. "Who is he?"

"Ronald Kirby," Joyce whispered back. "Black-and-white artist. I've met him. Quite nice, but enthusiastic."

Lina knew his work. He drew funny little men in absurd plights for *Punch* and other humorous papers.

Joyce just had time to introduce them before she too was claimed.

Kirby looked at Lina with a smile which she instantly thought one of the most attractive she had ever seen, a real smile that embraced his gray-green eyes just as much as his rather pronounced but sensitive mouth.

"I say," he said confidentially, "I believe I know a really good place, but it's rather a scramble to get there. Are you game to try it?"

"Yes, let's," said Lina at once.

They stood together for a moment, while the last men drew their partners, and then all the lights were put out. Kirby took Lina's hand and drew her confidently into the darkness.

She felt pleasingly excited.

Kirby led her up the stairs that rose from one end of the studio. Bodies bumped into them and were bumped by them, the air was full of hissing whispers, cigarettes glowed here and there. It was exhilaratingly mysterious. The really good place proved to be actually in a neigh-bouring roof. They had to climb out of an upstairs window and cross a few feet of leads, and there was a little door into a gabled roof.

"Isn't it rather dirty?" suggested Lina, peering into the blackness inside.

"No, there's a mattress to sit on, and I brought these." He showed two or three cushions which he had caught up as they passed through the studio. "I know this cubbyhole. It's the private resort of our host. But we'll have to talk in whispers, because it's over someone else's rooms. Or would you rather go back?"

"Of course I wouldn't. It's most exciting."

Kirby struck a match, and Lina saw the mattress stretched across the rafters. She sat down, and there was room for her feet where the level swept down to the door. Kirby closed the door and sat down beside her.

Lina's heart began to beat rather more quickly, though she did not quite know why. It was an adventure, in a way, sitting there in the darkness beside a strange young man.

"And what will you do if our host comes and demands his private resort?" she giggled, her glass clutched in her hand.

"I've latched the door on the inside," Kirby whispered simply.

"Oh!"

They sat for a moment in silence.

"You know, Mrs. Aysgarth, I chose your slipper on purpose."

"Did you?" Lina was conscious of a little flutter.

"Yes. I knew that old game, so as soon as hide-and-seek was suggested I had a good look at your shoes."

"Really?" Lina was too unsophisticated to hide her pleasure. "Why?"

"I thought you looked so nice."

Lina did not answer. She was not used to compliments, especially on her looks, and generally they embarrassed her; she felt them to be insincere. But this one had been so simply spoken that she believed it. He really had thought she looked nice. It was balm to her, after Johnnie's brutal words.

She put her glass down beside her, clasped her hands round her knees, and leaned gratefully against her companion. The movement was instinctive. Her usual self-consciousness, which scrutinized every action before she made it, had been dispelled by the drink she had taken.

"What did *you* think when you saw who'd chosen it? Were you disappointed?"

Lina knew nothing about the art of flirting. "No," she said clearly. "I was glad."

"You darling!"

The next instant Kirby's arm was round her, he had taken her chin in his hand, and was kissing her mouth.

It was so sudden that Lina was taken completely by surprise. She had expected perhaps a little verbal sparring, possibly even a tentative hand on her waist, which she would instantly shake off; but nothing more. Kirby's kisses astonished her.

They astonished her out of her senses: for the next thing that Lina realized was that she was returning them more fiercely than they were being bestowed on her.

"You sweet thing," Kirby muttered, holding her so closely to him that the thumping of his heart against her breast was almost the first thing that reached her returning consciousness.

She tore herself away from him. "I'm not—I'm not," she cried distractedly. What in heaven's name had happened to her? Had she suddenly gone quite mad?

Johnnie was standing now like a spectre at her elbow.
"Hush!"

Masterfully Kirby put his arm round her again, and
drew her to him. She resisted half-heartedly, and that
only for a moment. She wanted to be kissed again; wanted
it desperately.

He did kiss her, gently.

"Do you know," Lina heard herself saying, in a
strangely detached voice, "that was the first time I've let
anyone kiss me since I was married?"

"Is it?" Kirby's voice was caressing, but it had no conviction. Quite obviously he did not believe her. And how
could he, when she had just kissed him like that?

"Yes," she said flatly; and realized, with impotent annoyance, that she was beginning to cry.

At first Kirby did not notice her tears.

Lina lay limp against him, as she concentrated on trying to check the tell-tale sobs and heavings. Then her wet
cheek, as he brushed it with his, gave her away.

"I say—you're crying." His voice was dismayed.

Lina shook her head violently. "No, I'm not." She
tried to force a laugh.

"But you are. Your cheeks are wet." He felt them gingerly with the tips of his fingers.

"I'm not—I'm *not!*"

She gave way and collapsed on his shoulder, her body
shaking with sobs.

In its usual annoying way, alcohol had ceased to ex-
hilarate and become depressing.

3

Lina had told Kirby everything.

Encouraged by his kindness, she had poured out all

Johnnie's unfaithfulness, at first interspersed with tears and then indignantly.

Kirby was very sympathetic. His understanding surprised Lina. Complete stranger though he was, she felt that he was the first person who had adequately grasped what she was suffering. His condemnation of Johnnie was no less indignant than her own, although only this one side of Johnnie's rascality had been imparted to him.

"It's a damned shame," he kept repeating. "A really nice person like you. God knows there are few enough nice women in the world. He must be a plain idiot, your husband. Hurry up and divorce him and find someone who'll appreciate you. It's a damned shame."

"But you don't know me," Lina had to protest. "I may not be at all nice, really."

"You're a darling," Kirby declared, and sounded as if in his opinion there could be no possible doubt about that.

Lina felt immensely soothed.

Kirby kissed her, and stroked her hair, and went on telling her how nice she was, and how he had been attracted to her all the evening from the very first moment of seeing her, and how impatiently he had been waiting for hide-and-seek so that he could choose her slipper, and how much nicer she was now he knew her than he had even imagined before, and what a damned shame it all was. Lina found it most heartening to believe him. After all, she was quite nice; and it *was* a damned shame.

Then she discovered that they had been sitting up there for an hour and twenty minutes.

"An hour and twenty minutes!" she repeated, horrified. "We must go down at once."

"There's no hurry, dear."

"Indeed there is. An hour and twenty minutes! Really! What on earth will they be thinking?"

"What does it matter what they think? You hardly know anyone here, and your sister certainly won't mind. As a matter of fact, I don't suppose we've been missed at all."

The nervous exasperation seized her which opposition always provoked. "Don't be so absurd. Of course we've been missed. We must go down at once. Please open the door." Nerves made her voice sharper than she intended or realized.

"Oh, certainly, if you're so anxious to go." Kirby spoke stiffly, obviously hurt.

He opened the door.

Oh, dear, now I've annoyed him, Lina thought.

What was it that made her use that tone when she didn't really mean it? She must stop herself. But why couldn't he see that she didn't mean it? Why must all men behave just like children?

She was very contrite, because she ought to have realized by this time that men do behave like children and are just as easily hurt.

On the leads she caught his arm. "I'm sorry I spoke like that. It was horrid of me. You've been so sweet to me. Thank you, Ronald. But we must go down, really."

She held up her face to him, wondering at herself as she did so. Was this really she, offering her kiss to a man she had not known for a couple of hours? But the gesture had seemed completely natural.

Kirby's irritation, responsive as it had been to her own, was soothed at once.

Lina hurried down the passage and into the bedroom where the women had left their things, to repair her face. The sight of her childish frock in the mirror quite startled her, it seemed so ludicrously incongruous with her recent emotions. But that's how things are, she reflected, as she refixed the bow in her hair with rather unsteady hands; the comic mask so often has a tragic face underneath it; where would the films be if it hadn't?

Nobody seemed to have missed her and Kirby. Lina's self-consciousness as she came down the stairs with the feeling that a hundred eyes were glued on her was quite unnecessary. Only Joyce caught her eye as she swung past in the arms of her partner and drooped her own eyelid in knowing salute.

They were dancing in the studio now, and Kirby was waiting for her at the foot of the stairs. He took her without a word, and guided her onto the floor.

"You shouldn't," she smiled, as she moved into his arms. "Let me dance with someone else first."

He looked down into her eyes. "Do you think now I've found you I'm going to let you go?"

A thrill raced through Lina from head to foot.

For perhaps the first moment since she had met Kirby, Johnnie was completely forgotten.

4

"And how did you get on with Ronald Kirby?" Joyce asked, when they got home in the not-so-small hours of the morning.

"I liked him."

"I thought you did," Joyce said comfortably.

She asked no more.

CHAPTER X

THE next morning Joyce gave Lina more information about Ronald Kirby. She passed it over very casually, as if it were really of no importance at all.

"I don't know him well, of course; he's not in our lot; but I like what I do know of him. He's one of the few in that feeble artistic crowd who seemed really solid. He's never taken over anyone else's wife, or handed one of his own on to another man. And for an artist, he's intelligent."

"Aren't artists intelligent?" Lina asked innocently.

"Of course they're not. Most of them haven't got the brains of a mouse. They just have this odd knack of being able to put things on canvas, and that's all. They're the dullest of all the creators. Musicians are the nicest: you never hear a creative musician talk about himself at all. Then the really good authors. They don't thrust their work down one's throat; they've no need to. Then the second-rate authors, who do, and have. And then the painters, a long way bottom."

"Oh!" said Lina.

"But Kirby has got brains. He might have a future too. He's beginning to make quite a name with his portraits now. That's what he's really interested in, of course. His black-and-white stuff is only pot-boiling."

"I didn't know he went in for serious painting at all. He never told me."

"That's just what I mean," Joyce said. "Well, he does.

He paints nothing but women's portraits, and more unflatteringly than anyone else. He really is clever. He can show up his sitters more cruelly on a bit of canvas than Cecil could in a twenty-page description. Cigarette?"

"No, thank you."

"Oh, of course. I never can remember you don't smoke."

"But does he ever get any commissions, then?" Lina wondered.

Joyce laughed. "My dear, you really are refreshing. They love it."

2

At tea-time Kirby rang Lina up and asked her to dine with him that evening. She refused at first, and then accepted.

"Where shall I meet you?"

"Well, what sort of place do you like?" Kirby asked.

"I don't mind a bit."

"A nice place full of chattering women, with little pink lamps on the tables?"

"I don't mind, really. Where do you usually go?"

"I shall plump for a grill room, if you leave it to me."

"I do," Lina laughed. "So which grill room?"

They arranged to meet at the Monico, at seven.

Lina was ten minutes late.

Kirby jumped up from his chair in the vestibule. "Hullo, I was just getting quite certain that you'd been run over on the way."

"I am so sorry," Lina said penitently. "My bus got held up at every crossroads on the way."

"Oh," said Kirby, "you came by bus?"

"Yes."

Lina noticed that he looked a little surprised. She knew

why, and blushed faintly. His voice had held the same note as Joyce's did when Lina mentioned buses to her. Joyce never went in buses. Lina, who had not got the taxi-mind, always did.

"Well, let's go and have a cocktail," Kirby said magnanimously.

They went into the lounge.

Lina was not sure that she wanted anything to drink at all, after last night; what did Ronald think would be best for her? Ronald prescribed side-cars.

"Well, you extraordinarily nice person," he smiled at her, as soon as the waiter had gone, "how are you?"

"I felt a little morning-afterish this morning, but I'm better now," Lina smiled back, rather nervously.

She felt a little nervous. Ronald Kirby, in a correct blue suit, might be the same inside it as Ronald Kirby dressed as a sailor boy, but the atmosphere which it produced was not. Lina had difficulty in believing that she had wept on this man's shoulder last night—and kissed him as eagerly as he had kissed her. It had been an hour's natural madness, snatched out of the drab sanity of everyday life. What was he going to do about it? What was she going to do about it? She felt too unsophisticated, too provincial, too self-conscious. If he felt self-conscious too, their dinner was bound to be a failure.

Ronald, however, very evidently felt nothing of the sort. He began to chatter at once about the party and the people who had been at it, about other parties, about anything rather than Lina and her affairs. After a few minutes Lina realized that he had perceived her lack of ease, guessed its cause, and was engaged in remedying it. She smiled at him gratefully. He really was a most understanding person.

Ronald's tact, and two side-cars, restored her confidence. By the time he rose to lead the way to the grill room Lina knew that she was going to enjoy her evening enormously.

When he asked her after the oysters what she would eat next, she chose a fillet steak, very underdone. "I'm so hungry," she explained.

Ronald was delighted. "A woman who chooses an underdone steak in a restaurant when she might have *foie de volaille en brochette* must be sound at heart," he told her.

Gradually their intimacy returned.

Ronald, as if to show that he was not going to take advantage of any confidences which Lina might now regret having made, did not refer at all to Johnnie. Their conversation roamed over a large field. They discovered that they both liked travelling, René Clair's films, looking at cathedrals, chop-suey, and the novels of Mr. P. G. Wodehouse. Ronald told the inside story of a recent murder of an artist's model, and Lina told him how to cook little plums in red wine.

She tried to make him talk about his own work, but on that topic only he was shy. "I live among people who are always yapping about their work," he explained, "and I pray the good gods that I shall never get like them. It may be pharisaical, but it's a good deal less boring for one's friends."

"But I shouldn't be bored. I want to hear about your work."

"I expect when I know you better I shall bore you with it all right," Ronald assured her.

"So you're going to know me better, are you?" said Lina, quite archly.

The conversation took a different turn.

It appeared that Ronald was going to know her very

much better. He had decided that almost before they had gone off to hide last night. And now . . .

"Yes?" said Lina provocatively.

"Now," said Ronald with a rush, "I know you're the nicest woman I've ever met in my life."

"Nonsense!" Lina said; but the words had made her heart give an odd little jump.

"It isn't nonsense," Ronald declared fervently. "I tell you, I *know*. You're just exactly what I've always thought a woman ought to be and no woman ever has been."

Lina tried to keep her head. "It's sweet of you to say so, Ronald, but, after all, you don't know me, do you? You really don't know the first thing about me."

"If you're trying to persuade me that you're not the sweetest woman in London at this moment . . ."

Lina laughed skeptically, but an insane wish flashed through her mind that Johnnie could be there to hear.

She put her elbows on the table and leaned her chin on her interlaced fingers. "And what exactly have you always thought a woman ought to be, my poor Ronald?"

Ronald was not in the least nonplussed. He promptly rattled out a string of adjectives embracing, Lina thought, all the possible varieties of feminine perfection.

"Well, I'm afraid I'm hardly any of those," she laughed. "I'll tell you what I am. You might as well know now as later. Irritable, conceited, intolerant, bad-tempered——"

"You're not conceited!" Ronald interposed hotly. "I never saw a less conceited woman."

"—weak, lazy (*very* lazy), provincial, unpunctual (you saw for yourself!)——"

"That wasn't your fault. Your bus was held up."

"I ought to have come by taxi. Parsimonious too, you

see. Well, anyhow, I don't come very near that catalogue of yours."

Ronald smiled at her. "*I* think you're perfect."

Lina laughed with happiness. Ronald was absurd, of course; but it was delicious to be discussed like this.

There was no getting away from it: Johnnie never had appreciated her.

"And everything about you is perfect," Ronald added. "Except one. Your hat."

"My hat?" Lina knew only too well that hats were her weak point, but she had been sure that this was a success. She had bought it with Joyce last week, and Joyce, whose hats were certainly not a weak point, had very much approved. It was a little black Glengarry worn very much on one side. Lina had secretly thought that she looked quite dashing in it. "What's the matter with my hat?"

"It needs a feather over your left ear."

"My poor boy, don't you know feathers have gone out?"

"I don't care. It needs it. Besides, you'd look adorable with a naughty little feather over your left ear, Lina."

"Ronald, *really*. Anyone would think you were talking to a young girl of seventeen, instead of a matron of thirty-six."

"Are you really thirty-six, Lina? My goodness, you don't look it."

"Well, I am. How old are you?"

"Thirty-three."

Lina sighed. It was a pity that any man in whom she was interested must always be younger than herself.

Ronald took her back to Hamilton Terrace in a taxi. As soon as the more brilliant lights were left behind, he put his arm round her and kissed her.

"I've never been kissed in a taxi before," Lina said conversationally. "Isn't it supposed to be terribly vulgar?"

"That depends who's doing it," said Ronald, kissing her again.

"Well, certainly I don't feel vulgar," Lina remarked, rather wonderingly.

Ronald would not come in for a drink.

Joyce was reading in the drawing room. She looked up from her book. "You're back early."

"We sat on till the waiters nearly threw us out." Lina stood abstractedly in the middle of the room, pulling off her gloves. "Joyce."

"Yes?"

"Can you come down to Marshall's with me to-morrow morning?"

"Yes, I think so. What for?"

"I want to get a feather for this hat."

"My dear girl, feathers have gone out."

"I can't help that. It needs one."

"But nobody's wearing them now."

"It needs one," Lina said firmly. "Over the left ear. And what's more, I shall look adorable in it," she added: but not aloud.

3

Of course Lina visualized herself as Ronald's mistress. She spent most of that same night in doing so.

Here was the lover that Joyce had been counselling her so earnestly to take, for the raising of her little finger. She saw herself in his arms, under his kisses, in bed with him. The result both surprised and horrified her. That he attracted her strongly, and that he was the only man besides Johnnie who had ever attracted her physically, she knew already: what she had not realized before was that she actively desired him.

To desire a man whom one has known only for a bare. twenty-four hours! In spite of life with Johnnie, Lina was still old-fashioned enough to find that disturbing.

She wondered whether Johnnie's moral example had coarsened her. Lying alone in bed, with no man to touch by her side, she felt it rather depraved that she should want to have one there; and a man at that whom she had known such a preposterously short time—whom, in fact, she did not know at all. And when, too, she certainly did not love him.

(And Johnnie had called her a wet fish!)

Not that she loved Johnnie any more.

She hated Johnnie now—hated him bitterly and angrily and revengefully. He might have been her child once, but he had been a monster-child who had turned matricide. No, Johnnie would not stand in the way of her taking Ronald as a lover if she decided to do so in the end. She would not do so yet, of course. Ronald, who had such a delightfully high opinion of her, must never think that she was to be won too easily. It had been drilled into Lina from her early 'teens that no man thinks anything of a woman whom he can win easily. Somehow she had paid no attention to that admirable precept before she became engaged to Johnnie. And look at the result!

She lay on her back, staring up at the ceiling and worrying over whether she would ever take Ronald for a lover, or not.

Her thoughts turned to Janet, who had had the same problem to decide and had decided it.

She felt no bitterness against Janet. The bitterness that might have been felt against Janet had all been transferred to swell Johnnie's total. Janet must have suf-

fered a lot before she decided, and more still afterwards.
Lina could only be sorry for her.

Unlike most women, Janet was not a natural hypocrite. That was why Lina had liked her from the first.
She must have found the hypocrite's rôle very horrible.
But she had been helpless. One is helpless, when one
loves. Lina knew that. Janet must have hated Johnnie
for making her a traitress, even while she loved him.
Poor Janet: she must have suffered. She could not have
made Johnnie a very satisfactory mistress.

But Johnnie . . .

He had set out to get her, of course. Probably he had
been working to do so for years. Janet really had disliked him once, and Johnnie could not have borne that,
from a woman. It had been a challenge, which he had felt
bound to accept. Johnnie, the charmer: Johnnie, the irresistible. Johnnie, the blackguard.

Yes, Johnnie was the villain of Janet's piece.

Lina began to cry.

She always cried now when she thought of Freda
(common little upstart Freda, how she must have
laughed!), of Mary Barnard, whom she had hardly
noticed, of Olive Redmire, of the village girls—of her
own servants! She felt somehow that she had been a
pander for Johnnie's horrible amours, by her own blind
belief in him. She felt morally fouled, as well as
physically.

She forced her thoughts back to Ronald. Should she
become his mistress or should she not?

There was no possible need to decide that large question at any rate for the next two or three months, but
Lina invariably worried over her problems in advance.

She decided this one in two or three minutes. She

would become Ronald's mistress. That would be getting her own back on Johnnie with a vengeance. She exulted in the idea of getting her own back on Johnnie.

For Johnnie had not *minded*.

That was what upset Lina almost more than anything. Johnnie had thought those preposterous things about Martin Caddis—and he had not minded. Love must indeed be dead when a husband just does not *mind* the idea of his wife in somebody else's arms. But then Johnnie had never loved her. She had not been pretty enough for him. How she had wasted her time!

But she would make up for it now.

She was pretty enough, it seemed, for Ronald. She would give Ronald everything. Everything she could. *Everything*.

Lina, who had never before had an erotic vision in her life, plunged headlong into a series which a month ago would have left her appalled.

She saw herself with Ronald, and gloried in it. She *wanted* to be shameless. She wanted to do outrageous things—incredible, impossible, inconceivable things. And still more she wanted Johnnie to know that she had done them.

Ronald faded out. Lina was walking the streets, haunting bars, blatantly accosting men. Every woman wonders sometimes how she would shape as a prostitute. Lina had wondered, very vaguely, herself. Now she saw herself as one, in full detail: an extraordinarily successful one: a queen of prostitutes. What would Johnnie think about that? Would he mind then?

She turned over onto her other side. She never would and never could be a prostitute. Prostitutes are born, not made. Why waste time on an unproductive theme?

Ronald was recalled. Lina might never be a prostitute, but she would be a marvellous mistress. She could be. She wanted to be. She would be.

She wondered with interest whether Ronald had any abnormalities.

According to Johnnie, all men had some bias towards abnormality, greater or less. Johnnie had tried occasionally to hint to her of his own, but Lina would never let him.

"The normal's good enough for me," she always said.

She knew very little about the subject. It did not repel her; it simply did not interest her. She had read one book of Kraft-Ebbing's, and it had all seemed very childish and silly. A great deal of it she had not been able to understand at all, including the Latin bits. Certainly it had not encouraged her to let Johnnie open his mind on the matter.

She wondered suddenly if that was why she had lost him.

With her usual fairness she had to admit that she might have done more for Johnnie. At least she could have provided a sympathetic ear. And of course she had always known that men do go to other women for what they cannot get, or do not like to ask for, from their wives. Joyce had told her all about that, years ago. Joyce had said, very emphatically, that in ninety-nine cases out of a hundred it depends entirely on the wife whether she keeps her husband or not.

Lina noted with new interest that Joyce had certainly kept Cecil.

Well, she would not make that mistake again, if that had been her mistake. She almost hoped that Ronald had a few abnormalities, so as to give her the opportunity of not making the mistake. She didn't care. Ronald at least should never call her prim.

She tried to remember what she had read in Kraft-Ebbing.

Yes, she would do far more for Ronald than she would ever have done for Johnnie. Far more! And somehow—*somehow* Johnnie should learn just what she could do for another man.

That was quite settled.

Lina went to sleep.

4

The next day Ronald announced that he was going to marry her.

Early the next morning (a good deal too early, thought Lina, dragged out of bed to speak to him on the telephone) he rang up to ask her out to lunch. Lina refused, a little waspishly on account of her warm bed. He asked her to dine with him. She refused.

"Don't be so absurd, Ronald. I can't see you every day. Besides, we're going out this evening."

"You are going to see me every day," said Ronald.

Finally Lina promised to have tea with him in his studio, to see his pictures. Ronald lived in a service flat in Westminster, but he rented a studio in Chelsea. His sitters preferred to be painted in Chelsea.

Lina got there punctually at four-thirty. She had had to hang about for a quarter of an hour on the embankment in order to do so.

A little anticipatory thrill ran through her as she knocked on the door inscribed with Ronald's name.

A bigger one followed it when Ronald opened the door to her. For Ronald wasted no time. He took her straight into his arms, and kissed her as if he had been living for that minute all day.

"My darling!"

He held her away and looked at her.

"You enchanting creature! You've done it!" He had noticed the feather instantly. "It makes all the difference. I told you you'd look adorable, and you do."

"What nonsense," Lina said happily.

Ronald helped her off with her coat. He wanted her to take her hat off too, but Lina felt a curious reluctance. It seemed somehow more final.

The kettle was almost boiling, and Lina made the tea. They used a corner of the model throne for a table.

Lina walked about the studio, a bun in one hand, looking at Ronald's pictures. She was relieved to find that the modern influence in them was slight. Ronald did not paint his sitters with red noses, by way of a crude suggestion that they drank too many cocktails, or with no tops to their heads and enormous thighs. But he was not photographic either. No photograph could have done his women such justice.

Lina was impressed. Without doubt Ronald was clever. And he worked.

It was Joyce who had said, very significantly: "And he works."

"I'm going to paint you as soon as I can work off the commissions I've got on hand," Ronald told her. "Just like you are now."

"In this frock?" She was wearing a frock of green jersey with a white collar and very long white cuffs. The feather had been chosen to match it.

"Yes. I shall call it 'The Green Feather.' But I'm afraid it will blast my reputation forever."

"Then you'd better not paint me. Why should it?"

"Because I live on silly women who like to inform the world, through my portraits of them, just how fatuous or vicious they are. I seem to have a knack of showing it in their faces."

"Well," Lina smiled, "I don't think I'm vicious, but I often think I'm very silly, so that will be all right."

"If I painted you, Lina," Ronald said seriously, "it would be to show the world that there's one woman in it who's everything a woman could be. In fact," he added with a laugh, "if I go on knowing you much longer, Lina Aysgarth, I'm afraid you'll rob me of my livelihood."

"I shall? How?"

Ronald laughed again. "Well, let's put it, by destroying my lack of faith in women."

5

"Lina, I'll tell you one thing. I'm going to marry you." Ronald bent over her as she sat on a pouffe cushion between his knees, and kissed her hair.

Lina caught her breath. "Ronald—you frighten me when you say things like that."

"Frighten you? Why, my darling?"

"I don't know. You're so impetuous. What *do* you know about me?"

"I know you're the only woman I ever could marry. No, don't shake your head. It's part of my job to be a quick judge of character. I made up my mind at that party, as soon as I knew you were going to be free, that I'd marry you."

"Ronald! Did you really?" It rather took one's breath away to have one's future settled so decidedly without apparently any say in the matter at all, but undeniably it was exciting.

"Yes. You like me, don't you?"

Lina gave the knee she was holding a little hug. "Should I be doing this if I didn't? I can assure you, this sort of thing is quite out of my line."

"I know it is, you darling. That's why I want to marry you. You're so . . . well, there's no other word for it, *clean*. Most women have such unpleasant minds, you know."

"Do they?" said Lina doubtfully. It sounded rather a sweeping statement. "You have got a poor opinion of women, Ronald, haven't you?"

"Very."

"And yet it's so silly to generalize about them."

"I've got plenty of experience to speak from, my dearest. Anyhow, I can quite honestly tell you this: you're the first woman I've met who hasn't either bored or irritated me, or whom I've even wanted to see a second time."

"I don't think you can have met the right sort, Ronald. There really are plenty of nice women, you know."

Ronald held her to him. "There's one; and that's all that matters to me. And I'm going to marry her."

"Are you, though?" Lina laughed. "You haven't asked her yet, you know."

"Will you marry me, Lina?"

"No. I don't know you. I couldn't marry a man I didn't know. The registrar would have to introduce us, and think how awkward that would be. No, Ronald, seriously, it's absurd to talk like that now. Wait till we've known each other a few months, and then we'll see. But it was sweet of you to want to."

"Sweet of *me!* Listen, my darling. I know you're not in love with me——"

"No, I'm certainly not. But I do like you a lot, Ronald."

"You darling! No, of course you're not. You're still in love with that husband of yours; but——"

"I'm not that either," Lina said indignantly.

"I think you are. Anyhow, you certainly haven't got over the shock yet. But you're going to fall in love with me, so you may as well get used to the idea at once."

"I don't think I shall ever fall in love again," Lina said mournfully. "I might love you one day, Ronald. I believe I could. But not fall in love with you."

"You're going to do both," Ronald said firmly. "It's not fair that I should have to go through all this, and you escape scot-free. No, no, my lovely, you're going to do your share."

Lina looked up at him. "But you can't be in love with me. You can't possibly. Not so soon."

"Whether I can or not, I very certainly am," Ronald laughed. "I haven't thought about anything else but you for a single minute since I first saw you. Yes, my Lina, it was love at first sight all right, and a bad case too. And me, of all people! My goodness, I haven't been in love since I was seventeen, and swore I never would be. Swore it, I did. But then, of course, I didn't know you existed."

"You must be full of repressions, Ronald. You've been driven in very much on yourself, haven't you?"

"I suppose I have. But I liked it. I considered myself self-sufficient. I've always made a point of never having to rely on anyone for any single thing. And look at me now! If you say you can't meet me for lunch, the whole world turns black. You devil-woman!"

"Ronald, you mustn't rely on me like that," Lina said, really distressed. "You mustn't really, dear. Don't expect too much of me. I'm so afraid of letting you down."

"You're going to pull me up, my sweet," Ronald told her.

CHAPTER XI

NOT in her most visionary moments had Lina ever imagined so tempestuous a wooing.

As Joyce had said, Ronald had an enthusiastic nature. At first Lina had hardly believed it, but it really did seem that he had fallen insanely in love with her from that very first evening. He insisted on seeing her every day, and for no small part of every day too, putting off appointments recklessly to be with her; and every morning, no matter how late they had parted the night before, there was a rapturous letter from him on her breakfast tray. Lina found it unbelievably exciting to be wooed like this.

They lunched out, dined out, talked out, danced out; and when they were not doing any of these things out, Ronald seemed to be doing them in Hamilton Terrace. For Joyce of course encouraged him as hard, if as unobtrusively, as she knew how.

They talked interminably.

They talked about Lina, about Johnnie, about marriage, and about life.

Lina's views about marriage were undergoing a radical dissolution. "I can't quite get used to it, yet," she told Ronald. "I always took it for granted that when one got married, one was married for good."

"And yet people are getting divorced every day."

"Other people. Not one's self. Somehow one never thought of the possibility of divorce for one's self."

"You haven't got religious scruples, have you?" Ronald asked suspiciously.

"Oh, heavens, no. I may be old-fashioned, but I'm not mediæval. But all the same, I simply can't get used to the idea of being alone again."

"You won't be alone, my prettiness," Ronald would tell her.

One day he gave her, a little cautiously, his own ideas about marriage.

"You know, Lina, I've always said I'd never marry a woman until I'd lived with her for at least a year first."

"Have you, Ronald?" Lina smiled. She saw his caution and knew she was being sounded.

"Yes. Incompatibility of passion is the rock on which eighty per cent of marriages founder. Incompatibility of tastes is nothing to it. And how is one to find that out without experiment? Of course there should be a year's trial marriage for every couple. It would cut the work of the divorce courts down by half. But I suppose you don't agree with me there?"

"Why on earth shouldn't I agree with you?" A year ago Lina would most emphatically have disagreed with Ronald.

"Well, it doesn't seem the kind of theory you'd hold."

"Oh, I'm quite broad-minded. And I do agree with you. I think it's only common sense. If ever we do decide that we like each other enough, the ceremony wouldn't mean anything to me." Already Lina was considering marriage with Ronald as something more than just a possibility.

She really was astonished at the way, and the rapidity with which, her views had changed. She saw now that it is impossible to lay down moral rules to govern all cases.

They could apply to individual ones only; for what is right for one person can be quite wrong for another. It is a matter of conscience, and consciences differ. That is what the bigots never can understand. Lina did not think it would be in the least wrong for her to live with Ronald for a year to see if they would suit each other for marriage, simply because she would not consider it wrong; but for a Roman Catholic, who really believes in the sacred permanency of marriage, it would be wrong.

A year ago she would have accepted the convention that it was wrong for everyone. Now she was learning to think for herself.

In the same way she tried hard to look on unfaithfulness in marriage with a more understanding eye, though here she was not so sure that she had convinced herself.

"I wouldn't have minded if Johnnie had come to me and *told* me that he was going off with someone for the week-end," she would say to Ronald. "I'd have let him go. I shouldn't have minded a scrap."

"You would."

"I don't think I should, as long as it was all open and honest. What I can't get over is having been kept in the dark. All those women knew; and I never guessed a thing." At this point Lina would invariably begin to cry. "That's what I can't get over."

"That's just wounded vanity, darling."

"I don't care what it is. I can't forgive him for making confidantes of other women and never saying a word to me. I feel I've just been made to look a fool." That, when she came down to it, was really what had turned Lina's love for Johnnie into bitter anger against him: that she had been made to look a fool to her friends.

"My sweet!"

Lina would lift a streaming face to Ronald. "I've just been wasting my time. All these years I've just been wasting my time being faithful to him. That's what I can't get over. I could have been enjoying myself too."

"You'd never have taken a lover, Lina."

Even Ronald's complacent belief in her own decency would annoy Lina. "I probably should. Why shouldn't I? At any rate, he ought to have given me the chance."

Then Ronald himself would get angry. "I hate to hear you talking like that. Wasting your time! It's a damned good thing you didn't know, if you'd have been so silly as to give way to that childish tit for tat. Why do you want to make out that you're as petty-minded as other women, when you're nothing of the sort?"

"Oh, you don't understand." Lina's tears would burst out again. "I feel so battered. You don't know all I've been through. And when *you* speak to me like that . . ." She had never told him about her other troubles with Johnnie. That would not have been fair, yet.

Then Ronald would hug her and croon over her and say all the things she wanted him to say.

Lina did not know what she would have done, during this time, without Ronald and Ronald's shoulder.

Ronald himself told her plainly what he was trying to do for her.

"You *have* been battered, poor little thing. And my first job is to rehabilitate you in your own eyes. You're altogether too humble, my Lina. You think now that because Johnnie couldn't see what he'd got, you're no use to anyone. I never heard such nonsense! It's Johnnie I'm sorry for, for not realizing what he was throwing away. Not you. You're jolly well rid of him. And you're going to be happier with me than you could ever have been in a century of Johnnie. Aren't you?"

"Am I, Ronald?"

"You know perfectly well you are. My little beauty, if I were married to you, do you think I'd ever look beyond you for one single second? In any case, I'm not the promiscuous kind, for promiscuity's sake."

"No," Lina would say comfortably. "No, I don't think you are. But could I make you happy, Ronald? I wonder now whether I could make anyone."

Ronald's reply to that would be a physical one, and leave Lina squeaking a recantation of such heresy.

"So that, my lovely," Ronald would explain, "is why I tell you just what I think about you. Any other woman would become unbearable if she knew how much I adored her and how perfect I thought her. So conceited you're going to get if I'm not careful! You pretty little creature —stop just like that till I kiss the edge of your smile!"

"But you mustn't overdo it, Ronald," Lina would say, kissed. "No one knows better than I do that I'm anything but pretty."

Then Ronald would say, quite seriously: "When you smile like that, I think you're the prettiest thing I've ever seen." He would say it, too, with such quiet conviction that Lina would have to believe that he really did think so, deliciously absurd though it might be.

They discussed too, with astonishing detachment, whether Lina should become Ronald's mistress. They called it "the question." Afterwards Lina would wonder sometimes whether it had really been herself talking so calmly, and with such common sense, about such a revolutionary conception. Circumstances alter women.

Ronald of course was thoroughly in favour of the idea, though he did not want to stampede Lina into it before her mind was fully made up about himself.

"It wouldn't be just the ordinary surreptitious, rather

vulgar *affaire,* you see, darling," he pointed out. "It would only be in anticipation of marriage."

"Don't make it sound so dull," Lina laughed. "I'm not sure that I shouldn't rather welcome an *affaire,* just at present. Can't I ever be improper in my life?"

"No. Not you. You just couldn't, my loveliness."

"How half-baked you make me sound, Ronald." But it was a fact that Lina could never be deliberately improper. She detested smoking-room stories: not because of their rudeness, but on account of their manufactured artificiality; whereas a really spontaneous remark would always make her laugh, however improper. Joyce called her prim, which annoyed her. Lina did not consider herself prim in the least.

"Of course we should have to be careful, till your divorce is through."

"I should hate that. I shouldn't like to be hole-and-cornerish, Ronald. I'd much rather come and live with you openly, if it came to the point."

"You sweet thing! I know you would. But we just can't. So are we to waste the next nine months, on account of these incredible divorce laws of ours, or are we not? That's really the question."

"There's one thing I feel. If I *did,* it might make you feel that I'd got a claim on you; and that would be awkward if you got tired of me."

Ronald protested against such a ludicrous possibility.

"But you might," Lina insisted. "You say you're the faithful kind, but I don't know, do I? You've only known me for about a fortnight. I'm so afraid that this will all burn itself out when you know me better and realize I'm not nearly so perfect as you think now."

"If you're holding things up for anything so ridiculous as that . . ."

"No, I'm not. But it's no good forgetting the possibility. Besides, there's another thing."

"What?"

"I'm so afraid you might be disappointed in me," Lina said wistfully.

"Oh, my darling."

"I've been told so very plainly I'm no good at that sort of thing, you see. I thought I was all right, but apparently I'm not."

"My little thing, just give me the chance to tell you what you really are," Ronald said fervently.

Lina sighed. The spectre of Johnnie was at her elbow again.

They were both silent for a few moments.

"Lina," Ronald said, "come away with me for a week, to-morrow."

"No, Ronald."

"You don't like me well enough yet?"

"It isn't that. I do like you well enough. You're the only man I ever have, besides Johnnie."

"Oh, damn Johnnie! Darling, don't keep dragging him in with every other sentence. Do get him out of your mind."

"I can't," Lina said mournfully. "I do try, Ronald—honestly I do. And it isn't as if I still loved him. I hate everything to do with him. But it's no good going away with you until I can get Johnnie out of my mind, is it?" Lina did not want a spectre in her bed as well as at her elbow.

"No, I suppose not. Though I wish you didn't say you hated Johnnie. I'd much rather you were just indifferent to him. But, Lina . . ."

"Yes?"

"Don't keep me hanging too long. I'm no celibate, you know."

Lina gave his hand a squeeze. "I don't mean to keep you hanging. It's just that I must be sure."

"Yes, of course. But I'm not a celibate; and since I met you . . . Lina, sweetheart, they say there's nothing like a really good woman to drive a man who loves her to prostitutes. I've always said that was nonsense. Don't make me understand what they mean."

Lina sighed again. "You must do as you think best." It was a favourite observation of hers. It evaded responsibility.

But for all Ronald's hint, she could not make up her mind to that first, final step.

2

For a fortnight or more Lina was thrilled to ecstasy by Ronald's wooing.

During the third week she began to find him a little overwhelming. In the fourth a kind of mental claustrophobia set in. She felt that Ronald was stifling her.

They were sitting one evening in the Chinese restaurant, after a crab omelette, lobster chop-suey, and special rice with prawns; and Lina at any rate felt that her belt was uncomfortably tight. Lina had to take a good deal of trouble with her figure nowadays.

Ronald, upon whom the gargantuan helping provided by the restaurant appeared to have had no effect, was engaged in his favourite occupation of calling Lina's attention to her physical charms. He had just discovered, in the cinema which they had visited, that Lina's fingers besides being unbelievably soft had a fascinating tendency to curl, preferably round his own.

Usually Lina loved this sort of thing. After having been dismissed physically all her life and praised (when she was praised) only for her intelligence, it was delightful to have her intelligence taken for granted and to be told that, physically, she was the most attractive woman Ronald knew. She loved him to call her "my pretty" and "my lovely," because he so genuinely found her pretty. She was very ready to listen to Ronald on the subject of her smiles, of which it appeared that she had no less than four quite separate varieties: one when she was just amused, one when she was smiling at something which she thought she ought not to smile at, one when she was very much amused, and one, when she was very happy, in which her nose made three little wrinkles on either side of the bridge. That was very interesting and very gratifying.

But this evening Lina was not interested in either the wrinkles on her nose or the curling propensities of her fingers.

"Ronald," she said abruptly, "do you know we've seen each other every single day for nearly three weeks?"

"I do, my sweet. And I hope to go on seeing you every day for the next three years."

"Well, I don't."

"What?"

"I mean, it's quite time we gave each other a rest."

"I don't want a rest."

"Perhaps not a rest. A breathing space. I feel we're seeing each other too much."

"How can we see too much of each other?"

"I must have air. You must let me have some air, Ronald."

Ronald looked at her doubtfully. "You're getting bored?"

"No, no." Lina squeezed his hand. "It's just that I don't think it's a good thing for us to see so much of each other. You've never given me a minute to—to get adjusted to you. I've been very upset, you know. One can't switch over at a minute's notice from one person to another."

"I've always been afraid you were a one-man woman."

"I don't think I am. I don't know; I may be. I've always told you I'm a clinger."

"I love you to be a clinger. I want to be clung to. I love the way you always take my arm in the street. Do you know how I always see you when you're not there? On my arm, looking up under that wicked little hat of yours with the green feather."

"Do you, darling?" said Lina perfunctorily. She often called Ronald "darling" now. She had told him that she loved him, but she was not altogether sure that it was true. Anyhow, she had told him: because he had so much wanted it. "Do you? But you see what I mean, don't you? I must have air. I feel you're swamping me. Don't let's see each other for a few days, Ronald. Please."

"If you really feel that way," Ronald said gloomily.

"Yes, I do. Besides, it'll be much better for you. I feel I'm taking you from your work."

"Oh, damn my work. What's that matter, compared with you?"

"That's simply silly," Lina said, with a touch of irritation. "Of course you must work. I want you to. I'm interested in it. I want you to get on and make your name. Very well, that's settled, then. You can always ring me up, you know. And you'll go on writing to me, won't you?" She smiled at him, feeling much more amiable now that she had won her point.

"That's right. You're like all women, aren't you?

Must eat your cake and have it. I'm not to see you, but I'm to keep you amused with letters."

"Darling! I do love your letters so. They're more exciting than anything I ever imagined. They make my toes squiggle with joy when I read them."

Ronald laughed. "All right, you little wangler. But, Lina!"

"Yes?"

"Will this help you to make your mind up on *the* question?"

"I don't know. It might."

"Because it will help me very considerably to bear it, if it will."

"Oh, Ronald," Lina sighed, "do you want me so much?"

"More than I ever wanted anything, my lovely," Ronald said.

"I do wonder why," said Lina.

It was quite obvious why she should want Ronald: but why should Ronald want her?

3

Lina did find it a relief to be free of Ronald for a few days. It was as if an enveloping fog had been dispelled from around her and she was able to breathe freely again.

She did not understand herself. I suppose it must mean that I don't really love him, she thought; and yet I seem to love him much more now that I'm not going to see him.

It was all very perplexing. She would have liked to consult Joyce, but was quite sure that such mental acrobatics would be beyond Joyce's direct mind.

Ronald went on writing to her, but he did not ring up.

"Have you quarrelled with your young man?" asked Joyce.

"No," Lina said casually. "We're just not seeing each other for a few days. I felt I must have air."

"Air? What do you want air for?" Joyce demanded. "I should have thought you'd had all the air you wanted with Johnnie, and more. Don't you play fast and loose with Ronald, Lina. He's too nice for that silly sort of game."

"I'm not playing fast and loose with him," Lina retorted indignantly.

But was she?

She would not give him an answer on *the* question; she saw him when she wanted to, and not when she didn't; she had told him she loved him when she was not at all sure that she did. Was she insisting on all the jam on her bread, and none on his? The last thing she wanted to do was to keep a man on a string, in the usual selfish feminine way.

She went off and wrote a letter to Ronald, the first she had ever written him.

RONALD DARLING:

You must have a letter, after all the ones you've written me.

I'm trying to get things sorted out, but life still seems very complicated. Sometimes everything seems too much for me—Johnnie, the divorce, Joyce, Dellfield, and even you! I don't know what to do, or what to settle about things, and can't feel anything but oppressed and unable to breathe. I expect it's been the fog these last two days, too!

Now you've had time to think, are you sure you haven't been making a mistake? You're much too good to waste yourself in this way, on someone's cast-off wife. I'm furious for you. You should be more ambitious.

Think well, and look round, as I keep on telling you. There are plenty of nice women about, in spite of what you say. You ought to find some nice girl of twenty-five or so, who would make you work and work herself for you socially—not an elderly matron of thirty-six, three years older than you, who has to worry about her figure.

You must *look round, Ronald.*

Yours,
LINA.

But I would love to look after you properly. Your flat is a disgrace.

The next morning Lina was awakened by the housemaid ten minutes before the usual time.

"Yes?" she said sleepily. She had had a bad night, worrying.

"Mr. Kirby wishes to speak to you on the telephone, madam."

Lina scrambled out of bed, put on her wrapper, felt for, rather than looked for, her shoes, and went downstairs. It really was exceedingly annoying of Ronald to ring up when he *knew* she would be in bed.

"Yes, Ronald?"

"Oh, hullo, darling. Good-morning. I got your letter."

"Yes?"

"And I'm not doing any looking round, thank you. And how dare you belittle your sweet self like that?"

"Have you got me out of bed just to tell me you'd got my letter?"

"Hullo, what's the matter, darling? You sound a little terse."

"I was asleep," Lina said, not without bitterness. "I'm hardly awake yet."

"Well, wake up, because I want to ask you a question. Do you love me?"

"Was it really necessary to wake me up to ask that?"

"No, perhaps not. Sorry. Well, will you lunch with me to-day?"

"I thought we weren't going to see each other for a bit?" The possibility of being overheard by anyone outside the dining-room door increased Lina's exasperation.

"Well, it's three days now. Surely you've had all the air you want."

"Three days isn't much. Do be sensible, Ronald. No sooner do we get clear than you want to tangle everything up again."

"Clear?"

"Well, you know what I mean. Anyhow, I can't lunch with you to-day, or any day this week. We're booked every day."

"Oh! Then what about dinner?"

"And dinner. I do wish you'd leave me alone for a little, Ronald. I did ask you. And I know as soon as I see you, you'll be on to me again about—about what you always are on to me about. Oh, what is the good of talking like this on the telephone?"

"On to you?" Ronald said slowly. "I should hate to be 'on to you' about anything."

"Well, you have been. You know you have. You must give me time."

"All right." Ronald's voice was cold. "Anyhow, you're

engaged every day this week for lunch and dinner. Is that right?"

"Yes. Good-bye."

"Good-bye."

Before Lina had reached the top of the stairs she was wondering whether she had not been a fool.

She wondered the same thing at intervals all day.

The next morning she was awake an hour before her breakfast tray arrived and drew a breath of relief as she saw the letter from Ronald upon it. Ronald had understood, as usual.

She opened it eagerly.

DEAREST:

I was evidently mistaken in believing that you cared for me at all seriously, or ever might. Anyhow, I'm no woman's pet dog, to be whistled out when required to amuse and pushed back in the basket when not wanted. Air you're screaming for, and air you shall have.

Yours,

RONALD.

Ronald had not understood.

4

"Yes?" said Joyce. "Come in."

"May I use your telephone, Joyce?" Joyce had an extension by her bed, which she always used when she wanted to make sure of not being overheard.

Joyce took one look at Lina's tear-marked face, and jumped out of bed. "Yes, of course you can. I'll go along to the nursery. It's not—Johnnie?"

Lina shook her head.

As soon as Joyce was out of the room, she gave the number of Ronald's flat.

"Hullo?" came Ronald's voice.

"Ronald, it's me. Lina."

"Oh, yes?" His voice had gone hard and dull.

"Ronald, how could you write to me like that? How could you?"

There was a long pause at the other end. "It seemed to me about the best way to write," Ronald said slowly.

"You made me cry. *You* made me cry, Ronald. Good heavens, as if I hadn't had enough to cry over already, without that. Listen, I'm crying now." She was crying, unmistakably.

"I'm very sorry, darling."

"I was going to write to you at first, and then I thought I might say things I'd be sorry for afterwards, so I'm ringing you up instead."

"Yes?" Ronald sounded more sympathetic now, but very, very cautious.

"Ronald, don't you love me any more?"

"That isn't in question, as you ought to know, my dear. But the other way round is. Very much so."

"But I do love you, Ronald. I told you I did. I only wanted a little air."

"Yes." Again there was a long pause at the other end. Lina waited fearfully.

"Look here, Lina." Ronald's voice was full of decision. "Look here, I quite see your point of view. All this hasn't been fair to you. I took you on the rebound, and that's never satisfactory. I won't have you like that, either. You've got to love me as much as I love you, or it's not the faintest use our getting married. And you're perfectly right: you must have time to see things in perspective. Very well. We won't see each other for three months."

"Three months!" Lina wailed.

"Is that too long?"

"Much too long."

"Well, a month, then."

"But, darling, I shall be *miserable*. I want to see you. I don't need not to see you to make up my mind. It's practically made up already. Besides, it's you I'm thinking of as much as me. I feel you ought to do so much better for yourself than marrying me. Ronald, take me out to lunch to-day."

"No," said Ronald. "You must have time to think things out. Good-bye, my darling. And remember: *I love you*."

The click of the receiver sounded in Lina's ear.

She made her way mournfully back to her own room.

She had been right: that cursed exasperation of hers had led her once more into making a fool of herself.

A whole month!

She felt absolutely alone and forlorn. And this time it was utterly and completely her own fault.

And the unbearable thing was that it was so unnecessary; for she knew now that she must love Ronald.

5

There had been another letter on her breakfast tray. Lina opened it now, mechanically.

It was from the detective, to report that he had been able now to collect enough evidence against Mr. Aysgarth to make a successful action for divorce inevitable and was forwarding same to her solicitors. He also took this opportunity of enclosing his account to date.

Lina crumpled it up and threw it on the floor.

Then she picked it up again and smoothed it out. Of course. A cheque would have to be sent.

Johnnie . . .

It had taken her some moments to realize that it was of great importance to her to divorce Johnnie.

She could not marry Ronald, and be happy at last, until she had done that.

CHAPTER XII

Joyce was giving a party.

The party was on Lina's account, and Lina knew that it was really to bring herself and Ronald together again. It was over a week now since Ronald had announced his intention of giving her a month to herself, and she had had no word from him during the interval.

Joyce, however, had.

She and Ronald had dined together, and Joyce had come back most indignant with Lina. Ronald, it appeared, was in a terrible state. He had now worked himself up into the belief that Lina never had cared a straw about him and had only been amusing herself with him to help her to get over the loss of Johnnie. He was in despair, and his work had gone to ruin. Joyce had soothed him as best she could and emphasized Lina's real affection for him, but she had some very outspoken things to say to her sister alone.

"I told you, you weren't to play fast and loose with Ronald, and look what you've done. He's positively maudlin about you, and all you can tell him is that you want air. What on earth do you want air for? You're being a perfect idiot, Lina."

"But I do want to see him! It wasn't I who made this arrangement. I told him I wanted to see him."

"He doesn't believe you. I tell you, Lina, you're being an idiot. Here you are, nearly forty and behaving like a young fool of sixteen in her first love affair. I tell you, my girl, one can't afford to be coy at our age. If you let Ronald go, you may not get another chance. Are you fond of Ronald, or aren't you?"

"I'm not going to let any other woman get him," said Lina, breathing rather quickly.

"Well, you're going the best way about it. Ronald's going to make some woman a damned good husband soon, so it might as well be you. You cling onto him, my girl, with both hands. If you knew as much about this crowd as I do, you'd realize Ronald's value. He's a coming man, and he's solid. You'd be an important person in a few years, as his wife, instead of being buried down in Dorsetshire with no one to talk to but the vicar and Johnnie's mistresses. Besides," Joyce added more calmly, "it would be nice to have you up here and hear you rasping your brains occasionally. You'd be quite able to hold your own with our lot as soon as you got accustomed to them, and it's an amusing life. You'd like it, wouldn't you?"

"I should love it." Lina bore no resentment against Joyce. She was used to plain-speaking from Joyce. Whenever it was possible, Joyce always said what she thought.

"Then don't throw it away. Anyhow, I'm going to throw a party for you next Friday, and Ronald's promised to come, as a special favour to me. And if you're not as nice to him as you know how, and put an end to all this childishness between the two of you, I'll never introduce you to a man again."

"That's all I want," said Lina. Given the chance to be nice to Ronald, she had no doubt of the result.

She wondered if it was horrid of her to feel pleasantly excited at the idea of Ronald in a terrible state because he thought she did not love him.

2

All day Friday they were very busy. In spite of it being a scratch affair, everybody of any interest or importance in Joyce's set seemed to have found it possible to come. Nearly eighty people had accepted her hurried invitations.

Gunter's were doing the refreshments, so there was no need to bother about those, but there were a hundred other matters to be seen to. Like all the rest of the household, Lina got up an hour earlier than usual.

In her own home Lina quite enjoyed the preparations for a party. There she was efficient, swift, and decisive. In Joyce's she felt rather lost. She wanted to help, but could not help feeling she was more in the way than anything.

"Can't I do the flowers for you?" she asked Joyce.

"Yes," said Joyce gratefully. "You do the flowers."

Like all women, Lina was convinced she could arrange flowers just a little better than anyone else. Joyce had ordered bundles and bundles of tulips, and Lina spent a really happy hour putting them in their vases.

"Thank you so much, dear," said Joyce, called in to approve. She passed a frowning eye over the massed vases. "I never think tulips look really nice mixed, though, do you? I think I'll have the mauve ones in the drawing room, the pink ones in here, and . . ." With swift movements of her small brown hands she pulled Lina's work to pieces and began to rearrange it.

"I tell you what you could do, though," she said over her shoulder. "Open those bottles I put in the morning room, for the cup."

Lina went off, somewhat dispirited.

She could not find the corkscrew.

"Cecil will have one in his study," said Joyce.

Lina had never been into Cecil's study before when he was working. She hesitated outside the door, wondering whether to knock or not. In the end she knocked and went in all in one movement.

Cecil was writing, at his desk. He jumped up and got the corkscrew. Lina felt guiltily that she had probably spoilt the very best passage Cecil might ever have written.

She went out, envying him his calm detachment, to open the bottles morosely in the morning room. She had not been trusted to mix the cup.

At six Gunter's men came, and the confusion grew worse.

Lina hung about, wearing a helpful face and feeling a nuisance.

Joyce was making cocktails.

"Let me help," said Lina.

"I tell you what you could do," said Joyce, over her shoulder. "Keep an eye on Armorel. Nurse is busy mixing the cup for me."

Armorel was discovered in the dining room, filching things off the plates with all the depravity of six years old, as the men put them out.

Lina, having no children of her own, knew that she was better able to manage them than any infatuated mother. She reasoned with Armorel.

"You didn't quite realize you oughtn't to do that, dear, did you?"

"No, Auntie Lina."

"I know if you thought, you'd never do a thing like that when Mummie's back's turned, would you?"

"No, Auntie Lina."

"So now you understand, you won't do it again, will you?"

"Oh, *no,* Auntie Lina."

Joyce's voice floated down from the drawing room. "Lina, will you bring the mauve tulips up here?"

Lina took the mauve tulips up, secure in the knowledge that Armorel could now be safely left.

She came back to find Armorel filching things off the plates, to the open encouragement of Gunter's men.

At seven o'clock the soda water had not come, and Lina was able to make herself useful by telephoning for it.

They ate a scrap meal off the corner of Cecil's study table, and went up to dress afterwards.

At nine o'clock Joyce came into Lina's room.

"Ronald's here. I told him the party was at nine. Go down to him as soon as you're ready. You've got a clear half hour to do your grovelling in. And grovel! You owe him that."

"All right," said Lina. "All *right.*" She was not going to grovel for a moment. But she would forgive Ronald very nicely.

As she put on her frock she looked forward to forgiving Ronald.

It was a charming frock, if a trifle candid: white satin, cut as low as possible in front, and a good deal lower than that at the back. Women were being candid that season. Lina looked at herself in the long glass from every possible angle. Her face was all right; her fair hair, brushed tightly to her head and unwaved, only curled at the ends round her neck, inwards at the sides and outwards round the back, gleamed under the light; her frock, worn this evening for the first time, was admirably slimming.

"Well, I'm damned if I look a minute over thirty" observed Lina contentedly to her reflection, and went downstairs.

Ronald was waiting in the empty drawing room.

"Hullo, Lina," he said casually. "Look here, am I the first or is the party off?"

Lina went up to him and held up her red mouth. Lip stick could go to hell. "Is that all you've got to say to me, darling?"

"No, not by a long chalk it isn't." Ronald put his hands on her bare shoulders and rocked her to and fro. "I want to know what the devil you mean by playing me up like that?"

"Playing you up, darling?"

"That's what I said. I know I played my cards badly. I know I let you know how infernally fond I was of you; so you just thought you could take me for granted and do what you liked about it. Isn't that right?"

"I suppose it is, really. Darling, I'm sorry. I won't take you for granted again. Kiss me."

"No, you won't." Ronald was rocking her more violently. "I tell you, I've had a hell of a time these last few days, and I'm not going to have it again. I know your sort. What you need is a good spanking."

"Ronald! You wouldn't dare!" Lina thought he looked almost as if he meant it.

"Wouldn't I?" Ronald said grimly. "Wouldn't I! Let me tell you, that's just exactly what I've come here to do."

"Ronald!"

Three minutes later Ronald said, a little breathlessly: "Now I'll kiss you."

He hugged her to him, crushing the breath out of her.

Lina had never had such a painful kiss before. But she did not protest.

"That's the stuff!" she said to herself exultantly, as she ran up the stairs to her room five minutes afterwards. One's face can always be redone, and three minutes with a needle would repair the tear in her frock quite well enough. "That's the stuff! That's the *stuff!*"

The name of Miss Ethel M. Dell did not enter her mind: so she could not wonder if it had occurred to Ronald's.

Lina had made up her mind at last.

3

Lina did not go to tea at Ronald's flat the next day.

In the morning, Joyce had a telegram. It was from Robert's school in Surrey.

Robert taken ill not serious but would like you both to come. ASKRIGG.

Lina had never seen Joyce so upset before.

Nevertheless, upset though she was, she lost none of her efficiency. The car was ordered up from the garage, a telegram dispatched in answer, and within twenty minutes Joyce and Cecil were on their way to Surrey.

With the empty feeling that follows somebody else's departure, Lina went up to her bedroom with the idea of washing some stockings. She was worried on Joyce's behalf and felt tired after only four hours' sleep instead of eight.

She had barely put the stockings into the water when the housemaid appeared at the door.

"There's a gentleman to see you, madam. I showed him into the drawing room."

"Oh, thank you, Mary."

Lina went downstairs. It did not occur to her that the gentleman could be anyone else but Ronald, though she did wonder vaguely why Mary had not announced him by name.

She opened the drawing-room door and went in.

It was Johnnie.

4

"Hullo, monkeyface." Johnnie's engaging grin was uncertain and wavering.

"Johnnie!"

Lina's knees had gone almost powerless. She managed to get to a chair, and clung to its back, struggling for self-possession. "What on earth do you want?" Her voice at any rate sounded cold.

"You! Monkeyface, it's no good. I can't live without you. I simply can't. Listen—I love you. No other woman means anything to me. I haven't seen another woman since you went. They make me tired. You're the only woman in the world for me. I know I've treated you rottenly. I swear I'll be different if you'll come back to me. Won't you have a shot at it, monkeyface?"

He tried to take her in his arms, but Lina resisted him.

"This is a rather different tale from the one I heard from you last," she managed to get out, with a fair enough semblance of calm.

"I know. Darling, I was mad that evening. I can't think what made me say those things to you. They weren't true, hardly any of them. I just wanted to hurt you. I was crazy."

"Some of the things you said were crazy, certainly."

"About Caddis?" Johnnie said shrewdly. "Darling, I know. But I was so infernally jealous."

"Jealous! Even if it had been true, you said you didn't even mind."

"I *had* to pretend not to mind. But you gave me hell over Martin. I was mad with jealousy. Honestly I was."

"And so you find you love me after all, do you?" Lina said slowly. "You're sure it isn't just that you're running short of cash, Johnnie?"

"Oh, damn the money. Lina, if you'll only come back to me you can dock that infernal allowance altogether. Honestly, I mean it."

"That doesn't sound very like you, Johnnie."

Johnnie poured out a torrent of protestations. Lina did not know him, Johnnie had not known himself, he had not realized what she meant to him, he had been utterly wretched since she went, he could not stand it any longer, wouldn't she give him just one more chance?

"I'll be absolutely honest with you, Lina. I *did* marry you for your money. But, my God, I fell in love with you afterwards. On our honeymoon. I thought you were wonderful. And more every day since. I've been in love with you for years. You must know I have. I couldn't have acted all that time. I've been trying to do without you, because I knew what a rotter I'd been to you, and it was only fair to let you have your freedom. But I can't. I simply can't."

"Sit down, Johnnie. We've got to talk this out."

They talked it out. But it all came back to the same thing. Johnnie couldn't do without Lina. Would she not give him one more chance?

At last Lina said:

"I'd better tell you, Johnnie. There's a man here in

love with me. We intend to get married as soon as I'm free."

Johnnie turned rather white. "Are you in love with him?"

"Yes."

"Have you . . . ?"

"Not yet."

Johnnie got up. He looked very tired.

"Well, I suppose it's no good my staying. Good-bye, monkeyface. Good luck. I hope he's a good 'un, that's all. You deserve one."

He walked past her to the door. Lina saw two tears ooze out of his eyes and run ludicrously down his cheeks.

"Johnnie!"

"Hullo?"

"I will come back to you."

She knew now that Johnnie must love her.

She had known, from the very first moment she saw him, that she loved Johnnie, desperately, and had loved him desperately all the time.

During the whole interview, Ronald had hardly crossed her mind.

5

Lina did her best to keep her head. It was difficult, when all she wanted was to get inside Johnnie's arms and stop there for good, but she tried hard.

She did not give way too easily.

She would go back to Johnnie, but only on terms. He was to find another job, his allowance was to be cut down to two hundred and fifty pounds, he was to be completely faithful to her until or unless he found he could be so no longer; then he was to tell her honestly and allow her to divorce him. If he would agree to that she would take him back.

Johnnie did agree. He would agree to any damned thing, he told her, if only she would come back to him.

He gloated and capered over her return like a small boy.

"You won't half catch it from Joyce," he exulted. "I shouldn't have stood much chance if she'd been here, should I? Monkeyface, we've got to get out of here before they get back. I've got the car outside; go on— shove your things in your trunk now, this minute. Off with you! I'll give you just twenty minutes to pack."

Lina actually sang as she went upstairs. Johnnie wanted her: she wanted Johnnie: everything was wonderful. And this time everything was going to be all right. Johnnie had had his lesson.

As she packed, hurriedly and unmethodically and rapturously, she thought of Ronald. She had not the courage to ring him up herself. She would ask Mary to do so. And she would write to him from wherever it was they stayed that night.

She was sorry for Ronald. He had been right all the time, when he said she was still in love with Johnnie. She had known it herself, in her heart. That explained such a lot which had puzzled her during the last few weeks— her throwing herself at Ronald's head, her dithering, the way she had let him and anybody else influence her, her inability to make up her mind, the dull pain that was with her all the time even when she had thought herself at her happiest. She had simply been drifting, not caring really what did happen to her, because she thought she had lost the anchor of Johnie's need for her; and Ronald's need had seemed so—well, unimportant, compared with that.

She was sorry for Ronald. Very sorry. But he would get over it. She would write to him.

Somehow she got most of her things into the trunk; the others could be sent on later. She put on her hat and coat, and went down.

Johnnie himself carried down her trunk, with exaggerated caution like a conspirator, grinning at her, over the top of it. He put it on the grid, fastened the straps, and they set off. It was two months since Lina had come to stay in Hamilton Terrace, but she felt that she was leaving nothing of herself in London. She felt it was not she at all who had ever come to stay there, only a pale, gutted ghost of the real Lina.

Johnnie drove with her hand in his. When he had to release it to manage his gears, he put it on his knee.

When they were clear of London Lina said to him:

"Yes, my lad, you were right. If Joyce had been there you wouldn't have had such an easy job of it. It was just your luck that you came on the very day she had that telegram."

"Luck?" Johnnie grinned at her with ingenuous triumph. "I sent that telegram."

PART THREE

CHAPTER XIII

Not until she had been back at home for more than three months did Lina discover that Johnnie was a murderer.

They had been three very excellent months.

Johnnie had been charming to her, completely devoted. Lina, very suspicious at first and fighting instinctively against his charm, had become convinced. Johnnie did love her. He could not possibly have pretended like that. When at last she allowed herself to believe it, Lina thought she was happier than she had ever been before.

She had made it up with Janet, in an emotional scene when Janet, the unemotional, wept against Lina's cheek and implored her forgiveness. But Lina did not see nearly so much of her as before. It was almost impossible now to get Janet to the house at all. She was positively terrified of encountering Johnnie.

The Newshams Lina had cut clean out. Luckily they lived nearly five miles away, so there was little difficulty there.

Everyone in Upcottery had been delighted to see her back, but Lina felt that their welcome was tinged with bewilderment. No one ever said so, but it was plain that everybody had thought her quite mad to part from Johnnie, even temporarily. Lina talked brightly about her holiday in London, but she knew that it had been more than rumoured round the neighbourhood that she and Johnnie had parted for good.

To Ronald Lina had written the very first evening, from Bournemouth, where they stayed a few days while Dellfield was being opened up again and new servants engaged. She had written as nicely as she could, and without saying anything that she knew would make Ronald's despair worse. She did not tell him that she loved Johnnie and not himself; she let it be inferred that her return was due to duty only. She did tell him plainly that if this last experiment failed, she would become his if he still wanted her. She let it be gathered that in her opinion it probably would fail. It never occurred to her that, given the choice between cake and bun, she was seizing the cake and telling the bun to stay fresh just in case.

Reading the letter through, she found it cold comfort for Ronald. Ronald had been very, very good to her. And he wanted her so badly.

Her emotion boiled up, and she added a postscript. Whatever happened, whether she stayed with Johnnie or not, she would go away with Ronald for a week during the summer, if he would like that. Lina, hating to be dishonest, felt she owed him at least that.

The question of morality troubled her very little. Johnnie, she thought, deserved payment of this debt no less than Ronald did. Besides, love Johnnie as she might, Lina still felt that she could never wholly forgive him until she had got her own back on him. Why should he have had all that amusement, and she no experiences of her own at all? Let her have those, and they could begin again fair. Not for a moment did she look on it as tarring herself with the same brush.

Influenced by this new outlook, she took a good deal more freedom for herself. Those two months at Joyce's had unsettled her. She found now that she was no longer content to let Dellfield, Johnnie, and Janet form the boundaries of her life. She went up more than once to London alone, staying at a hotel (Johnnie neither objecting nor questioning), and of course dined with Ronald.

They discussed the situation very earnestly, and when she was with him Lina still found herself very much attracted to Ronald. It was comforting, too, to feel that she had him to fall back on if ever Johnnie did let her down again.

For Ronald, in the end, had become resigned into sense, as Lina considered sense.

He took it hardly at first, as was only natural, and poured out a torrent of protests and appeals to Upcottery, threatening to come down there and carry Lina off from under Johnnie's nose if she persisted in this insane altruism. Lina had managed to stop that, but Ronald had remained difficult for some time. In the end, however, he did become resigned, gave the experiment six months, and supposed he could wait that time extra; especially if Lina would go away with him during it. He wrote to her every day for the first month, and then two or three times a week.

Lina told Johnnie she was going away for a fortnight in July.

She fully intended to spend a week of this fortnight with Ronald. They talked it over and talked it over, dates were arranged, a room almost booked. Yet somehow or other it came about that Lina took Janet with her for that fortnight, to Corsica. She was not quite clear herself how it happened: just that, when it came to the point, she went to Corsica with Janet.

Ronald was naturally most disappointed, but Lina told him that it had not proved quite convenient after all. They would have their week together later on. No, no, of course they would. It could not be arranged just at present, since she had only just come back after a fortnight's absence, but they would have their week later on.

Except for Ronald, and Johnnie's reduced allowance, Lina might never have been away at all.

Johnnie never asked her for extra money now.

2

Johnnie, it turned out, had plans of his own.

He had been unable to find the job for which Lina had stipulated, but Lina had to admit that that had not been for want of trying. Johnnie had pulled every string he knew; but it was the summer of 1932, when England at last had to atone for the third-rate minds that had been governing her since the war by facing the fact that not even a nation can go on consistently living above its income to keep a political party in office; and jobs were impossible to obtain. So Johnnie came out with plans of his own.

He had got into touch with Beaky Thwaite to finance them, he told Lina exultantly; Beaky had agreed, and they were going to clean up a fortune between them. Johnnie's eyes sparkled as he expatiated on the fortune they were going to clean up.

Lina thought the plan sound, but she did not think there was a fortune in it.

Briefly, Johnnie had been struck by the fact that in a world of tumbling prices, the most catastrophic of all were those for a commodity which above anything else should have remained unaffected. The commodity was property and land.

"It's like this, monkeyface," he explained excitedly. "When the pound goes down, you see, it goes down.

It isn't worth so much. A hundred pounds in notes, or a hundred in stocks and shares, aren't worth the old hundred ever again; they're only worth about seventy. You see that, don't you?"

"Yes, of course," said Lina, who didn't.

"That's because money isn't money at all, really. I mean, it isn't *wealth*. It's only what you change for wealth. Wealth is based on something solid, that you can buy or sell. And, hang it all," said Johnnie triumphantly, "there isn't anything more solid than land, is there? I mean, you see that?"

"Oh, yes," said Lina, who did see that.

"And what's more, as soon as the pound is stabilized at a lower value, the very first thing that's bound to find its real value (I mean, become worth more of these not-so-valuable pounds) is land—sooner than diamonds or anything. Isn't it?"

"Is it?"

"But, darling, I'm telling you it is. So as soon as the pound went down, you'd have expected anyone with any spare cash to plunk it all into land, because that's certain to recover quicker than anything. But nobody did. I can't think why, but they didn't. Nobody wants land. You can't sell land at all to-day. And the consequence is that land's gone down more than anything else. It's worth actually less of these old, not-so-valuable pounds as it was a year ago. Well, the thing's obvious. Buy land—and you'll double your money in a year. Do you see now?"

"Yes, darling. But will you double your money in a year?"

"Sweetheart, I keep telling you you will. Do try to understand. Land's the goods. Land and bricks and mortar. You *can't* lose: you must gain. Look at the back page of *The Times* any day now. They're simply *giving* country houses away. You can buy a house that would have cost ten thousand three years ago, for four now. And less. Why everyone doesn't snap them up, I can't think."

"Will they double in a year too?" asked Lina intelligently.

"Well, I don't know about that. Not so certain as land," Johnnie said sapiently. "Anyhow, we're not going to risk them. We're going out for building-sites."

"Building-sites?"

"Yes. I know a fine site in Bournemouth that they were asking twelve thousand for a year ago. Right in the centre of the town; simply asking for a block of shops; couldn't be safer. We're getting it for seven. And we'll sell this time next year for fifteen!"

"That sounds very good."

"Darling, do be a little more enthusiastic. I don't think you understand even now. Look here—we buy the site for seven; it's worth, say, eleven; along comes the trade recovery next year, everyone screaming for more shops, more business, more everything, people beginning to build everywhere, and—we've got the best site in Bournemouth! Now do you see?"

"Yes, I think it looks a very good idea. But will the trade recovery come along next year?"

Johnnie threw his hands in the air and began all over again.

"How much money is Mr. Thwaite putting up?" Lina asked, when Johnnie had proved his case once more and she had approved it.

"Twelve thousand. And twelve thousand will make twelve thousand, so that's six thousand apiece. How's that?"

"Very good, darling. I hope it comes off."

"Of course it'll come off. And there'll be a few more pickings than that," Johnnie added, with a grin.

"Will there?"

"Yes, it's like this. Old Beaky got tipped the wink that the pound was going to crash and what to do about it, so he sold out twelve thousand pounds worth of shares, sent the money over to New York, and had it turned into dollars. On the sly, of course. Nobody knows a thing about it except himself and me. It's in a bank over there. One of us is going over there to get it, and bring it back in cash and bearer securities, so that it can't be traced."

"Why mustn't it be traced?"

"Oh, better not," said Johnnie vaguely. "As a matter of fact, Beaky's windy. Thinks he might get into trouble over having sent the money out of the country and all that. Anyhow, the joke is that old Beaky did what he was told, but he hasn't the vaguest idea why he was told. Beaky always was a bit batty, but he's got so much money it doesn't matter. He hasn't realized at all that his twelve thousand in dollars will be worth over fifteen thousand when it's turned back into pounds again, owing to the exchange having gone up in the meantime. He thinks he's still got only twelve. And," exulted Johnnie, "he's going to give me a cheque for the whole boiling in dollars, *and* I'm going over to New York to collect it, *and* he only expects twelve thousand pounds out of it, and I'll get you a new hat when I come back, you funny little monkeyface."

"Wait a minute," Lina worried. "I don't understand. You're going to bring back fifteen thousand, and only give Mr. Thwaite twelve? You don't mean that, surely?"

"Commission," said Johnnie glibly. "Always done. You don't understand these things, darling."

Lina could only laugh. Johnnie was so transparent.

"I understand that you're intending to cheat Mr. Thwaite out of three thousand pounds, Johnnie, and you mustn't do anything of the sort. You'll give him his full fifteen thousand. After all, you say you're each going to make six out of it."

"All right, monkeyface," Johnnie said, in a resigned voice. "I suppose, if you say so. I was an idiot to tell you."

"You'd have been a bigger idiot if you'd done it and he'd found out. Is that a promise, Johnnie?"

"It is, you little Puritan," Johnnie smiled. "Lucky for us you're not in business, isn't it?"

"Very well," said Lina. "It's a promise. And I shall ask Mr. Thwaite myself if you gave him the whole fifteen thousand."

Johnnie's face fell so suddenly and so completely that Lina laughed again.

Johnnie was exceedingly transparent.

Lina took Johnnie's tendencies quite for granted now.

3

So Johnnie went to New York.

And Lina, having quite decided to give Ronald a week of Johnnie's fortnight's absence, altered her mind at the last minute and decided instead that this would really be too unfair to Johnnie.

She was sorry for Ronald, who was very disappointed.

4

It was in September that Lina found the notebook.

Johnnie had been back from America about three weeks. He had not been at home very much, owing to the requirements of his new business. The owners of the building site in Bournemouth were being difficult, scenting Johnnie's keenness to buy, and had raised their price, necessitating a procession of telegrams and conferences. Johnnie was touring about a lot too, with Beaky Thwaite, looking for other promising sites. He assured Lina, with as much enthusiasm as ever, that everything was marvellous, but these things took time.

One morning, having seen Johnnie off to Bournemouth once more, Lina decided with reluctance that she really must look out the things for the jumble sale. She had promised the vicar some old clothes of her own and Johnnie's, but had put off from day to day the task of sorting them out. Before her resolution, induced by a pleading postcard that morning from the vicar, could ebb, she went upstairs as soon as she had finished her morning talk with the cook.

There were a couple of hats, some well darned stockings, two or three pairs of old shoes of her own, and a frock or two, which she made into a pile in the middle of the bedroom floor, and then went through her drawers for oddments of ribbons and underclothes and ornaments to add to them. It was surprising, when once she had made up her mind to part with things, how much she found she could spare. It always was.

Then she went into Johnnie's dressing room.

Johnnie had told her what clothes of his she could take. She looked them out, added them to the pile, and looked into Johnnie's wardrobe. She decided that he could be very well rid of an elderly mauve suit which she had never very much liked and which she was quite sure Johnnie had not worn for at least two years. She took it off its hanger, and felt in the pockets.

There was an equally elderly handkerchief in the

breast pocket, and nothing else at all but a little cheap black notebook in one of the side pockets of the coat. Lina opened it idly, to see whether Johnnie would want it preserved or whether it could be thrown away. Most of the pages were blank, but a few at the beginning were filled with writing, Johnnie's writing, in pencil. The first one was headed: "Arterio-sclerosis."

Lina was interested. Arterio-sclerosis was the disease, she knew, which had caused her father's death. Arterio-sclerosis combined with mild angina pectoris. She read on.

As she read, the coat which she was still holding dropped from her hand on to the floor. She sat down on the edge of the bed.

ARTERIO-SCLEROSIS

Arterio-sclerosis may be defined as a condition of thickening of the arterial coats, with degeneration, diffuse or circumscribed. The process leads, in the larger arteries, to what is known as atheroma and to endarteritis deformans, and seriously interferes with the normal functions of various organs.

In the early stages, the patient should be enjoined to live a quiet, well-regulated life, avoiding excesses in food and *drink. Alcohol in all forms should be prohibited.*

ANGINA PECTORIS

Whatever the cause, arterio-sclerosis predisposes to angina. A majority of the patients have sclerosis, many high blood pressure.

The patient may drop dead at the height of an attack, or faint and pass away in syncope.

An attack may be induced by emotion, or toxic

agents (*e.g.* *alcohol*), increasing the tension of the heart walls. Emotion is of less importance. The angina of effort that follows any slight exertion is, as a rule, far more serious.

CEREBRAL HÆMORRHAGE

Cerebral hæmorrhage is apoplexy.

Individuals with arterio-sclerosis are particularly liable to cerebral hæmorrhage. Violent exertion, particularly straining efforts leading to overaction of the heart, may cause a rupture.

So far the entries were obviously extracts copied from some medical work. The few that followed, written in a more hasty hand, seemed to be jottings added from time to time in Johnnie's own words.

High blood pressure. Increase it, and you get apoplexy.

Three dangerous things—too much to eat, too much to drink, and violent exercise.

?Running upstairs after dinner?

Port. Ha, ha!

Cecil?

What about old days in the mess? Excitement.

Got it! The three-chair trick.

Ha, ha. Try it, anyhow.

After that there was a page of figures. Lina did not do more than run her eyes over them. They seemed to consist of calculations of the income to be derived from fifty thousand pounds at various rates of interest. Evidently they referred to the time when Johnnie was

trying to persuade her to sell out her government stock
and invest her capital in more adventurous schemes.

She frowned her puzzlement, flicking through the
pages again. Why should Johnnie have gone to the
labour of studying these diseases after her father died,
even to the extent of copying out notes about them?
She did not remember that he had shown such interest
in the medical details at the time. And what on earth
did those extraordinary observations at the end mean?

She felt oddly disturbed. There was something almost
sinister about those two "ha, ha's" in such a connection.
It almost seemed as if Johnnie had been rejoicing over
her father's death.

As she added the mauve suit to the bundle on the
floor and set about collecting Johnnie's other remnants,
her mind was busy recalling the details of her father's
death nearly three years ago.

They were still quite clear to her.

General McLaidlaw had died, tragically, on Christmas night, after dinner, while the men were still in the
dining room. He had seemed quite well during the meal,
and had eaten the usual Christmas dinner, and, in the
usual way again, probably a little too much of it. A very
special sherry had been got up from the cellar, and a still
more special hock, and the General had had his full
share of them. It was remembered afterwards that Mrs.
McLaidlaw had reminded him, not without anxiety, that
his doctor had warned him to be very sparing in his use
of alcohol in any form, but the General had robustly
damned the eyes of all doctors and retorted that Christmas came but once a year.

And after dinner there had been a very, very special
port.

The doctor had had no doubts about the cause of

death. He had not put his conclusion so bluntly to the family, but its gist was that the General had drunk a great deal too much. The decanter of port was, in fact, almost empty; and Cecil said he had had only one glass, while Johnnie had been sure that he had not drunk more than two. The General must have had something like four. The doctor had been just a little surprised, not that the General should have drunk four glasses of port but at their effect upon him. He had not considered his condition so dangerous, or he would have forbidden him alcohol altogether. But there the General was, patently dead of apoplexy, and all the doctor could do about it then was to sign the death certificate to that effect.

Johnnie had been very much upset.

The General *had* drunk a lot of port, and Johnnie was upset to think that he might perhaps have stopped him and never did. And the General had got excited too, talking about old times in his regiment when he was a giddy lieutenant and the pranks they used to play in the mess on guest nights. But the fault was equally Cecil's. Cecil might have stopped him too, and never did.

Actually, however, Cecil had not been in the room when the General died. He had gone out about five minutes earlier, to get something for the General from the library. Johnnie had come to him there and told him that the General had had a stroke, and what ought to be done about it? When the two of them got back to the dining room the General was dead.

Johnnie had been very much upset.

Still sitting on the bed, Lina read through the pages again. Johnnie must have been interested, as well as upset. The notes at the end seemed to be jottings of what the General had been doing to bring on his attack. Johnnie must have hurriedly written them down, to tell the doctor. But why those horrible "ha, ha's"? And what did "Try it, anyhow" mean?

Lina knew about the three-chair trick. It was a favourite trick of Johnnie's, requiring a good deal of strength and fitness. You put your head on the seat of one chair, your heels on another, with a third underneath your back; then, supporting yourself on your heels and your head, you took the middle chair away from under you, passed it over your body, and slipped it underneath again on the other side.

"Got it! The three-chair trick."

That could only mean one thing. Johnnie had suddenly realized what had caused the General's stroke. He had been trying to do the three-chair trick, and it had been too much for him.

But it would have been madness to do such a thing—madness! He had been warned not to take any great exertion. The three-chair trick was a tremendous exertion. Johnnie used to say it was the biggest physical strain he knew.

Of course the General had had a good deal to drink. And having knocked it off to a great extent during the previous year or two, it might have gone to his head. That could have made him forget the doctor's warning and try the three-chair trick.

But it was inconceivable that Johnnie could have let him do it. Johnnie knew all about his condition. Everyone knew. It had been common knowledge for a year or more that the General, though not in a state which could possibly be called dangerous, had yet to begin to take care. Johnnie could not possibly have let the old man do such an insane thing.

Lina thought she knew what must have happened. They had been talking about the three-chair trick, and then Johnnie had gone to help Cecil look for the General's spectacle case in the library, and during his absence the old man must have tried it. Probably Johnnie had heard him fall before he reached the library and hurried back.

But if he had told the doctor what he suspected, the other had never passed it on to the rest of the family. It was the first time Lina had heard of the three-chair trick in connection with her father's death.

She got up and slipped the little notebook into a drawer in Johnnie's chest of drawers. At first she thought she would ask him if her father had really done this preposterous thing—had practically killed himself like that. Then she decided that it would serve no purpose after all. Lina always preferred to remain ignorant of a possibly unpleasant fact than be forced to acknowledge it.

Mechanically, for her thoughts still persisted in playing round the notebook, she began to do up the bundle for the jumble sale.

CHAPTER XIV

"Not much hope of tennis this afternoon. Hell's bells!" Johnnie, standing at the window with his hands in his pockets and contemplating the drizzle outside, breathed on the glass and drew a cross in the result with the end of his nose.

Lina looked up from the stocking she was darning. "Johnnie, did Cecil ever find Father's spectacles in the library the night he died?"

"Good heavens, monkeyface, I don't know. Why?"

"I just wondered."

Lina went on with her darning. Johnnie began to walk restlessly about the room.

Her head bent over her work, Lina asked:

"Why did he want his spectacles, in any case?"

"I don't know. Oh, to read a newspaper cutting I wanted to show him, I believe. Why?"

"Oh, nothing. I just wish it had been you who went to look for the spectacles, not Cecil. That's all."

"Why on earth do you wish that, you extraordinary little monkeyface?"

"I don't know. I just do. Then it would have been Cecil who was with him when he had that stroke, not you."

"But Cecil couldn't have done any more for him than I could."

"No, I suppose not."

"That's about the fourth time this week you've asked me something like that," Johnnie said idly.

Lina started ever so slightly. "Is it?" She uttered a nervous little laugh. "How silly of me. I seem to have been thinking about Father lately, for some reason or other."

"Well, it's all more than three years ago now."

"Yes," Lina agreed, with an odd feeling of relief. "Nearly four." Four years is a long time. Somehow, things that happened nearly four years ago are not nearly so important as things that happened last week.

But she really must not give way again to this nervous prompting to ask Johnnie details about her father's death.

It was true that Lina had been thinking a lot about her father, and her father's death, during the last week. She had tried hard not to do so, but all the time it was there in her mind, refusing to be thrust into oblivion.

That little black notebook was haunting her.

On the very first afternoon she had removed it from the drawer in Johnnie's room to a drawer in her own dressing table. A dozen times since then she had pored over it, with the fascination of repulsion. But for those "ha, ha's" she would have asked Johnnie about it with directness. But they prevented her, those appalling little written-down chuckles. She could not bear to confront Johnnie with them, and listen to his glibly lying explanation. For of course Johnnie would lie.

Why was she so sure that Johnnie would lie?

Lina put the stocking back in the basket, took up another, and spread out her hand in the foot. It was the hundredth time she had asked herself this question. For the hundredth time she refused to answer it honestly. Johnnie would lie because to lie in the face of embarrassment was Johnnie's nature. She would not ask herself why Johnnie might be embarrassed.

Lina knew that the General's spectacles had not been in the library at all. She remembered that they had been found, the next day, in a drawer of the dining-room sideboard, of all unlikely places. She remembered that quite clearly.

Yet she had asked Johnnie if Cecil did find them in the library.

It was absurd to have asked a thing like that.

It was absurd to ask anything at all: to keep giving way to this morbid feeling that she *must* speak to Johnnie about the details of her father's death, and force him to speak to her about them: to keep hoping that he would lie, so that she could make herself believe his lies, and yet hoping that he would not lie, so that she could believe that he never had lied.

It was most absurd of all to go on brooding like this, just because Johnnie had written down a few interesting facts about her father's diseases . . . to go on brooding until the preposterous fancies which she absolutely refused even to form in her conscious moments came crowding on her, fully and grotesquely grown, in her dreams.

She dropped her hands and stared at Johnnie.

The epitome of boredom, he was picking out on one finger on the piano a popular fox trot, *Guilty*.

2

Two nights later the Aysgarths were dining at Whinnies. Lady Fortnum had a small house party for the week-end, and after dinner the men had been trying who could put a half-crown furthest on the floor with one foot off the ground.

"Johnnie," Lina said suddenly, "do your trick with three chairs."

"That?" Johnnie smiled at her. "Oh, I haven't done that for years."

"Try it," Lina persisted.

Johnnie shook his head. "Getting too old for that sort of thing. Besides, muscles have got soft. Why, I haven't done that trick since—oh, since before your father died."

3

Lina was packing.

Blindly, haphazard, almost hysterically she threw her clothes into a big suitcase, just enough things to last for a week or two. Johnnie had gone out, and she could relax at last.

How she had got through the rest of last evening she hardly knew; still less how she had got through that interminable night, with Johnnie sleeping at her side till it was all she could do to hold herself back from screaming and screaming and throwing herself out of the bed, out of the room, and out of the house; while all the time there beat on her brain, as if it were the drum in some never-ending jazz band, the same refrain—"No, not since *two minutes* before Father died, no, not since *two minutes* before Father died, no, not since TWO MINUTES before Father died . . ."

She had had to bite the sides of her hands to fight down her hysteria.

As soon as Johnnie was out of the house she had telephoned her wire to Ronald and then run straight upstairs to pack.

In the train she regained some of her control.

Upcottery was left behind, definitely now and forever.

Upcottery and Johnnie. Johnnie the J. P. Johnnie the murderer of her own father.

Of course, now that she was calmer, she could understand how Johnnie's mind had worked.

To have called Johnnie a murderer to his face would have upset him very much indeed. Johnnie of course had never looked on what he had done in that light, not even when it was in contemplation. He had used no poison, he had employed no "blunt instrument," such a thing as murder had never entered his thoughts.

Besides, gentlemen don't murder. But they may, quite permissibly, help another gentleman out of life.

Johnnie's reasoning would have been perfectly simple. "General McLaidlaw might die at any moment. It would suit me extremely well if he would die at this one. If General McLaidlaw did certain things at this minute, he actually would die. Well, if he does them, that's his own lookout; no one's going to force him."

And so Johnnie filled up the old man's port glass and gone on filling it, hidden his spectacles so that Cecil could be sent to find them, led him on to excite himself with the memory of youthful exploits, and then . . .

"How could anyone call that *murder?*" Johnnie would have demanded, in surprised as well as hurt tones.

Lina called it murder.

She did not shirk the word or the thought.

Johnnie had murdered her own father as certainly and as carefully as if he had shot him through the heart across his own dining table.

She could not cry, yet. This shock was too great for tears.

Johnnie . . .

And she—incredibly *she*—could have Johnnie hanged. Hanged by the neck until he was dead. Johnnie . . .

She had only to take that notebook out of her suitcase, into which she had thrown it, and go with it to Scotland Yard. They would not refuse to recognize what she had known in her heart all the time but would not admit to her reason—that those notes had been made before and not after her father's death: that they were not the jottings of an interested novice of science, but a murderer's deliberate plan for his crime. Not they! They would . . .

Lina tugged the heavy case down from the rack, delved into it to find the notebook, pulled out the pages and tore them into little bits, and threw the scraps out of the window.

4

Or was it, legally, not murder at all?

Lina, thankful she had the carriage to herself, pulled off her hat and passed her hand over her hot, aching forehead.

When you incite a person to do something which both of you know will probably kill him—is that legally murder or not?

Oh, what did it matter? The legal aspect did not count. Morally it was murder. Morally, Johnnie had touched bottom at last.

Lina would have liked to cry, but could not.

For the really heartrending thing was that Johnnie could never recognize it as murder. Johnnie, with his infantile moral blindness, could never see those things as any ordinarily decent person sees them: as Lina herself saw them. Lina saw Johnnie as a murderer. Johnnie saw himself either as one driven by circumstances to a certain unconventionality of action, or else as a rather clever person. Probably he had managed to persuade himself, too, that he was doing his father-in-law quite a kind turn. Relieving pain. Euthanasia.

Lina shuddered.

Yet she could not hate Johnnie. She was horrified, even appalled; but one cannot hate a moral defective. But one cannot, equally, go on living with him.

She forced herself to think of Ronald.

Her flight to him had been instinctive. Ronald, with his solidity and dependability. Lina wanted desperately now to depend on somebody else at last. It had been part of the irony of her marriage with Johnnie that she, so unfitted to be the responsible partner, had had to support Johnnie in character as well as in purse. Well, that was all over now. Love is very decidedly not everything. Lina did not know whether she still loved Johnnie or not. She very much feared that she might go on loving him, whatever he had done. And four years is a long time.

Loving him, but not living with him. She had found that she could live with a thief, a cheat, a forger, a reprobate even; but not with a murderer.

A murderer . . .

It was still almost impossible to believe that Johnnie was a murderer.

Murder is always a thing apart from one's own life. People murder and are murdered, yes; but not the people one knows; certainly not the people one loves. Lina thought bitterly that, just as the last person to realize a husband's promiscuity is his own wife, so the last persons to believe in a man's murderous possibilities are those who are closest to him. "What, George!" they cry, horror-stricken. "Impossible! He was always so kind to the cat."

But Johnnie was a murderer. There was no getting

away from it. Though in this case the last person to believe it would certainly be Johnnie himself.

She was still thinking about Johnnie.

Lina changed to the other side of the carriage, though sitting with her back to the engine always made her feel rather sick. She wished it would make her feel sick now, to give her something else to think about; though ever since last night there had been a horrid empty feeling in the pit of her stomach, as if she were eternally descending a headlong lift, which was worse than any genuine nausea.

Ronald . . .

Lina's mind reached forward from the quicksand of its emotions to his rocklike solidity. She had not treated Ronald very well. She had disappointed him, too severely and too often. She had been a feckless little idiot, unable to make up her mind, unable to decide what she really wanted, drawing back each time she approached the brink of a decision. No wonder his letters had become fewer and less impassioned. It was in fact nearly a fortnight now since she had heard from him at all.

No, she had not treated Ronald well. But she was going to make up for that now. The tears came into her eyes at last as she thought of Ronald's delight when she told him that she had made up her mind at last: that she had come to him for good, without any reservations at all. It was wonderful to be wanted like that.

Johnnie had wanted her like that. . . .

But no. That was finished. There could be no possible weakening this time.

Besides, within a few hours she would have made any return to Johnnie impossible. Once he had got her, Ronald would never let her go again. Lina knew that.

And she knew that this time she would not want to go.

No, she was not in love with Ronald. She could never be in love with anyone again. But she did love him. And she was going to try, thankfully and with all her power, to be a good wife to him.

She wondered, would he kiss her on the platform?

5

Ronald met her at Waterloo, but he did not kiss her on the platform.

Lina's heart jumped as she saw him waiting for her. Yes, she loved him a lot. More than she had thought.

She clung to him, with both hands clutching his coat sleeves, in gratitude and relief. She felt safe at last. Ronald would look after her now.

"I've come to you, Ronald."

"Yes."

Ronald was looking down at her. She noticed with surprise that he seemed very much embarrassed. She thought it was because she was clinging to him in public, but she did not care: Ronald was there to be clung to.

He cleared his throat.

"I've got something to tell you, Lina."

She smiled up at him affectionately. "Yes, darling?" It was good to be with Ronald, so safe and dependable.

"I'd better tell you at once. I—well, you kept me on a string too long."

"I—what?"

"You kept me hanging too long. I decided you didn't care for me, *really*. I made up my mind you were in love with your husband all the time. I—I couldn't go on standing by indefinitely. So—well, I'm engaged to some-body else."

"You don't—love me any more?"

"No," said Ronald miserably.

They looked at one another.

Lina became conscious that people were beginning to stare.

"My suitcase," she muttered.

Ronald got her suitcase out of the carriage. He asked her if she wanted a taxi.

"No," said Lina. "Will you get me a porter?"

Ronald hailed a porter.

Lina held out her hand. "Good-bye, Ronald."

He took her hand awkwardly. "If there's anything I can do . . . ?"

"No," Lina said. "Good-bye."

Ronald hesitated a moment, then lifted his hat and shambled away. Lina knew that he was feeling the worst possible cad, and she was sorry for him, when it was not his fault at all.

"Taxi, miss?" said the porter.

Lina looked at him stupidly.

"Put it in the cloakroom, miss?"

"Oh! No, thank you." She looked mechanically at the watch on her wrist.

Three minutes later she crept into a train that would take her back to Upcottery.

There seemed nothing else to do.

CHAPTER XV

BEAKY THWAITE appeared to have no relations, few friends, and nothing at all to do. When Lina asked him, as she often did, how he spent his time, he did not seem very sure even of that.

"Oh, I don't know. Wander about, you know. Look up some old bean occasionally, and all that sort of thing."

"Don't you ever go to your house in Yorkshire?" Beaky was the not very willing owner of a large mansion and estate, including several thousand acres of grouse moor, in Yorkshire.

"Oh, yes. I take some old bean up there now and then, you know. Don't stop there alone, though, if I can help it. Bores me stiff."

"What you want is a sensible wife to look after you. Why don't you get married, Beaky?"

Beaky would laugh hugely. "What? Married? No, thanks. Not me. What? Besides, there aren't any sensible wives, what? Oh, sorry, Lina. Put my foot in it again. You're sensible, all right. Damned sensible. I don't know what the old bean would have done without you. Toddled off to the bow-wows, I expect, what?"

"Why do you say that?"

"Oh, I don't know," Beaky would answer vaguely. "Old Johnnie always was a bit of a lad, what?" But Lina knew that even Beaky had no idea how much of a lad old Johnnie had been.

Beaky stayed at Dellfield a lot now. Johnnie, rather

surprisingly, encouraged him to do so; and Beaky needed very little encouragement. It was obvious to Lina that Beaky was enormously fond of Johnnie. The worship which had been accorded him when they were schoolboys was still hardly diminished. In his admiration of Johnnie, Beaky was never tired of relating to Lina episodes and escapades in which Johnnie had played the principal part, to the enthusiastic audience of Beaky. Beaky admitted that his own schooldays would have been distressingly dull but for the way Johnnie had dared him into sharing his adventures.

Lina was interested in these stories, for the light that they threw on Johnnie the fledgling. The actual friendship between the two was illuminating. It was plain from Beaky's remarks that Johnnie had been one of the most popular boys in the school, even before he reached the glories of the first eleven and the first fifteen. He might have chosen anyone as his particular friend; and he had chosen Beaky, the unathletic (though persevering) and the not-too-popular. Lina thought she knew why Johnnie had done this. For one thing, the abundant admiration which Beaky offered him, and the ability to twist his Jonathan round his little finger, had appealed more to Johnnie than a more equal friendship with someone of his own standing in the school. That was usual enough, when the more spectacular character of the two lacked ballast. But Lina thought there had been a little more in it than that. Beaky had probably applauded escapades which a less infatuated friend would have denounced. Even now, for instance, he seemed to think it only a joke that Johnnie should have been asked to leave two terms before he should have done so, owing to certain petty thefts of money from trouser-pockets in the changing room having been traced to him.

Lina did not like Beaky. But it was impossible to dislike him. He was the most vacuous person she had ever known.

The land scheme in Bournemouth still seemed to be hanging fire. Johnnie reported fresh difficulties from time to time. Always, just when things appeared to be going smoothly at last, some new trouble would crop up. However, Johnnie's spirits did not suffer. He remained just as cheerful, whatever happened.

Beaky left everything to him. He took no part in the negotiations whatever, confining his activities to sitting beside Johnnie occasionally in the car when they went out to look for new sites. The prospect of making a few more thousands did not excite him at all. He had more already than he could spend. Lina thought his only interest in the affair was the excuse it offered of seeing Johnnie and staying a great deal at Dellfield.

She wished that something could be settled, so that Beaky should not have to stay quite so much at Dellfield.

From time to time she hinted as much to Johnnie.

But Johnnie unexpectedly seemed to want Beaky to stay at Dellfield as much as possilbe. Lina was sure that Beaky bored Johnnie almost as much as he bored her, and she could not understand why he should want him about the place.

Johnnie, however, could not help her there. He did not seem to know himself. Or, if he did, could not explain.

"Oh, I don't know," he would say carelessly. "I like old Beaky, you know."

"Yes, but he's so boring. Sometimes I feel I simply can't *bear* him a minute longer."

"We must put up witn him for a bit, till this thing's over. He's going to be damned useful to us, after all. Be a good little monkeyface and help me out."

And Lina would remember the early resolutions of her married life and make up her mind to bear Beaky a little longer, in order to help Johnnie.

But when Johnnie was tackled upon the question of how much longer he would need helping in this way, he was still more vague. Things weren't going well. But things might suddenly go better. One never knew. One just had to see.

Lina, deploring her inferiority in matters of business, was unable to find the searching questions which she felt must be waiting somewhere, if one only knew from experience where to look for them.

2

Four years is a long time.

Even three months is enough to turn the most mind-haunting horror into something that neither haunts nor horrifies.

Lina could hardly believe, when Joyce and Cecil brought Robert and Armorel to stay at Dellfield for Christmas, that four years ago on that day Johnnie had brought about her father's death. With the little note-book scattered from the train, she had even managed to persuade herself that she might have imagined the whole thing. In any case, she no longer thought of it as "murder."

And whether it, rather improbably now, were true or not, it had all happened four years ago. It was absurd, Lina was now convinced, to upset one's life for something that had happened four years ago.

She had gone back to Dellfield with the knowledge that Johnnie, who had cheated and stolen and forged, had now been proved to have murdered too. He had touched bottom. Things could never be worse. She had found a kind of grim consolation in that reflection. Whatever Johnnie did in the future could never be worse than he had done already.

And in spite of what Johnnie had done, Lina loved him more than ever. That was why she had never even considered seeking refuge with Joyce. At times she thought, with some perturbation, that what Johnnie had done had, in a way, actually increased her love for him, at any rate on its protective side. Certainly it had not diminished it. Lina wondered whether she too might be learning to turn a short-sighted eye on moral realities.

She enjoyed her Christmas.

Beaky she had firmly refused to invite, in spite of Johnnie's urging, and she was able to have several long and satisfactory conversations with Joyce.

It gave her a good deal of pleasure to be able to tell Joyce, with complete truth, that she really was happy, and to see that Joyce believed her. She was rather superior towards Joyce, adopting the idea that Joyce had very nearly managed to persuade her into making a mess of her life and that only by her own finer perceptions had she saved herself at the last minute. Joyce quite acknowledged now that Lina had not been such a weak fool as she had thought, in going back to Johnnie.

It gave Lina still more pleasure to hear Joyce admit, as Joyce, with her usual honesty, did admit, that Johnnie undoubtedly did love his wife. Johnnie was very sweet to Lina all the time they were at Dellfield, and his attitude was not lost upon Joyce. She asked Lina penetrating questions about Johnnie's behaviour during the last eight months, and could find no loopholes in it.

"Well, perhaps it all happened for the best after all," she delivered judgment. "I don't pretend to admire your Johnnie, and I'd much rather have seen you go off with Ronald; but you weren't such a fool as I thought. Johnnie certainly does love you. He's had his shock, and it's improved him. And so long as he makes you happy, I don't care. But if he ever slides again, my girl . . ."

"He won't," said Lina. She had no doubts about that now.

And of course Joyce knew nothing of any other possible directions in which Johnnie might slide. Though of those too Lina had few doubts now.

But she did catch herself once or twice looking at Joyce across the table at Christmas dinner.

Or rather, Joyce caught her.

"Why so solemn, Lina? What are you thinking about?"

"Oh, nothing," Lina answered, and smiled quickly. Actually she had been thinking: what would you say, Joyce, if you knew that my husband had killed our father?

But the fact that Johnnie had, only distressed her now when she remembered it. It distressed her almost as much to realize how seldom she did remember it.

And as things turned out, the only lasting difference that her discovery of the notebook made to Lina was the loss of three hundred pounds a year. In a fit of panic at the remembrance of what Johnnie had once done when he was short of money, she had raised his allowance again to five hundred a year.

So Johnnie scored.

3

After Christmas promptly arrived Beaky, for a week's visit. Johnnie had invited him, without saying anything to Lina about it. Lina was annoyed and told Johnnie so.

"It won't be for much longer," Johnnie soothed her.

Lina, who had meditated a week's banting following the usual Christmas overeating, had to content herself with buying a most expensive belt instead. She had to be really careful about her figure now.

It was during the first day or two of this visit of Beaky's that a faint suspicion crept into Lina's mind. She began to fear that Johnnie's real reason for keeping Beaky in such close touch with him was that, having a rich man at his disposal, he was determined not to let him go; so that if the land scheme did fall through, he could find some other way of separating Beaky from some of his unneeded thousands. And as soon as the suspicion was really lodged in her mind, she began to fear too that Johnnie was actually meditating some such plan already. Knowing Johnnie, Lina took it for granted that the plan, if plan there was, would be an unscrupulous one.

She did not know quite what to do about it.

Of course it was quite useless to ask Johnnie outright, but she did ask him one night in the bedroom if he was short of money.

"Short?" said Johnnie. "How do you mean?"

"Well, have you run up any more debts, or anything like that?"

"Are you offering to pay them for me, if I have?" Johnnie grinned.

"No, I'm not. I just wondered. Have you?"

"Not a one," Johnnie said blithely. "Your husband's

a reformed character, Mrs. Aysgarth. Thanks to you."

"Darling!" said Lina, almost mechanically fond.

But she was not altogether satisfied. There was a glib air sometimes about Johnnie which she mistrusted.

She debated whether she ought to warn Beaky.

It is not a pleasant or an easy thing, to warn a guest that one's husband is not quite to be trusted in matters of finance; but Lina, nagged at by her conscience, did her best.

One morning when Johnnie was busy with his cows she tackled Beaky about it.

"Beaky, how are things getting on with you and Johnnie?"

Beaky looked up from the book he was reading by the drawing-room fire. "Eh? Oh, I don't know. Leave all that to the old bean, you know."

"Yes; that's what I mean. Why are you so slack, Beaky? You shouldn't leave everything to Johnnie like this. You ought to keep an eye on things yourself, too."

Beaky laughed his enormous laugh. "Hullo! What's this? Pi-jaw, what? Reminds me of being hauled up in front of the old chief. 'You're getting slack, Thwaite, what?' What? Eh? Damned good."

"No, I'm serious, Beaky."

"Are you? What? Top-hole. I say, have you read this muck? What? Got it off your shelves. Can't make head or tail of it. Friend of yours, I expect. You know all these comic birds, don't you? Good God! What?"

"Beaky," Lina said patiently, "do you mind just listening to me for a moment?"

"Rather. Like to have these things explained to me. Bit weak in the top story, I expect, what? Don't be too highbrow, though. Well, what's it all about, what?

Sorry I called it muck. Friend of yours, and all that sort of rot, I expect. What? Eh? Well?"

"I'm not talking about that book."

"Oh, aren't you? Sorry. Thought you were. Here, I say! Not carrying on with the pi-jaw still, are you? What?"

"You can call it a pi-jaw if you like. Beaky, I want to know. How much money are you putting into this scheme?"

"Oh, I don't know. The old bean said we'd want about fifteen thousand. Probably lose it all, but who cares? Here, I say. You at a loose end this morning, Lina? What about a walk or something? I feel a bit lousy myself, too. Eh? What about it?".

"No, thank you," Lina said with forbearance. "I don't want to go for a walk. I want to talk to you."

"Carry on, sergeant," said Mr. Thwaite amiably.

"Beaky, I don't think you're being fair to Johnnie," Lina began, and paused to admire the inspiration of this opening. By pretending to put the blame on Beaky himself, she would be able to convey her hint much more delicately. "I don't think you're being *fair* to him," she repeated. "You must remember that———"

"Here, take a pew, what?" interrupted Mr. Thwaite. "I know some old beans yap better on their pins, but it puts the wind up me. What? I mean, standing over me like a beak. What? Sorry. You know what I mean. Take a pew, what?"

Lina sat down and began again.

It was unfair to Johnnie, because Johnnie, compared with Beaky, was a poor man.

"Oh, rot," protested Mr. Thwaite. "Here, I say. Draw it mild, what?"

A poor man, repeated Lina firmly; and it was not

fair to put on a poor man the responsibility of a very large sum of money belonging to somebody else. Supposing things went wrong. Supposing Johnnie made an error of judgment. He was not a business man. He might quite possibly lose a large proportion of the money. And how would he feel then? Very perturbed indeed. Very upset. Especially since, if the error was a particularly gross one, he would not be able to repay what he had lost.

It was not fair. Beaky ought to take an equal responsibility. He must look into things for himself, and decide for himself whether Johnnie's advice was always sound or not. Now did Beaky understand?

"I get you," Beaky nodded sagely. "I get you, old bean. Sorry! Lina, I mean. What? You mean, the old bean's a proper old mutt, what? You're afraid he'll be twisted right and left."

"I don't mean anything of the sort," Lina snapped, wishing Beaky were not quite so obtuse.

She tried to explain herself further, but still without giving Johnnie away.

An hour later, when she was powdering her nose before lunch, she heard Beaky and Johnnie in conversation just under her window. Beaky's loud tones carried themselves without difficulty to her dressing table.

"Hullo, old bean. Been looking for you. Here, I say, what's the matter with Lina? What? Eh?"

Something inaudible from Johnnie.

"Why, she's been trying to persuade me for the last hour that you're soft in the head. What? Good God! I mean, all the land sharks in Bournemouth are going to see you coming a mile away. She says I'd much better pull out while the cash is still there, before you've been twisted out of it. Eh? Damned good. What? Good God!

Thank the Lord I'm not married. What? Oh, sorry. Putting my foot in it again, what? Didn't mean that. Lina's one of the best, and all that sort of rot. But she seems to think you've got a screw loose, old bean. Suppose all wives think that about their husbands, though, what? Otherwise they wouldn't have married 'em. Eh? Good God!"

4

Johnnie was very angry.

"What business is it of yours?" he demanded. "That's what I want to know. What business is it of yours?"

Lina was never slow to flare up when someone else was already alight. "*You* ought to know what business it is of mine."

"What do you mean?"

"Well, would you rather I asked Captain Melbeck to say a word to Beaky?" Lina was sorry for the sentence as soon as she had uttered it.

It seemed, however, to roll off Johnnie's back. "Good Lord, if you're going to be forever bringing up that old stuff," he said with angry disgust.

Already Lina was penitent for bringing up that old stuff. "But, Johnnie, you remember what you used to be like."

"Oh, yes, I know all that. But have I been like it lately? That was years ago. You know I'm quite different now. And here you are, practically warning Beaky that I'm not fit to be trusted with twopence-halfpenny of anyone else's."

"Johnnie, I didn't put it like that. You know what an idiot Beaky is. He got it all wrong. All I said was that it isn't fair of him to leave everything to you: he ought

to take responsibility for the decisions too. That's all
I said."

"Are you sure?"

"Of course I am. You *know* what an idiot Beaky is."

Johnnie grinned. "All right. Sorry I blew you up,
monkeyface. I thought you'd got it into your head that
I was trying to twist him, or some damned nonsense.
Kiss me!"

"Darling!" said Lina. "Now come along. We must
go down to lunch."

Not for quite a couple of hours did she realize that
this was precisely what she had imagined—and still did.

CHAPTER XVI

THE Aysgarths' position in the county was a curious one, typical of the transition period in which they lived.

Connected as Johnnie was with most of the old families living in Dorsetshire, the Aysgarths were on intimate terms (so far as it is possible for terms among old families to be intimate) with houses into which Lady Fortnum was not received at all. On the other hand, the Lady Fortnums of the county, and there were plenty of them, looked down on Johnnie as definitely below their social level because he had worked for his living. He and Lina were invited to Whinnies on little more than sufferance. And yet it was on little more than sufferance that they went.

The Aysgarths, in fact, at Dellfield, were neither quite of the old order, nor of the new. The more the land of England is changing hands, the more do the former holders by right of birth look down on the new owners by right of purchase; and the more do the latter scoff at the former. For one who takes pleasure in despising his neighbour more than himself, the English countryside of this decade offers exceptional opportunities.

When, therefore, Lady Fortnum found herself short of a man for the party she was taking over to a regimental ball at Poole she had no compunction in ringing up Beaky, whom she had met twice, and inviting him to dine and go on with the party, without thinking it necessary to include Beaky's host and hostess in her invitation.

"Here, I say," observed Mr. Thwaite, coming back from the telephone in much perturbation. "Here, this is a bit thick, you know. What? I mean, look here, old bean, what the devil am I to say? What?" He explained the dilemma.

"A sweet piece of impertinence," Johnnie grinned. "And what did you say, Beaky?"

"Well, dash it all, old bean! I mean, I hedged. What? Told her I'd have to find out if you had an engagement. I mean—well, dash it all! What? Look here, I say, she's hanging on. What shall I say?"

"Go if you want to, Beaky," said Lina. "Don't if you don't. Do you?"

"Oh, draw it mild. I mean . . . Good God! Well, after all, I suppose a dance is a dance, isn't it? But look here, I say, if she's got the nerve not to ask you too . . . Well, I mean, dash it all!"

"You go, Beaky," Lina advised.

So Beaky went.

"I think that about reaches even her limit, for downright impudence," observed Lina, but without rancour. The absence of rancour was due to the fact that at any rate she would have an evening without Beaky, which was a relief.

During the course of it she said tentatively to Johnnie:

"Johnnie, I don't want to be a nuisance or interfere with your plans, but need we really have Beaky to stay again for a long, long time?"

Johnnie grinned at her. "Getting a bit fed up?"

"Yes. He's *so* dull."

"I'm getting fed up too. We won't have him again."

"What, never?"

"I hope not."

"You can manage the business without him?"

"Oh, Lord, yes." Johnnie paused. "As a matter of fact," he said airily, "it's all a washout."

"What, the land scheme?"

"Yes. The price of land has gone up. We couldn't make a good enough profit. Don't tell Beaky that, though," Johnnie added quickly.

"Why not?"

"I'll tell him myself, by letter, when I call the whole thing off."

"Why not tell him before he goes?"

"Oh, I don't know. He'd want to ask a lot of fool questions. It'd be easier by letter."

Lina felt her heart give a little leap. Johnnie had spoken far, far too glibly. She thought: There's something wrong here, my lad.

Quite casually she asked: "What's going to happen to the money, then?"

"The money?" Johnnie looked his artless surprise.

"The fifteen thousand that you brought back from America."

"Oh! Well, I suppose Beaky will use it in some other way. *I* don't know."

"Has he got it now, or have you?"

"He has. You're very curious this evening, monkey-face."

Lina forced a laugh. "Am I? I didn't mean to be. I suppose I want to talk to you, now we've got an evening to ourselves for once."

"Well, don't let's talk about that business. I'm sick of it. And of course it's been a great disappointment to me." But Johnnie did not look disappointed in the least: though he obviously tried.

Lina hid her alarm as she thought to herself: Johnnie's made up his mind to get that fifteen thousand somehow. I'm *certain* he has.

She felt suddenly very miserable and dispirited.
Johnnie had relapsed.

2

But she had no evidence that Johnnie had relapsed.

On the contrary, Johnnie had spoken the truth.

Not for a moment had Lina believed that the fifteen
thousand pounds was in the possession of Beaky.

Wrapping up her question as much as possible, though
careless of what Johnnie might say did he discover that
it had ever been put, she found out from Beaky the next
morning that the fifteen thousand really was in his own
keeping. It was lodged in a bank in Paris, under an alias.

"Why do you have to be so secretive about it?" asked
Lina, worried.

"Good God, I don't know. Ask the old bean. Agin the
law, or some rot."

"Johnnie would know, of course," Lina said quickly,
doing her best to prevent this conversation from being
repeated too. "Did he advise secrecy?"

"Rather. Half the fun, what? Don't want to be copped
and jugged, eh? I mean, what?"

"No, of course you don't," Lina said brightly.

But the conversation had not eased her mind.

If anything it worried her still more that Beaky should
have the money himself.

For how in that case did Johnnie contemplate getting
it except by some scheme that would be quite flagrant?

3

There were two whole days left of Beaky's visit.

Lina did not know what to do.

She did not see how she could warn Beaky more than

she had done already. If he had been too stupid to take her hints, then she had done all she could for him. Besides, it was not the possibility of Beaky losing his money that worried her in the least. That prospect meant nothing to her at all. What terrified her was the unmasking of Johnnie as the dishonest agent of Beaky's loss.

She did not know what to do.

The thought occurred to her of asking Johnnie outright *why* this suspicious secrecy was necessary: of questioning and pestering him until she got at some clue to the plan that Johnnie must have in his mind. But Johnnie, she felt sure, would not allow himself to be questioned and pestered. And in her ignorance he could so easily put her off with a plausible answer. In any case, she did remember vaguely something about a prohibition against the removal of funds from England during the crisis; though whether it was still in force or not, she did not know. But such a prohibition there seemed to have been; and Beaky seemed to have contravened it; so the employment of secrecy would, according to Johnnie, be quite plausible.

Sitting in front of her dressing-table mirror as she curled the back ends of her hair before dinner, Lina laid down the tongs and stared sightlessly at her own reflection. *Why* had Johnnie called the land scheme off so suddenly? And *why* had he been so anxious that Beaky should not know yet?

And why, for that matter, had he told her?

Had it been by way of preparation for some surprise later?

Why, why, why?

"Oh, God," Lina breathed wretchedly.

It was all beginning again; and she had thought it all finished. The old load of unfair responsibility, enormous responsibility which she hated so much and with which she felt herself so unfitted to cope, was pressing down on her again.

She took up her tongs from their little nest of fire in the Meta holder and went on with her work. Whether one's husband is meditating larceny on a grand scale or whether he is not, one's back-hair must still be curled.

She worked mechanically, her mind busy.

The tongs slipped and burnt the side of her neck. She uttered a little squeak and searched hurriedly for cold cream.

As if the physical stimulus had jogged her mind, her thoughts became less despondent. After all, what evidence had she? None at all. There was nothing whatever really to show that Johnnie was meditating any such crime. It had just been her intuition; and Lina had read enough books by men to know how fallible feminine intuition is.

She had probably been imagining the whole thing.

Yes, that was it. Her imagination, stimulated by fear and the knowledge of Johnnie's old weakness, had carried her away. Johnnie had assured her only a couple of days ago that all that kind of thing was dead and buried. She must have more faith in him. Johnnie had not relapsed at all. She had imagined the whole thing.

While she finished dressing Lina was very busy persuading herself that she had imagined the whole thing.

4

But in the drawing room after dinner her fears returned.

Johnnie was so very attentive to Beaky.

Uselessly Lina told herself that it was absurd of her

to be suspicious because Johnnie was attentive to Beaky.
She remembered only too well how attentive Johnnie
had been to herself when he was about to rob her. And
here was Johnnie behaving in exactly the same way to
Beaky: laughing at his silly jokes, encouraging him to
the reminiscence that Beaky loved, pressing drinks and
cigars on him, quite ignoring his wife in his concentra-
tion on his guest.

"Ho, ho!" roared Beaky, already rather drunk. "Here,
draw it mild, old bean. You'll have me tanked soon.
What? I mean, won't Lina have a spot?"

"No, thank you," said Lina coldly. She really disliked Beaky now, for being about to be robbed by Johnnie.

Too restless to sit down, she moved to the piano,
which she had not opened for months. Johnnie meant to
rob Beaky. How was she going to stop it?

"Going to strum?" inquired Beaky, superfluously.
"Tophole. Here, I say, old bean, remember those songs
old Hardy had on that gramophone of his? Pretty
ghastly, what? *Carolina Brown*. Eh? Good God! Play
Carolina Brown, Lina."

Lina played Debussy.

She thought:

"My husband's going to rob you. You *idiot!* My husband's going to rob you of fifteen thousand pounds Why
the hell can't you stop him for yourself?"

She got up from the piano.

Beaky, egged on by Johnnie, was consuming yet another whisky-and-soda. He would probably be drunk
soon. Was Johnnie trying to make him drunk? Why?
Johnnie would certainly have no difficulty in making
Beaky drunk if he wanted. Beaky did anything Johnnie
suggested. And if he demurred, it only needed an adult
version (and not so very adult either) of the old school-

boy "dare" to bring Beaky up to scratch at once. But why should Johnnie be trying, apparently, to make Beaky drunk here and now? The money in any case was in Paris.

"I think I shall go to bed," Lina said.

Johnnie nodded. Beaky rose, not too steadily.

Lina looked at him with distaste. She thought, again:

"Yes, my husband's going to rob you. He's going to rob you of that fifteen thousand pounds as sure as eggs are eggs. He's going to get that money if he has to kill you for it—if . . ."

"Darling—what's the matter?" exclaimed Johnnie.

"Hullo! Here, I say . . . Good God!" said Beaky. Lina had fainted.

5

Johnnie meant to kill Beaky.

Lina knew it.

She could not prove it, she could not argue it, she could not defend her conviction in any way. She simply *knew* it.

And what was she going to do about it?

All night long, after Johnnie had carried her up to her bedroom, she lay awake, trying to force her distracted mind to deal with this dreadful emergency; and in the morning she still had no plan.

Beaky was going the next day but one. And some time after that, unless she prevented it, Johnnie would kill him. She had two whole days in which to find a means of preventing it.

What was she going to do?

Stray remarks of Johnnie's had taken on a new significance now. It was the last time Beaky would stay at Dellfield; the failure of the land scheme was a great dis-

appointment, when Johnnie had not looked disappointed
at all—when Johnnie had tried to look disappointed and
failed. Lina saw now why Johnnie had abandoned the
land scheme. It was horribly true that there was not
enough profit in it. There would be far more profit in
getting rid of Beaky altogether: there would be fifteen
thousand pounds' profit in that. And the reason for all
that secrecy about the money was now only too plain. It
would never be traced to Johnnie, because nobody at all
except their three selves knew of its existence.

But Johnnie had insisted on secrecy from the very first.
Did that mean that from the very first he had meditated . . . ?

Lina buried her burning face in her hot pillow. It was
too horrible.

And only she could stop it.

And what was she going to do?

6

In the end she did nothing.

As the morning drew on she saw more and more
clearly that she had been making a colossal, a perfectly
hideous mistake. A single stab of preposterous inspiration had led to a whole night's nightmare; and that was
all. It is ridiculous to take seriously the bogies that sit
on one's bed when one's head is splitting and one cannot sleep. Indigestion! From indigestion of the stomach
to indigestion of the mind is only a short step after all.
The whole thing had been indigestion, and nothing more.

Ordering the meals, doing the flowers, washing out a
pair of stockings, among normal tasks and normal sights,
Lina rapidly became normal herself. It was, she saw, and
even smiled at herself for ever having failed to see it,

quite impossible for murder to connect itself with such a very ordinary household as Dellfield.

Murder!

Johnnie contemplating the murder of Beaky!

Husband Johnnie contemplating the murder of friend Beaky!

What could be more impossible?

Of course there had been that incident four years ago. But that had not been *murder*. Not exactly *murder*. And it might very well not have been anything at all. Lina had never known. And nowadays she did not want to know. But more and more she had been taking it for granted lately that her imagination had created the whole thing. Nothing like that scene which she had visualized had ever taken place at all. She practically believed that now. She did believe it.

So of course there simply was no precedent.

And without a precedent this new piece of idiocy would naturally never have entered her mind at all.

So there one was.

But just to prove to herself how mistaken she had been, how wickedly mistaken, she noticed Johnnie very carefully during that evening; and Johnnie was perfectly normal.

Johnnie was normal, Lina was normal, Beaky was as near normal as he ever could be: everything was normal. And too much imagination is a great curse.

Fortunately Lina was far too worn out that night to exercise the curse. She slept for nine hours without opening an eye.

7

But in the morning her doubts returned.

She felt heavy and depressed, as one does when one

has slept too long. The breakfast tray seemed to weigh her down in bed; she did not even open *The Times*.

Sipping her coffee, she tried to tackle the problem. This was no fit of silly panic; she ought to be able to see things in their right perspective now. Lina was quite sure (she kept telling herself how sure she was) that everything was quite all right; but the problem was, ought one not, with Johnnie, to be *prepared* for the worst?

Lina felt dispiritedly that one ought. Everything was quite all right, of course. But one *ought* to insure against the worst by speaking the right word now.

But to whom should one speak it, Beaky or Johnnie?

How on earth could she say to Beaky: "Just be careful of Johnnie. Keep your eye on him. It's quite on the cards that he's made up his mind to kill you." Impossible.

And even less could one say to Johnnie: "I know you were responsible for Father's death. I've a suspicion that you may be planning something of the same kind against Beaky. You'd better not; that's all."

No. That would mean the end of everything between herself and Johnnie, if he once knew what she thought he had done—whether he had really done it or not. Their marriage could not continue.

On the other hand . . .

"Oh, God," said Lina wretchedly.

She wished she had a stronger mind. She wished she was one of those people who always know exactly what to do, whatever the emergency.

In her bath she tried to persuade herself that there was no emergency at all. She tried to recapture her happy conviction of yesterday. But it would not come. There was probably no emergency, but there *might* be. That was as near as she could get to it.

And all the time she was busy stifling the horrid, heart-pumping dread, growing nearer to certainty every minute, that there *was* an emergency—a terrible emergency. And that she herself was too cowardly to face it.

All the morning the feeling grew on her. What was she going to do? The normal tasks, which yesterday had restored her sanity, to-day seemed grimly ironical, in comparison with the horror that was fermenting.

She was alone in the house, except for the servants.

Johnnie and Beaky had gone off in the car, to look at some land that was for sale on some cliffs somewhere by the sea. They were to be back for lunch.

Suddenly the thought pierced her: *why* had Johnnie taken Beaky to look at more land, when he had already decided that the land scheme was a failure?

Why had he taken Beaky to some cliffs?

Lina started up from the chair on which she had been sitting. Her sewing was strewed, unregarded, on the floor. She pressed her hand to her aching forehead. She knew now. The time had come. Johnnie was going to push Beaky over the cliff.

The time had come, and here was she in Upcottery, unable to prevent it. She did not even know where they had gone. But she must do something. Anything. She could not sit here while somewhere else Johnnie was committing murder. Johnnie *must* be saved from committing murder. What was she to do—what was she to do?

In a panic of indecision a dozen hopeless plans flashed across her mind. She would ring up the police; she would borrow someone's car and drive like mad to the likeliest place; she would get the B. B. C. to broadcast an S O S, she would . . .

She made little darting runs, towards the telephone, towards the front door, towards the kitchen.

This would not do. This was utter idiocy. If Beaky was to be saved, she must keep calm. She *must* keep calm. She must think, calmly and coolly, what was best to do.

She could not keep calm. Across her distracted vision the whole scene passed, in a series of horrid little vignettes: the car running smoothly over the turf as it drew off the road, Beaky, appreciative and loudly old-beaning, Johnnie inviting him to look over the edge of the cliff at the rocks below, that sudden thrust in the small of Beaky's back, Beaky dropping, dropping, dropping, turning leisurely over in the air, until . . .

Lina screwed her knuckles into her eyes. What was she to do?

It was half-past twelve.

She could do nothing.

In an apathy of despair she sat down again. Well, she would know soon enough now. They were to be back for lunch. If within the next half hour they had not returned. . . .

They did not return within the next half hour.

At half-past one Lina, pale and trembling but with a composed face, lunched alone, for the benefit of the servants. She had thought it all out. At the inquest it would be fatal, quite fatal, if there appeared any hint that she had been anticipating what happened. That would at once throw doubt on its being an accident at all. Lina quite understood that. She was calm now, and she knew that Johnnie's life depended on her keeping her head.

As she drank her soup she thought:

"Beaky's dead now."

It was strange that she could think that with so little emotion.

At ten minutes to two Johnnie and Beaky drove up to the front door.

Lina ran out to meet them and fell into Johnnie's arms, sobbing.

"Oh, *Johnnie!*"

"Sorry we're so late, darling. Hullo, what's up?"

"I've been imagining the most *dreadful* things," Lina wept, with truth.

8

Actually the truth was just as far as it could have been from Lina's imaginings. So far from Johnnie ever having contemplated killing Beaky, he had saved Beaky's life; and at the greatest danger to his own.

"The old bean won't tell you a word about it himself, I'll bet," Beaky bubbled, "so you can have it straight from the horse's mouth, what? Damned close shave. We both of us nearly conked, I can tell you. Good God! Bit of a hero, old bean, aren't you? What?"

"Oh, shut up, you ass," Johnnie grinned.

What had happened was that they had run the Bentley onto the turf bordering the cliffs, exactly as Lina had imagined, while they looked round. When they were ready to leave Beaky, who was driving, had turned the car round while Johnnie stood by the edge, idly watching the waves among the rocks at the bottom. He had glanced up, to see Beaky still backing and Beaky's back wheels within a foot of the edge. With completely characteristic asininity, Beaky was manœuvring on the very limited piece of turf without even looking towards his rear.

Johnnie had to act in a flash. There was no time to warn Beaky. Before his shout could penetrate Beaky's understanding, the car would be over the cliff. He leapt forward, bounded onto the running board, and clutched the hand brake. The engine stalled, there was a lurch and a thud, and the car had come to rest with its back wheels spinning free in the air. It was half over the cliff, but it stopped there. Johnnie and Beaky climbed very gingerly out, to find labourers and a horse to drag the car into safety.

The chances had been about even whether Johnnie, clinging desperately to the hand brake, might not have gone over the cliff with the car.

"I tell you, the old bean's a pukka hero!" spluttered Beaky.

Lina looked at Johnnie, her eyes wet. How could she have thought such things about him? It would have served her right if Johnnie had been killed in trying to do the very opposite from what she had so wickedly thought.

"Oh, *Johnnie!*" she muttered.

9

That evening the rescue of Beaky was celebrated.

Never had Johnnie been merrier or Beaky more boisterous.

Lina felt as if years had been taken off her age.

10

"Well, cheer-oh," said Beaky, extending a large hand. "Thanks frightfully, and all that sort of rot. What?"

Johnnie was peering into the radiator of Beaky's Bentley. "Hullo, you're a bit short of water. I'll get a can while you're making your farewells to Lina."

"Will you really? I say, thanks frightfully."

"And you're going straight up to Yorkshire?" Lina said conversationally.

"That's the idea."

"But you'll never do it in a day, from here."

"What? Oh, I say, draw it mild. Only about three hundred, to my place. Bit boring though, alone. May stay a night in some pub. See what happens. What? Here, I say, don't stand out here. Too parky, what?"

"I'm quite all right," Lina smiled. "And when are we going to see you again, Beaky?"

"What, me? God knows. I mean. . . . Oh, I'll tootle along sometime, I expect. Depends when you ask me, doesn't it? What? Eh?" Beaky evidently considered this a joke and paid tribute to it heartily.

Something said clearly in Lina's mind: "You'll never see Beaky again. Never! Unless . . ."

The blood drained from her face. She stared at him.

A terrible thought had come to her.

Johnnie had saved Beaky's life because he had not been ready for him to die.

The money was in a Paris bank, under an alias. Only Beaky could draw a cheque for it. Until Johnnie had Beaky's cheque, Beaky must not die.

Lina knew that this revelation meant that she could delude herself no longer. She had two minutes in which to act. And if she did not act, Beaky's life might be the price of her complacence.

It was her last chance. And his.

Johnnie *did* mean to kill Beaky—sometime. Lina knew it. She always had known it, really.

Once Beaky drove away from here . . .

"Beaky!" she gasped out. Her teeth were chattering, and the skin of her face felt as if it had been drawn tight, like parchment on a drum.

"Hullo? Here, I say, you are cold. I knew you were. What? You hop indoors."

"Yes, but Beaky . . ." She must stop him going—detain him somehow, till she could decide what to do.

"Consider it said," replied Beaky firmly, and propelled her through the doorway. "Anyhow, here comes the old bean with the water. I'll be pushing off in a minute. Well, good-bye, and all that sort of rot. I mean, cheer-oh. What?"

Through the morning-room window, a minute later, Lina watched him drive away.

II

The next morning Johnnie had a telegram.

It came over the telephone, and Lina herself received it.

It was from Johnnie's brother, Alec, asking Johnnie to meet him in London for dinner that evening on urgent business.

"Damn!" said Johnnie. "That's a bit inconvenient. I've been putting off a lot of jobs till Beaky went. Think I ought to go, monkeyface?"

"Yes," said Lina. "Of course you must. How long will you be away?"

"Oh, not more than a couple of nights, if that. Well, I suppose I'd better pack."

Lina was not sorry that Johnnie was going away for two days. She wanted to be alone. It would help her to get things into their right perspective and rid herself of the lingering shadow of the bogey. She knew now that that moment of absurd panic on the doorstep yesterday morning had been caused by a last flick of the bogey's tail. It had been extremely lucky that Beaky pushed her indoors before she said anything too dreadful.

And in any case Beaky was safe enough in Yorkshire, with Johnnie under Alec's eye in London.

Not of course that there was any question of safety, really. Had not Johnnie actually saved his life?

Still, Beaky was safe.

She went upstairs to see what Johnnie was forgetting to pack.

12

Lina forced herself to read the little paragraph again.

PARIS TRAGEDY

ENGLISHMAN DEAD

The Englishman who was found dead in a house of amusement in Paris, as reported in our later editions yesterday, has now been identified as Mr. Gordon Cochrane Thwaite, of Penshaze Court, Yorkshire. Further details are now to hand of the manner in which the tragedy occurred.

It appears that Mr. Thwaite visited the resort, which has a questionable reputation, in the company of another Englishman. Both men had evidently been drinking during the evening, and on arrival Mr. Thwaite ordered a bottle of brandy. They then passed into a smaller room, together with two young women belonging to the establishment, and all four partook of the brandy. According to the statement of one of the girls, the brandy being of a good brand, Mr. Thwaite's companion asked for it to be served in large beakers, and these were provided. In a spirit of bravado, Mr. Thwaite filled one of these to the brim and drank it off. Owing to the fact that neither of the girls understands more than a few words of English, it is not clear how Mr. Thwaite came to perform such a foolhardy action, but their impression is that the men were having a bet on whether Mr. Thwaite would do it or not.

Mr. Thwaite's companion was not present when the tragedy happened, having left the house a few moments after the incident of the brandy. The French police have not yet succeeded in establishing his identity. They would be grateful if he would communicate with them, in order that he may confirm the young women's account of what took place. His name would appear to be Allbeam, or Holebean.

We understand that Penshaze Court is entailed and will pass to a distant cousin of the deceased.

13

Lina was searching feverishly in Johnnie's desk in the morning room.

Johnnie was out. She had not seen him since she had read the paragraph in the newspaper in bed, after her breakfast.

How she had managed to get up, dress, talk to the cook, and perform her other routine jobs just as if this was a morning exactly like any other morning, she hardly knew. She hoped dully that the servants had got no inkling of the panic, the horror, and the sick despair through which her mind had had to fight as she talked with them.

Now she was free; and, outraging every canon of her upbringing, she was searching Johnnie's private papers. She searched partly in a desperate hope that she might find proof that the man in Paris had not been Johnnie, and that it really had been Alec himself and not poor, unsuspecting Beaky who had sent that telegram; partly in a still more desperate fear that she would find proof of quite another sort. In any case she must know.

She found her proof.

Among the old receipts, the letters, and all the other unsorted rubbish of years, in a little drawer by itself, there was a small black account book. Lina looked at it cursorily at first, and then, because she did not understand the entries, more carefully. It was full of lists of curious names, preceded each by a date and followed by a sum in pounds; and in front of the pounds there was a plus or a minus sign, in red ink.

One or two familiar names in the lists caught her eye, and she realized at what she was looking. It was Johnnie's betting book.

There was no need for her to do any calculations. Johnnie had done them for her, on the opposite pages. At the time of Beaky's death Johnnie had been nearly thirteen thousand pounds on the wrong side. He had been betting continuously, ever since he had first begun nearly eight years ago. There was no gap shown even after Lina had come back to him at the beginning of last summer.

In another drawer Lina found the rest of the story: demands from bookmakers, letters from moneylenders, threats of proceedings, and all the rest. Her mind had been so bludgeoned that it hardly felt the extra blow of learning that Johnnie had actually borrowed money on the strength of his expectations under her own will.

But the thing was plain enough. There were letters dated within the last month whose tone was unmistakable. Their writers meant business. If Johnnie did not pay, Johnnie would be jailed. Johnnie had been desperate.

And Johnnie had taken desperate steps.

There could be no glossing over the thing this time: no finding smooth words to veneer plain facts. This was murder. Lina knew that in whatever light she might have persuaded herself to regard her father's death, she could not do the same thing now. This was murder.

With mechanical neatness she put the papers back in the drawer exactly as she had found them and went upstairs to lock herself in her bedroom.

She had been wrong. Johnnie had not touched bottom before. He had found yet another profundity to plumb.

But this time it did not even enter Lina's head to run desperately away from him.

14

For a fortnight or more Lina lived in almost continuous panic.

Her terror was so great that it very nearly swamped every other emotion. Horror and despair were almost lost in fear.

Her panic was lest Johnnie should be caught.

At first it seemed to her impossible that Johnnie should not be traced. Every time there was a knock at the door, every time the telephone bell rang, she lived through Johnnie's arrest and conviction for murder. In Bournemouth she found herself hurrying past policemen. Even the village policeman at home ceased to be a rather quick-witted rustic and became a figure of sinister significance.

Her nerves were worn into rags. She would look at Johnnie, sitting there so merry and unperturbed, and could hardly stop herself from screaming.

She felt herself and Johnnie cut off from the world:

outcasts from humanity: marooned on a desert island of guilt. She and Johnnie, all alone.

For this time she was as guilty as Johnnie. Guiltier, because she was the responsible one of the two.

She had known——she had *known* that Beaky was going to be killed; and she had not uttered a word to prevent it. And Beaky had paid for her pusillanimity with his life.

Lina wept and wept for Beaky and her own cowardice till she could hardly use her eyes for anything but weeping. Johnnie was much surprised that she should show so much feeling for a man whom she had always professed to dislike.

Bitter, self-accusatory remorse was the only feeling which could struggle through the panic to the surface of her mind.

There was scarcely any repulsion against Johnnie. Lina knew exactly what had been the process of his twisted mentality. "*I* know that half-a-pint of brandy will kill a man. Beaky ought to know it. If Beaky, with the knowledge that he ought to and indeed may have, is such a condemned idiot as to swallow half-a-pint of brandy, then that's Beaky's funeral. Nothing to do with me at all."

It had been Beaky's funeral.

And Johnnie had merely profited by it, just as the distant cousin had profited by it. Murder? What an extraordinary idea!

If anything, Lina felt more protectively responsible for Johnnie than ever. Johnnie could not be held to account for what he did: Johnnie simply did not know. Lina's protectiveness did not extend to the world in which Johnnie was loose.

But if there was not repulsion, there were moments of horror. There was horror when Lina, watching the progress of Johnnie's betting book and Johnnie's drawers now every day, came across a batch of receipts five days after Beaky's death: receipts from moneylenders, totalling nearly fourteen thousand pounds. They underlined Beaky's death so dreadfully. Johnnie had been desperate, and now Johnnie was square again. Beaky had fulfilled his purpose.

But there were no more entries in Johnnie's betting book. Perhaps Johnnie too had known something about panic.

There was more horror when Lina remembered that evening in the drawing room, when Johnnie had seemed to be trying to make Beaky drunk, for no reason at all. Lina knew now that there had been a reason. She knew now that she had been present at a rehearsal of Beaky's murder.

Gradually her panic subsided.

There were no further references at all in the newspaper to Beaky's death. The French police had probably despaired of finding Beaky's companion. Slowly Johnnie's complete confidence had its influence on Lina. She became calmer; her nerves rehabilitated themselves; her trembling fits ceased; she could pass the policemen in Bournemouth without averting her head.

But she still had that curious cut-off feeling, as if she and Johnnie ought not to be mixing at all with decent, law-respecting people.

However, there were still no more entries in Johnnie's betting book. Lina almost cried again, with relief, about that. She was ashamed to catch herself thinking quite seriously, that if only Beaky, so useless in life, had by his death cured Johnnie of that terrible fever, he had not died for nothing.

When she felt better, her conscience would not let her rest till she had tackled Johnnie on that point. To tackle him on that other, and so much greater point, had never once entered her mind. She could not have done it.

"Johnnie, look here, I want to speak seriously to you about something. I've got more than a good idea that you've been betting a lot lately. No, don't say anything. I know you have. Well, darling, I just want to tell you this. I can't *bear* that any more."

"As how?" Johnnie grinned—the carefree grin of one who owes money to no man.

"What I want to tell you is that if you ever make a bet on a horse again, Johnnie, I shall leave you. I mean that. And I shall know."

"You would, would you? How?"

"Never mind. I should. And you ought to know me well enough to be sure that when I tell you I should, I should. And if you do, I'm finished. That's all."

"Well, darling, I don't see how the devil you can know, but it's perfectly true: I have had a bet or two lately," Johnnie said seriously. "But I'll swear to you, if you like, that I never will again. Never! The game isn't worth it. My God, no!"

"Oh, do please stick to that, Johnnie," Lina cried.

She really believed that this time Johnnie would stick to it. There had been a look on his face as he said that the game wasn't worth it. He meant that.

Lina had not the least doubt that Johnnie must have killed Beaky only with the greatest regret.

CHAPTER XVII

LINA wished sometimes that there were a few more people of her own age in Upcottery; they all seemed so much older or so much younger. Lina felt herself at least a generation more youthful than anyone at all older than herself, for in the country people age so quickly; and of the younger ones, like Marjorie and Joan Boldron, the very knowledgeable daughters of the vicar, she was almost afraid; they were so very much more sophisticated than she could ever be. Lina felt uncomfortable when people made sex abnormalities a subject of drawing-room conversation, even among their own sex.

Now that Martin Caddis was permanently away and Janet, fleeing, as Lina suspected, from Johnnie, had got work with a business firm in London, Lina found herself very much alone. Her mother, too, of whom she had always been very fond, had died the year before. But Lina was interested in her house and actually liked housekeeping, so that she was seldom really lonely. And she still read a great deal.

Nevertheless, she had been very glad to get a letter one day from Joyce, after she had been back with Johnnie about two years.

DEAREST LINA:
Did you ever meet Isobel Sedbusk when you were with us? I hear she has taken a cottage for the summer quite close to you, at Maybury. You might like to get in touch

*with her. Don't be alarmed if you haven't met her before;
she's not nearly so formidable as she looks. In fact, she's
a very good sort. No nonsense. And intelligent; but keep
off religion. I've written to her that you may look her up.*

Your affectionate sister,

JOYCE.

*P. S.—In case you didn't know, she writes detective
stories.*

Lina had known that, of course. Anyone who ever read
anything knew that Isobel Sedbusk wrote detective
stories.

She did not, however, think that she had met her in
London, and when she went over to Maybury to call
she was sure of it. No one who had once met Isobel Sedbusk could ever have any doubts on the point afterwards.
Miss Sedbusk impressed.

That had been at the beginning of the previous summer, and Lina, who had liked Miss Sedbusk at sight, had
seen quite a lot of her. Johnnie was delighted with her,
too. Miss Sedbusk, who boasted of weighing fifteen stone,
and boomed in proportion, was a very easy person to get
to know. She was inclined to talk a little too much about
her own line of work, and liked showing her familiarity
with the tools of her trade, such as blood and *rigor mor-
tis;* but she was amusing and had plenty of other interests
as well. In spite of the fact that she wore black sombreros
and had a masculine cut about her clothes, she was an
ardent feminist.

Within six weeks she was calling Johnnie "old man"
and rating Lina for not trying to write detective stories.

"Anyone can," affirmed Miss Sedbusk. "It's just a
matter of hard work, that's all. Lucky for us that more

people don't know that, though. The market's over-crowded enough as it is. My publisher tells me . . ."

The next summer Miss Sedbusk took the same cottage again. Lina was surprised to find how pleased she was to hear it.

Within two days of her arrival Miss Sedbusk appeared in person, demanding tea. She had walked the four miles from Maybury, and quite intended to walk them back again.

The two women bumped cheeks.

"Well, how are you, Lina? Fit?"

"I am glad to see you, Isobel. I've missed you."

"Have you? Good. I like people to miss me."

"I'll tell Ethel to bring tea at once. Shall we have it in the garden? It's such a lovely day."

"Anywhere you like," acquiesced Miss Sedbusk. "What I want is the tea itself. Well, how's Johnnie?"

"Johnnie's very fit. He's in the garden somewhere. He's taking up roses this year in real earnest."

"Well, I suppose we all come down to it one day," pronounced Miss Sedbusk.

Lina took her guest into the garden, and they sat under the cedar by the tennis court. It came into Lina's mind that it was on this spot that Lady Fortnum had lost her diamond pendant so many years ago. (How many was it? It must be nearly nine.) She no longer had any illusions about that loss. It was lucky that there had been no writer of detective stories present then.

"How's the new book going, Isobel? I suppose you're in the middle of one, as usual."

"Not yet. I've been putting it off till I got down here. I'm held up for an idea."

"Oh? You usually have so many ideas."

"I want a new method of murder. You wouldn't believe how hard it is to think up new methods of murder. Everything's been done." It was a favourite complaint of Miss Sedbusk's: the difficulty of finding new methods of murder.

Something prompted Lina to say:

"How about one man persuading another to drink a tumblerful of neat whisky, the first man knowing it will kill him and the second not knowing it?"

"Been done," said Miss Sedbusk briefly.

"Oh!"

"Been done in real life too."

Lina started. "Has it?"

"Palmer got rid of one of his victims that way. Abbey."

Miss Sedbusk knew the names of all the historical murderers and their victims. She really was interested in murder, besides making it, vicariously, her profession.

"Really?" Lina tried to make her voice sound disinterested, but her heart had begun to beat rather quickly. "Was he—hanged?"

"Eventually."

"Not for that?"

"Oh, no. He killed at least a dozen people after Abbey."

"In the same way?"

"No; he went on to real poison afterwards."

Lina produced quite a creditable laugh. "And I thought I'd found such an original idea. But after all," she added, very nonchalantly, "I suppose that wouldn't count as murder at all, would it? I mean, it isn't *real* murder, like giving the man poison, or shooting him, or anything like that."

It was a question Lina had wanted very much to put for more than two years now. Her own answer to it had quite crystallized by this time, but she had always wished to hear the opinion of someone else. All last summer she had tried to take the plunge and ask Isobel, but had never found the courage. Now it had just come out, quite naturally.

"That's rather a nice point." Miss Sedbusk's voice had taken on its debating tone. It resounded heartily through the garden of Dellfield, till Lina wished that Isobel was fitted with a volume control, like the wireless.

"No, I'm inclined to doubt whether it would be murder, from the legal point of view. The legal definition of murder is 'to kill with malice aforethought.' Still, you've got the malice aforethought all right. And if he knowingly incited the man to commit an act which would result in his death . . .

"Take a parallel. Supposing it was a footbridge over a torrent that he'd sawn through, and he incited the other man to cross it. That would certainly be murder, wouldn't it?"

"Yes," said Lina unwillingly.

"The distinction's a very fine one. Wait, though!" commanded Miss Sedbusk. "That isn't a true parallel. I see the flaw. The brandy turns on a question of *general* knowledge, whereas the footbridge is a piece of particular knowledge. The man has just as much chance of knowing that a tumblerful of neat brandy will kill him as the other has."

"Yes," Lina nodded eagerly. "That's just what I thought—think."

"But with the footbridge, of course, he hasn't," firmly pursued Miss Sedbusk. "Yes, that's the difference. And in a matter like that, of general knowledge, even if he did knowingly incite the other man, I should say the chances are that, legally, it wasn't murder."

"No," Lina agreed comfortably.

"But I'll ask my lawyer friend whom I always pester with this kind of thing, to make sure, if you like."

"Oh, no; don't bother," Lina said hastily. "I'm really not in the least interested. In fact, I can't think how you can wallow in all that kind of thing, Isobel. Personally, I couldn't *bear* it."

"Well, I got the information about Abbey from your own book on Palmer," returned Miss Sedbusk.

"Mine?"

"Or Johnnie's. He lent it me last summer."

"Oh! Oh, yes," Lina murmured. She had not had the least idea that Johnnie had a book like that. She made a note of the name: Palmer.

Usually Lina found a curious and rather horrid fascination in encouraging Isobel Sedbusk to talk about murder; though it made her shiver at times to hear Johnnie discussing it with her, in the bantering way he had adopted towards Isobel. But this was sailing rather too near the wind. She changed the subject.

When Johnnie had taken Isobel back to Maybury in the car, she went into the morning room and searched the book-shelf.

There it was. *The Life and Career of William Palmer, of Rugely;* on the same self as *Jorrocks* and *Ruff's Guide to the Turf.* She felt quite angry with Johnnie. He really was too confidently careless.

She took the book away and hid it in her bedroom, to destroy later.

But she would read it first.

2

Of course Isobel had said that it wasn't murder.

Lina had come to that conclusion herself, a very long

time ago. It had been a great consolation to her. If one's husband has not committed *murder,* then one's husband cannot reasonably be considered a murderer. Poison, and pistols, and Isobel's "blunt instruments," are the ingredients of murder: not a silly bet between two drunken men.

It was the first time that Lina's heart had beaten at all rapidly over that subject for months.

Not that she had come in the least to condone what Johnnie had done. It was horrible, even now, to think about. But it had not been murder; and that does make all the difference. It was surprising, too, how little she did think about it, consciously.

But in her subconsciousness Lina knew that it remained, and always would remain, as vivid as ever. Subconsciously it influenced all her thoughts, and most of her actions. The feeling that she and Johnnie were cut off from the rest of the world had now become natural to her. Other people did not know it, but she did, and took it for granted. It no longer distressed her, really. It just meant that Johnnie was not responsible for what he did and she was his keeper, with a trust that she must never relax for an instant; and no one else must ever, ever know anything about it. She still had her moments of rebellion against the responsibility that had been laid on her, but they were not many. Time can accustom one to anything.

And of course she had her compensations.

Johnnie had not relapsed again. This time he had stuck to what he said. The pages of the betting book remained blank. Johnnie had made no bet for nearly two-and-a-half years. Lina felt that to have caused such a reformation nothing could really have happened in vain.

At times Lina surprised herself with the way in which

she had come to accept what had happened. She refused to suspect that she was taking the letter for the law. She was determined to believe the casuistry with which she consoled herself and defended Johnnie. And she did believe it. Johnnie, who could not distinguish right from wrong, had not thought that he was doing wrong; and therefore he had not done wrong. And in any case he had not committed murder, and that was a very great consolation.

Moreover, Johnnie did love her, devotedly; and that was a very great consolation too.

Johnnie and she had been married now more than ten years, and Johnnie still loved her devotedly. Lina knew that. Johnnie had not looked at another woman since she came back to him. He had got over all that sort of thing. Lina knew that too. She was no longer the blind wife; unconsciously she was now on the alert the whole time for Johnnie to stray. If he had strayed, she would have known at once. Johnnie had not strayed.

Lina loved him more than ever.

She loved him tenderly, maternally, and passionately. She loved him so much that sometimes, alone, the tears would come into her eyes at the thought of loving so much, and being so much loved. She actually loved Johnnie all the more for the terrible things he had done. It proved that she was so necessary to him, and she adored being necessary to him, even though Johnnie could never know just how necessary she was. Lina knew that she could never have loved Ronald like that.

Johnnie was such a model husband now too. He hardly ever left Dellfield at all. He gardened, played with his prize bulls and his roses, attended the county council, sat on the bench, and pottered. The complete country gentleman. Johnnie was absolutely no trouble at all.

But Lina never left him. She had not set foot in London since Beaky's death, except for one or two visits with Johnnie. Her patient might be quite well again, but Lina knew she dared not leave her post. She did not want to leave it.

She was happy.

Incredibly, she thought sometimes, remembering everything; but she *was* happy. Johnnie needed her, and she needed Johnnie; and she was happy.

It increased her happiness to know that Johnnie was happy too. He was merrier in public, and more affectionate to her in private, than ever before. There was still more than a touch of the schoolmistress about his views of her, she knew; but that did not matter. Johnnie's nature needed a schoolmistress; perhaps unconsciously welcomed one. It was far too inert to be able to remain upright without such a prop.

And being accepted as a schoolmistress, Lina could not help behaving rather like one. She tried not to speak sometimes too peremptorily, or even dictatorially; but it was now she who took all the decisions, as a matter of course. Johnnie did not seem to mind. Lina thought he preferred it. His mind was lazy too. Hers had been disciplined; Johnnie's never would be.

So Lina now said what Johnnie was to do; and Johnnie, still with his schoolboy grin, did it.

Lina never realized quite how much, and how often, she said what Johnnie was to do.

3

Lina considered it a measure of Johnnie's regeneration that he should suddenly, in the autumn between Miss

Sedbusk's two summers, have begun to take such an interest in insurance.

The old Johnnie had never thought beyond the moment. To skimp the present by safeguarding the future would have seemed to him madness. And yet here was the new Johnnie, his desk littered with the pamphlets of various companies, poring over them day after day, comparing, taking notes, working out premiums and figures, all as if insurance were one of the most absorbing things in the world.

Lina, coming into the morning room one rainy October afternoon, had to kiss the little new bald patch on the top of his head in order to bring him down to earth again.

"Yes, but there's a lot in this insurance stuff," Johnnie had told her earnestly. "No, there is really, monkey-face. Look here, for instance. Supposing I died to-morrow . . ."

"Darling!" said Lina fondly.

"No, but supposing I did. You'd be left without . . . Oh, no, you wouldn't. I was forgetting the boot was on the other foot. Well, supposing *you* died to-morrow."

Lina sat down on the arm of a chair. Johnnie really did mean business.

"I hope I shan't. But all right, suppose it."

"Well, *I* might be left penniless. Mightn't I?"

"Not quite penniless, darling. I'm leaving you enough to buy the matches for your cigarettes." Lina had made a will when she first inherited her money, leaving everything to Johnnie. She had never told him so.

"No, but I might. *I* don't know what's in your will. And as I've always said, I don't want to. That's your pigeon. But for all I know you may have left everything to Robert and Armorel. And even if you haven't, there are the death duties. Everyone ought to insure against death duties. You ought really, monkeyface, you know."

"Ought I, Johnnie?" Lina smiled.

"Yes. I mean it. Seriously."

Lina knew perfectly well that she ought to be insured against death duties. Her solicitor had told her so repeatedly. She had never bothered to take the steps.

"I suppose I ought," she said reluctantly. She did not at all like the idea of parting with income to save somebody else capital after her death, even Johnnie.

"Well, it's about time, if you want anything like a decent premium. They get pretty high when you're over forty."

"I'm not over forty," Lina said indignantly. "I'm not forty at all yet, as you very well know." She was thirty-nine.

Johnnie began to explain the figures. A policy payable at death was very much cheaper than an endowment policy; it was not necessary to have a profit-bearing policy; and so on. Johnnie seemed to know all about it.

"I see," said Lina, as intelligently as possible. "And how much ought I to take a policy out for? A thousand?"

"A thousand? Ten!"

"Johnnie! The death duties couldn't come to anything like that."

"I bet they would. Or pretty nearly. Wait a minute. I'll look it up in Whitaker." Johnnie fetched Whitaker from the shelf and ran through the pages. "Here we are. It's fifty thousand, isn't it? The duty on fifty thousand is—yes, I thought I was right. Ten per cent. Ten thousand. And a policy for ten thousand will cost—yes, you can get one for just over two-fifty a year."

"But, darling, we can't afford two hundred and fifty a year. It's out of the question."

"Can't we?" Johnnie scratched his head. "Look here, monkeyface, it is important, you know. I tell you what you can do. Dock me a hundred off my little lot, and that will leave you with only a hundred and fifty to find."

"Johnnie, that's very sweet of you." Lina was touched. "But you couldn't manage on four hundred, could you?"

"It'd be a bit of a squeeze," Johnnie said nobly, "but, after all, it's only fair, isn't it? I mean, considering it's my advantage. That is," he added, "if you are leaving me anything."

"Oh, yes," Lina smiled, "I am leaving you something. But I won't take a hundred from you. I'll manage it myself somehow." She knew that really she could manage it quite well. She had never lived quite up to her income. The house was not expensive to run, and there were no children. "But what you shall do," she added, "is to take out an endowment policy for yourself too. With a premium of about forty pounds a year." Johnnie's face fell.

"It won't do you any harm to learn to save a little, my lad," Lina laughed unsympathetically.

A few days later she paid the first premium on her policy. Johnnie could be business-like enough when he liked.

But Lina soon had cause to wonder whether she had been wise in forcing Johnnie to save against his will.

Chancing to be in the morning room a week or so later, she remembered that she had not looked at Johnnie's betting book for some time. During the last year her examinations of it had become more and more perfunctory. She opened the little drawer and took it out.

There was a new entry, dated three days ago. It was only for ten pounds, and the horse had won, at four to one; but the danger was there. Johnnie had begun betting again.

4

Lina wasted no time.

She went at once to find Johnnie, potting bulbs in the greenhouse.

"Johnnie, do you remember my telling you nearly two years ago that if you ever had another bet I should leave you?"

"Did you, monkeyface? I believe you did say something like that. Look here, I'm putting the Grands Maîtres in this blue pot, for the drawing room. That all right?"

"And do you remember my saying that if you ever did bet again, I should know?"

"What's the matter?"

"Only this. I'm leaving you."

"What?"

"I gave you every warning," Lina said angrily. "I told you I wouldn't have it. Well, I won't. I'm going."

"But what the devil . . . ?"

"Do you deny that you've begun betting again?"

"Certainly I do," said Johnnie with dignity.

"Then what about Attaboy last Wednesday, at four to one?"

"How the blazes," gasped Johnnie, "do you know anything about that?"

"Never mind. I do know." Lina knew too that Johnnie would never suspect her method of knowledge. Tampering with another person's private papers, even one's own husband's, is one of the things that simply do not occur.

"Well, I'm blest! Anyhow," said Johnnie candidly, "you're perfectly right. I made forty quid on Attaboy. Got the tip from a man who really knows. It would have been a sin not to use it. I'd offer to blue it with you, monkeyface," Johnnie grinned, "but it's going to pay for my insurance premium."

"Johnnie, did you hear what I said just now?" Lina was annoyed that Johnnie did not seem to be taking her threat in the least seriously.

"I heard you pulling my leg."

"Indeed I wasn't pulling your leg. I meant it. Still," said Lina, with what dignity she could, "I'll give you one more chance. And the next time I do go. Remember, Johnnie: I mean it. I don't care who gives you the tip; I don't care whether the wretched horse wins or loses: *you are not to bet*. If you do, I shall go."

"Right," said Johnnie. "And now we've settled that, tell me if the Grand Maîtres are all right for this bowl."

5

Lina was worried.

Johnnie had been so offhand. He had not taken her threat seriously, and he had given no promise. She was very, very much afraid that Johnnie did intend to take up betting again. And if he did, she did not know what she would do. The bare thought was a nightmare.

But Johnnie, it appeared, was not going to take up betting again after all.

In her anxiety, Lina visited the little drawer in the morning room every single day. If she did not get an opportunity during the daytime, she went down specially from her bedroom at night. And there were no more entries.

As the time went on, her worry ceased. Johnnie had not taken up systematic betting again after all. It had been just a single bet, no doubt on the strength of the good tip he had mentioned. One bet does not make a sinner. The new Jekyll had not lapsed into the old Hyde.

By the time Isobel Sedbusk arrived for her second summer, Lina had almost forgotten all about the incident.

She had never noticed, on her first visit to the drawer after tackling Johnnie in the greenhouse, the piece of black cotton fastened across the face of the drawer, which her opening of it had dislodged.

CHAPTER XVIII

LINA was putting on a new hat.

She had bought it the day before, in Bournemouth; a little woven wisp of soft black Chinese hemp, and it was the most daring one she had ever possessed. One wore it completely on the side of one's head, right down to the left eyebrow, showing all one's hair on the other side.

"Really," Lina had said, "I think this one's a little *too*."

"It suits you wonderfully, madam," the shopgirl had assured her. "You have such a small face. And your hair . . ."

Now Lina was delighted with it.

She drew it on very carefully: one had to have one's hair just exactly *so*.

With it she was to wear her new blue woollen frock, her silver fox fur, and a pair of black kid gloves, also bought yesterday in Bournemouth, cut very wide and gauntlet-like at the wrist. The June afternoon was cold and gloomy.

Lina wriggled and smoothed her fingers into the new gloves and then studied the whole effect in her long mirror. It was good.

"I bet there aren't many women of forty who could carry off a hat like that," she meditated: and then corrected herself quickly, even in her thoughts, "thirty-nine," because there is a very great difference between thirty-nine-and-a-half and forty.

Lina did not feel anything like forty. Forty marks an epoch in one's life. At forty one cannot escape the suspicion that one is approaching middle age. Other people one considers definitely middle-aged at forty. And yet Lina felt less middle-aged now than before she had married. She had been an elderly young woman, she knew; she now felt an exceptionally youthful one.

And her looks had not let her down. At that distance from the glass, only a few feet, she still looked comparatively young: certainly no older than when Ronald had fallen in love with her so desperately. At that distance one could not see at all the faint clefts that ran from her nose to the corners of her mouth, and from the corners of her mouth down on either side of her chin. And when she held her head up, the little bagginess under her chin disappeared completely. She must remember to hold her head up.

Mechanically she moved her head sharply from side to side and up and down, in the chin-reducing exercise which, with further exercises intended to tame the other more exuberant parts of her anatomy, she performed now very seriously every single morning, naked, in her bedroom, only smiling faintly in response to Johnnie's ribaldries. Lina never locked her bedroom door against Johnnie, and never refused to say "come in" whenever he knocked; but she did wish he would not knock when she was doing her exercises.

She looked at herself again in the glass, turning this way and that. No, she did not look the tiniest bit different from when Ronald had fallen in love with her.

Lina still thought of Ronald, quite often. She felt very tender about him. Ronald had helped her over a terrible period; even now she did not know what she would have done without him then. But she was thankful, *thankful,* that she had not gone away with him. Ronald had been right. She was a one-man woman.

Nevertheless, she still wondered, at times, what Ronald would have been like in bed. Lina had not a very good imagination, except, like most women, as concerned herself, and she could not quite picture Ronald in bed. She thought he would probably have been much too respectful (he always had kept her on a pedestal), and then she would have had, very tactfully, to educate him up to being less so, which would have been a bore. Johnnie had spoilt Lina for respect in love.

She hoped Ronald was very happy with his wife; for Ronald was married now. Lina was not jealous of her in the least.

She resettled her fur on her shoulders and went downstairs.

"I'm ready, Johnnie."

Johnnie looked at her. "This the whole outfit? Fine!"

"Do I look all right?" Johnnie had seen the new hat already, last night, surmounting a pair of pale-green step-ins, and had pronounced it with much enthusiasm the best ever.

"All right? I'll say you do. A little bit of all right. That hat's going to knock 'em flat in Upcottery. Monkey-face, you're a marvel. Come and be kissed this minute."

"Careful, then," Lina smiled.

"Isn't it kiss-proof?"

"No lipstick's kiss-proof against you, Johnnie," Lina retorted.

She kissed him with carefully pursed lips, holding him from clasping her too closely with her palms against his chest, and mindful of her powdered nose, which was just a fraction of an inch too long and made kissing difficult after her face had been done. But it was wonderful of

Johnnie still to want to kiss his wife in the middle of the afternoon . . .

"The car's outside," Johnnie said.

Lina was going to pay a first call on some new people in the neighbourhood, upon whom report had been favourable. Johnnie was to drive her over, and she intended to walk back. The call was entirely an excuse to wear the new hat.

2

Lina called in for tea on old Lady Royde, a connection by marriage of Johnnie's, who lived all alone in a large house, most of it shut up, little more than a mile from Upcottery. Lina was very fond of the old lady, and made a point of going over to see her at least once a fortnight.

"My dear, how nice of you to call in. And what a charming hat!"

"I'm rather pleased with it. You don't think it's a little *too?*"

"No, I don't. It suits you so well."

Over tea Lina recounted where she had been.

"Ah, you *have* called? Then I will. I hear they're very nice. You liked her? Yes. She was a Langthwaite, I understand; one of the Gloucestershire lot; but I don't seem to know his name at all. However, my dear, if *you've* called . . ."

Lina walked back to Dellfield with the happy consciousness that she had had cream with her tea and did not care. Cream is good for one. It wraps up the nerves.

Isobel Sedbusk and Major Scargill were coming to dinner, and she was looking forward to that.

Life seemed very peaceful and very pleasant.

3

Miss Sedbusk was talking about murder. As usual. She talked emphatically, thumping her fist on the dinner table.

"I *believe* in murder," declaimed Miss Sedbusk. "All sorts of people ought to be murdered. It's a great pity one isn't allowed to do it."

Lina smiled nervously. She knew that Isobel was only talking nonsense, but she did wish that Miss Sedbusk would not talk nonsense about murder in front of Johnnie.

"I saw in the paper this morning," she said, "that income tax ought to come down again in the next budget. I hope——"

"As things are, of course, it needs an amount of nerve that few of us have got. I don't know," said Miss Sedbusk to Major Scargill across the table, "whether you ever read a book of mine called *Ruddy Death?*"

Major Scargill looked guilty. "Er—I don't know . . ."

"Well, it doesn't matter," Miss Sedbusk forgave him. "The point is that I dealt with the idea there. I wrote . . ." Miss Sedbusk explained at some length what she had written.

She also explained other views.

"Very interesting," said Major Scargill. "Lombroso, eh? Very interesting."

"I thought Lombroso was quite exploded now, Isobel," put in Lina perfunctorily.

Miss Sedbusk leaned impatiently aside while the parlourmaid removed her plate.

"So he is. But I still think there might be something in his premises, though not in the deductions he made from them. For instance, there may not be a murderer's face, but there certainly is a degenerate's face. And a good many degenerates come to murder. In other words, some murderers can be detected from their faces, but not all."

"Ha," said Major Scargill.

"But what I do think," pursued Isobel, "is that one can often tell from a person's face whether he or she is capable of murder; though not, of course, whether he'll ever commit it. I find it quite amusing to look up and down a tube carriage and think: 'Yes, old man, *you* could commit murder, if it came to the point.' "

"You do, eh? Well, what about dinner tables? What about us, eh, Miss Sedbusk? Could our hostess commit murder if it came to the point?"

Miss Sedbusk shook her head regretfully. "Lina hasn't the nerve, any more than I have. It's a pity in a way, but very few women have. After all, murderers are comparatively rare birds, you know. You couldn't, Major, for instance."

"Well, that's comforting."

"And as for you, old man," said Miss Sedbusk to Johnnie, "you couldn't commit a murder if you tried for a hundred years."

Lina caught her breath and waited for some bantering reply. Instead Johnnie said, quite seriously, and almost regretfully:

"No. I don't believe I could."

Johnnie really thought that. He could not commit murder if he tried for a hundred years. Well, no doubt he was right. After all, he never had committed murder. Lina was quite sure that Johnnie never could have murdered Beaky in cold blood. He had not got either enough or too little moral strength.

She glanced down the table at him. His eyes were on her, but for once there was no twinkle in them. He was looking at her with an odd mixture of gloom and affection, quite unlike his usual expression.

Her heart gave a little jump.

Surely, she thought, Johnnie hasn't been taking Isobel's nonsense *seriously?*

4

In the drawing room after dinner Lina had a curious experience.

The men had remained in the dining room only a very short time. They came into the drawing room for coffee. The tray had been put on a small table near the piano, and Lina had poured it out there. Johnnie handed the cups round and brought Lina hers.

She sipped at it, unthinkingly, and noticed that it tasted a little peculiar. Instantly the thought jumped into her mind: Has Johnnie put arsenic in it?

She sipped it again. It was peculiar.

Johnnie would get hold of a lot of money if he had put arsenic in Lina's coffee; and Johnnie nearly always wanted money.

She thought, in a detached way: "Am I going mad?"

She drank off the rest of her coffee.

5

June passed into July. There was a spell of dry, hot weather, and Lina played tennis almost every day. Johnnie was very good to her about tennis. It must have bored him very much, but he was always ready to play a set or two with her. Indeed, he came and asked her nearly every morning whether she would like a set. Lina enjoyed pottering about a court when there was no one to see her mistakes. Johnnie did his best to coach her too, very patiently; but Lina never seemed to improve.

"No, it's no good. I must be getting too old," she laughed, after half an hour's failure of the new, whizzing service that Johnnie was trying to teach her.

"You *are* patient with me, darling," she added, with sudden gratitude for Johnnie's wasted time.

"I like doing things with you, monkeyface," Johnnie said: rather wistfully, Lina thought.

"Well, I like doing them with you," she smiled.

It was true that Johnnie liked doing things with her nowadays. He did everything with her. He never went out anywhere without her, except, of course, on business or duty, and for the last month or two Lina had noticed that he was continually coming to her and asking if she wanted him, or if she would like to do anything with him. Lina was delighted. Never had Johnnie been more attentive to her. And that really was saying something, in Johnnie's case. He was completely cured of his old fever for new women.

In fact, Lina thought, since Beaky's death her marriage had been practically ideal. There had been little quarrels, of course; and once, at the beginning of the present year, Johnnie had asked her to lend him five thousand pounds of her capital for some new scheme of his own, which Lina had refused with decision, not unjoined with one or two hard words; but on the whole things had been just about as good as they possibly could be. But for Johnnie's moral weakness, their marriage always would have been ideal. Lina was thankful that the idyll had come later instead of at the beginning.

For it really was an idyll, now. Lina thought, with

a little giggle, that lately Johnnie had taken actually to following her about, just like a lovelorn boy of seventeen. It was extraordinary. And *most* gratifying. Lina was so much touched that she could not find the heart to hint to Johnnie that at times he was becoming a positive nuisance.

The only odd thing was that Johnnie was not nearly so merry now.

Lina had noticed him, at that dinner with Isobel Sedbusk and Major Scargill, looking at her down the table in an odd, most un-Johnnie-like way; and since then she had intercepted much the same sort of look several times. It was a peculiar look, as if Johnnie could not make up his mind whether he liked what she was wearing, but liked *her* so much that it did not matter what she wore. Lina had asked him once, with a smile, what he was thinking about; and Johnnie had seemed to give himself a mental shake, grinned, and replied that he was wondering whether to put on a clean pair of white trousers that afternoon, or make the others do once more. Lina had been quite disappointed.

Johnnie's maudlin behaviour had given Lina a new sense of that power which women feel when they are very much loved, and soon take for granted, and so often abuse. She had not had quite the same feeling ever since she had kept Ronald Kirby on his string. She had never been quite sure of Johnnie before, and any feeling of power there had been over him had been the influence of a steady mind over a shiftless one, and much resented. Now at last she was convinced that Johnnie would never again do anything that would upset or hurt her, not merely because he respected and was even a little frightened of her, but because he adored her. It was a very comfortable feeling.

She tried hard not to be impatient, or snap at him, as she so often did when any suggestion, even of the most unimportant order, did not encounter her approval.

6

Isobel and Lina were talking about investments. Isobel had just sold the film rights of one of her books for a thousand pounds, and she was undecided what to do with the money.

"I'd like to spend it on going round the world, but I suppose I'd better not. I can save up for that out of income, and this ought to be treated as capital. The rest of my money's in War Loan, but I think I'd like something more exciting. What's yours in, Lina?"

"War Loan, too. A safe five per cent," said Lina knowledgeably.

"H'm, yes! Till the Bolshies take the country over." Miss Sedbusk was inclined to take a gloomy view of England's future: perhaps not more gloomy than the governors of England's present warranted. "You wait and see what income tax will be then."

"Income tax is bad enough, but it's the death duties I think are so monstrous. Do you know that when I die Johnnie will have to pay ten thousand pounds in death duties? Ten thousand!" said Lina with pain.

"Nonsense," replied Miss Sedbusk robustly.

"Why nonsense?"

"Because it is nonsense. Twenty per cent?"

"Ten per cent."

"Hullo, you're a richer woman than I thought. I didn't know you'd got five thousand a year."

"I haven't. Barely half that."

"Then your arithmetic's wrong, my dear girl. Ten per cent. of fifty thousand is five thousand."

"Is it?" said Lina. *"Is* it?"

By the time she got home she had thought it out. It must have been a genuine mistake, because Johnnie had not benefited; Lina had made the cheque out to the insurance company, not to Johnnie. Johnnie could not possibly have benefited. After the first horrid apprehension, that had been a tremendous relief.

But it was a nuisance, and extremely careless of Johnnie to have led her into paying just twice as much for her insurance as she need have done. Of course the policy would have to be cancelled.

"Johnnie," she said crossly, "you really are an idiot. What's ten per cent. of fifty?"

"Five, of course," said Johnnie in surprise. "Why?"

"Because in that case ten per cent. of fifty thousand is five thousand, of course. How could you have been so careless? You made me waste a hundred and twenty-eight pounds too much on my insurance premium last October. We don't want a policy for ten thousand at all. It ought to have been five. Really, you ought—what's the matter?" Johnnie had become quite white and was staring at her in the utmost alarm. Lina thought she had spoken most mildly, considering how foolish Johnnie had been. "What's the matter?" she repeated more sharply. It annoyed her that Johnnie should look at her, when she had to remonstrate with him, like a schoolboy awaiting a caning.

"Nothing's the matter," Johnnie said, rather gutturally.

"Oh, I'm not going to stop it out of your allowance, if that's what you're frightened about," Lina snapped, "though you certainly deserve it. You'd better write to-day and get that policy cancelled and take one out for me for five. Do you understand, Johnnie?" she added impatiently.

"Yes, all right, I will," Johnnie mumbled.

A week later Lina said to him:

"By the way, what about that insurance policy of mine? Have you written?"

"Not yet," Johnnie said glibly. "No hurry. The premium's not due till October."

"But I asked you to write last week."

"Much better to let it stand till it expires. Then there's no question. You leave it to me, monkeyface. I'll look after it all right."

Lina left it to him.

7

Johnnie had acquired a passion for detective stories.

He had always read them, but only sporadically. Now he seemed to be always deep in one. Lina was kept quite busy ordering new ones for him from the library. How-ever, she did so willingly enough. Any innocuous amusement of Johnnie's was to be encouraged.

He was forever discussing them with Isobel too: getting her recommendations, listening to her criticisms on the work of her fellow authors, just as eager as she was to find flaws in detection or method.

"Hullo, Isobel," he would greet her whenever she appeared at Dellfield, which was two or three times a week at least. "Hullo, begun the new book yet? Look here, I've thought up a new method of murder for you."

"Have you? Good man. Let's have it."

And then they would plunge into discussion.

It seemed to Lina that whenever she found Johnnie and Isobel together now, they were talking about new methods of murder. She did not altogether like it.

Indeed, she did not like it at all. It seemed to Lina supremely ironical that Johnnie should be trying to find new methods of murder for Isobel. It seemed to her worse than ironical that he should listen so interestedly to Isobel's own ingenious schemes. Of course it was absurd to wonder. Quite ridiculous. But still . . .

Lina did not like it.

What she particularly did not like was that the method of murder, to meet Isobel's requirements, had to be practically undetectable.

One afternoon, as they were sitting in the garden of Miss Sedbusk's cottage, Lina's nervous exasperation caused her to burst in on the discussion. She had been annoyed, because it was she who had been going over to tea with Isobel, and Johnnie, in his doglike way of this summer, had insisted on going with her.

"But you'll only be bored. We shall talk about women's things," said Lina, who felt as if she had hardly seen Isobel alone for weeks and had been looking forward to doing so that afternoon.

"I think I'll come along," Johnnie had replied airily. "I'd be much more bored alone here, without you."

"Really, Johnnie, can't you bear to let me out of your sight for a couple of hours? I really can't understand what's the matter with you this year."

"I like being with you, monkeyface," Johnnie said pathetically. "You don't *mind* if I come along, do you?"

"Oh, come if you must," Lina snapped.

So Johnnie had come.

And of course the conversation very soon came round

to the usual subject. Miss Sedbusk never minded talking her own particular shop, and she did so with gusto.

"Why must you be so complicated?" Lina burst in at last. "Live electric wires inside the springs of an easy chair, indeed! Why not use arsenic and have done with it?"

"Because, my good woman, arsenic of all poisons is the easiest to detect. Arsenic remains in the body——"

"Well, that's what people do in real life. Why don't you try to keep your books somewhere near real life, Isobel?"

"They are near real life," snorted Miss Sedbusk, stung. "As near as the conventions of the detective story allow. What you don't seem to realize, my dear girl, is that the kind of method I'm always looking for—perhaps the electric wires are a bit too complicated—is precisely what hundreds of people *do* use in real life: the people we never hear about, because they're never caught out."

"I—I don't think murder's as common as all that," Lina said weakly. Why *must* Isobel be always talking about murder?

"Huh! Well, all I can say is, you don't know much about it. Believe me, *hundreds* of people walking about to-day have put somebody out of the way in their time. Why, it's as easy as falling into a bog. Just a nudge with the elbow as they're walking along the edge of a cliff; just a—— Hullo, what's up?"

Lina was standing up. "I must be getting home."

"But you've hardly finished your tea."

"I know. But—I've got rather a head. You don't mind if I go a little early, do you? Are you ready, Johnnie?"

"Me? Oh, well, I think I'll sit on a bit here and smoke a pipe, monkeyface."

"I'd rather you came with me," Lina said palely. Seeing Isobel's puzzled face, she added: "I do feel a little queer."

"My dear woman, lie down for a bit here, on my bed."

"No, I think I'll get home. Are you ready, Johnnie?" Lina bore Johnnie away.

This was really beginning to be too much of a good thing.

8

Once a year or so Lina glanced at her will.

She kept it in a sealed envelope, in a drawer in her bureau. Her solicitor had told her she ought to keep it at the bank, but Lina liked to have it under her hand.

Each year she took it out of its envelope, read it through, and put it back in a fresh one.

On the day following her visit to Isobel's something prompted her to perform the annual rite for the present year.

She did not know why, but her heart beat rather oddly as she took the long envelope out of the drawer. For the first time, she scrutinized it with minute care before she tore it open. She pretended she did not know what she was looking for.

She found it.

Not at the flap end but at the other, whose fastening was less secure, she discovered the tiny wrinkles and the smudgy appearance of an envelope that has been steamed open.

9

She went straight into the morning room.

Johnnie was not in the house.

For some minutes she stood stock-still, looking at Johnnie's desk.

Then she pulled open the little drawer at the side, and examined Johnnie's betting book. The last entry was still the Attaboy of last October.

Lina drew a breath of relief.

But her relief was only for a moment. Almost instantly the thumping of her heart began again.

She stood uncertainly by the desk, her hands clenched at her sides.

"It *is* all right," she whispered, half fiercely and half distractedly. "It *is* all right."

With a little swoop she pulled open the drawer in which, three years ago, she had found the moneylenders' letters.

It was full of papers. Lina pulled them out and, laying them on the desk, turned them rapidly through. They seemed harmless enough. Bills, letters from friends . . .

DEAR SIR:

We thank you for the acceptance of the eight thousand pounds (£8,000) signed by Mrs. Aysgarth. This will be perfectly satisfactory.

Yours faithfully,
p.p. S. V. PRITCHETT & CO.

Lina pressed her hand to her forehead. Her mind seemed numb. She could not understand. What acceptance? What did it mean? What was an "acceptance"?

With shaking fingers she searched further.

DEAR SIR:

In reply to your inquiry, we beg to state that an acceptance signed by your wife, in respect of the three

*thousand pounds for which you are indebted to us, will
quite meet our requirements.*

> *Yours faithfully,*
> *p.p.* MORLEY BROS.

There were others too, but it was enough.

A sudden flaring illumination had at last seared its
way into Lina's mind.

CHAPTER XIX

JOHNNIE was going to kill her.

Huddled on her bed, Lina was trying to realize that. Johnnie was going to kill even her.

She could not realize it. It was more than incredible. It was a conception which her distraught mind could not yet grasp at all. Johnnie, her child—Johnnie, her whole life, was going to kill *her*.

Never for a moment had it entered Lina's wildest fears that she herself could ever be in danger from Johnnie. Johnnie, driven to desperation, might have planned the deaths of other people, if only they could be led into killing themselves: but not hers. Never *hers*. Johnnie loved her. Johnnie adored her. Johnnie could never get on without her. It was just inconceivable that Johnnie could possibly contemplate killing *her*.

But it was true. Johnnie could contemplate even that.

Lina might not be able to realize it yet, but she knew it. Unable still to think clearly, her mind leapt from one to another in a series of distracted little pictures that carried their own conviction: Johnnie so attentive to her, just as he had been to Beaky before he killed him (and she, blind idiot, so pleased with Johnnie's attentions, and latterly so bored with them!); Johnnie trying to get hints from Isobel on murder; the way she had caught Johnnie looking at her sometimes; oh, a hundred things. Yes, she knew it. For weeks now, perhaps for months (the insurance, as long ago as last October!), Johnnie had been planning to kill her.

Johnnie . . .

Lina flung herself down among the pillows. Let him, then! Quickly! If Johnnie could do that, Lina no longer wanted to live.

She burst into a torrent of sobbing.

No, it was impossible. Johnnie could not be going to kill her. Not Johnnie.

2

But it was true.

As Lina bathed her eyes, a dull misery of certainty succeeded the chaos in her mind. The incomprehensible idea had become comprehensible. Without doubt Johnnie did intend to kill her.

And what was she going to do about it?

Curiously, there had been no panic. It was impossible to be *afraid* of Johnnie. Lina felt no terrified urge to get away from the danger: to flee helter-skelter to Joyce for safety. Not in the least.

Not of course that she was going to stay at Dellfield, for Johnnie to kill at his leisure. But she would go in her own good time. She was not in danger yet.

Or was she?

She began to tremble. Supposing at tea that very afternoon Johnnie put . . . Supposing at dinner . . .

Oh, God, she could not stand it. The panic which shock had so far held in check began to break loose. At any moment Johnnie might come in—break the door down and kill her in her own bedroom: throw her out of the window on to the flags below and say she had fallen—anything. At any moment Johnnie might come and kill her; and what was she going to do?

Lina tore a suitcase out of the cupboard and began

feverishly to pack. She must get away; she must get away; she must get *away*.

3

By tea-time the suitcase was back in the cupboard, her things again in their drawers. Lina was not going to run away. It was impossible to be afraid of Johnnie.

At tea she was exceedingly bright, in the hard, artificial manner she used to adopt towards strangers when she felt nervous. Johnnie looked at her with surprise as she prattled wittily from her dry mouth about this and that.

"What's the matter with you, monkeyface?"

"The matter? Nothing at all. What should be the matter?"

"I mean, why are you going on like this?"

"I thought you'd like me to talk to you," said Lina, with a bright smile. "Perhaps you'd rather read a detective story?"

She thought to herself:

How do I do it? I'd never have thought I was capable of it. Oh, God, let me keep it up. So long as he doesn't suspect . . .

Johnnie looked puzzled, but he did not suspect.

As tea went on, Lina had an odd sensation that she was living a play. It was the middle of the second act. The audience knew that at the end of the third act she was to be killed, to bring down the curtain; but she did not know it. She was to sparkle gaily and nonchalantly right up to the end. Unconsciously she found herself acting up to this nonexistent audience.

But this illusion of unreality led to a conviction of unreality.

It was impossible, really it was impossible, seeing Johnnie there so normal and unconcerned, to take seriously the idea that he was actually meditating her own death. What she had forced herself, when alone, to regard as an actual fact seemed now, in the presence of Johnnie himself, utterly fantastic. Johnnie could not be so inhuman. Not the Johnnie she knew and loved: the real Johnnie sitting there, so different from the monstrous Johnnie of her imaginings upstairs.

She looked at him. Johnnie smiled back at her.

No, it was fantastic.

She very nearly said to him:

"I had such a funny idea this afternoon, darling. I thought you were going to poison me."

Very nearly.

And yet she checked herself. Supposing Johnnie turned white, and . . .

She caught her breath. Johnnie had turned white, not long ago, when she taxed him with that mistake in her insurance policy; and . . . Mistake! It had not been a mistake, of course. She had forgotten for the moment that Johnnie was going to kill her. He had overinsured her life for that purpose.

But Johnnie was not going to kill her. She had just seen how fantastic that was. Johnnie loved her far too much ever to do anything again that would hurt or upset her. And as for *killing* her . . . Of course it was fantastic!

She cupped her chin on her palm, staring at him.

Johnnie shifted in his chair. "What on earth's the matter with you this afternoon, monkeyface? Just now you were chattering away nineteen to the dozen, and now you've gone all boxed up. What's the matter?"

"Nothing!" Lina jumped up and sat on Johnnie's

knee. She looked down into his eyes. "Johnnie, you do love me, don't you?"

"Of course I do." But Johnnie looked uneasy.

"You'd never do anything again to hurt or upset me?"

"What do you mean?"

"Just that. You wouldn't, would you?"

"Of course I wouldn't."

They stared at each other.

Then Johnnie caught her closer to him. "You know how I love you, my darling," he whispered, and there was a catch in his voice.

Lina did know it. She felt quite reassured now. One does not kill a person whom one loves like that, not even for her money.

How could she for one moment have imagined such a thing?

4

But it was no good.

Lina might persuade herself sometimes that it had all been a nightmare; she might have moments when, seeing Johnnie laugh, feeling Johnnie's arms round her, she was completely certain that it had all been a nightmare, just as she had been completely certain that her premonitions of Beaky's death had been a nightmare. But all the time, against persuasion, against conviction even, she *knew*.

Johnnie really did intend to bring about her death. And she did nothing about it.

But Lina was not frightened any longer. After the first shock she had seen how extremely simple her solution was. She had only to buy back her life from Johnnie. She had only to tell him that she knew he was in financial trouble, forgive him once more, forgive him once more too for forging her name again, and settle his debts. That was all. And that, in time, was what she would do.

But somehow she never did it.

At first, still shirking action even at such a juncture, she put off speaking to Johnnie from day to day. She shrank from it; she would do it to-morrow. Then actual resentment at having to buy back her own life and part with precious capital made her stubborn. Johnnie thought he was going to kill her, did he? Kill her, to cover up his own rottenness! Well, let him try. She was not going to help him out of his mess yet. Let him try what he damned well liked. She was ready for him.

Lina was not frightened now. She knew Johnnie's mind. He would never kill her outright, just as he had not killed her father or Beaky. He would only try to make her kill herself. All she had to do was to be on her guard against doing anything that might prove rash. That was where Johnnie would find the difference. Her father and Beaky had not been on their guard.

Lina felt so confident that she could never be led into killing herself that at times she would smile, though bitterly, at the mere idea.

So she did nothing.

For of course there was always the feeling that though Johnnie might possibly be going to try to cause her death to-morrow, it was out of the question that he should be doing so to-day.

5

Lina sat bolt upright in bed.

She had heard sounds. They had woken her up. Somebody was moving about. It must be in Johnnie's dressing room.

She strained her ears into the darkness.

Nothing.

But something—somebody was waiting, just as she was waiting. Something—somebody was crouching behind Johnnie's dressing-room door, listening just as she was listening.

Lina knew what it was. It was Johnnie, coming to kill her—*now!* She had left things too long.

Oh, God, she had left things too long. How could she have been so insane?

She stared through the blackness towards the dressing-room door. Since Lina had discovered what Johnnie was planning, she had made him sleep in his dressing room. Johnnie had grumbled bitterly, but Lina had not cared about that. She turned him out and locked both the doors of her bedroom. Without that she would never have got a wink of sleep at all.

And now Johnnie had got hold of a second key and was coming through, to kill her. Oh, why, *why* had she not thought to have bolts put on the doors too?

She jerked with terror, biting her knuckles to keep back the screams. Had that been a footstep?

She hardly drew breath, listening so desperately.

There was nothing. Johnnie was still waiting.

She had just one hope: to creep out of the room without making a sound, creep out of the house, and run over to Maybury and Isobel—just as she was, in her nightgown, even with bare feet.

Very, very slowly, inch by inch, she edged towards the side of the big bed, turned back the clothes, and crept out. Her breath made funny little whistling noises in her throat. Cautiously she felt for her mules and put them on. She glanced fearfully towards the dressing-room door. A sudden ray of moonlight had made its whiteness just discernible. And it was opening.

Lina screamed and collapsed on the floor.

She was paralyzed with terror. If Johnnie had come in at that moment he could have killed her by any method he liked and she could not have done anything but watch him.

But Johnnie did not come in, because he was so sound asleep that not even Lina's scream woke him up.

Lina did not realize till after her breakfast the next morning, when she saw the sun produce exactly the same effect, that when one of the window curtains was moved by the wind, its shadow on the dressing-room door gave a momentary illusion that the door was opening.

But that same day she had bolts put on both doors in her bedroom.

6

Things could not go on like that.

One cannot live under the daily dread of death and quite keep one's normal balance. Lina's courage wilted. She did dread death now, actively.

Slowly the acid of fear had bitten into her nerves until at times they were barely capable of control. Once or twice in Johnnie's presence she was filled with an impulse to scream out her terrors and accusations at him, and had to push her handkerchief into her mouth to keep silent. A dozen times she packed a suitcase, to run away from them; and then unpacked it again when her nerves came back once more to the normal, and she could not decide whether to run away or not. And since with Lina indecision meant inaction, she remained.

She actually did cry out one day at Isobel that she could not bear to hear the word "murder" again as long as she lived. Offended, Isobel now confined her conversation to matters of philosophy and dress.

Things could not go on like this. Lina began seriously to wonder whether she would not actually let Johnnie kill her and put an end to it all.

It was an idea that had been prompted by a book which Isobel had lent her before Lina flew out at her. It was a penetrating piece of work, about murder and murderers. Analyzing her subject, the authoress had suggested that just as there are born murderers so there are born victims: murderees, whose natural destiny it is to get murdered: persons who, even when they see murder bearing down on them, are incapable of moving out of its way.

Lina laid the book on her lap, and stared into vacancy. Was she a murderee?

She was not at all sure that she might not be.

For, after all, if Johnnie could find the heart to kill her . . . The tears would come into her eyes that Johnnie could have the heart to kill her, just for her wretched money.

She often came back now to that first reaction of all: if Johnnie could want to kill her, then Lina no longer wanted to live.

She would watch Johnnie broodingly. How could he —how *could* he, after all she had done for him?

"A penny for your thoughts, monkeyface," Johnnie would say.

And Lina would laugh and put him off.

Afterwards she would wonder how she had managed to laugh.

7

Lina took up the telephone receiver. It was Mrs. Forcett, on whom Lina had called that day she went on to tea with Lady Royde. Lina liked her.

Mrs. Forcett wanted to know if she and Johnnie could come to tennis next Wednesday.

"Next Wednesday? Yes, I think we're free. Will you just hold on a minute while I look in my engagement book? Yes, quite free. That will be delightful. Half-past three? Yes. Good-bye."

Lina was pleased. Not only did she like the Forcetts, but one met interesting people there. And Mrs. Forcett was a good hostess. She looked forward to Wednesday.

Before she had got through the morning-room door there had come, like a sickening thud between her shoulders, the remembrance of the horror that now lived with her. What was the good of making that or any other arrangement? By next Wednesday she might be dead.

It was odd that one could forget that by next Wednesday one might be dead. And yet this kind of thing was always happening.

8

July dragged into August, and August into September; and still Lina was alive and at Dellfield.

She and Johnnie even talked about their summer holiday.

Lina listened, with detached fascination, to Johnnie making plans—plans which she might be no longer alive to share. He wanted to go to a little village on the Mediterranean, just on the border between France and Spain.

"Not the seaside this year, Johnnie," Lina would say, wondering at her own calm. At the seaside one could be capsized out of a boat; or held under the water while bathing, under the pretense of a rescue; or . . .

"Well, what about a walking tour in the Pyrenees? I hear one can have quite a good time there."

"No, no," Lina shuddered. So that had been Johnnie's plan all the time! To push her over . . .

But Johnnie did not seem to press the Pyrenees. Perhaps it had not been his plan after all.

Lina kept wondering, with a sick sensation, what Johnnie's plan really was. She thought he had found one now. He no longer discussed methods of murder with Isobel. He no longer pored over detective stories. Where had he found his plan? Could Lina trace it out and so forestall it?

But did she want to forestall it?

Oh, God, what did she want?

She was wretched, and she wanted to die. Johnnie did not want her any more. He only wanted her money.

No, no, no. She did not want to die. She wanted to live. Johnnie loved her.

It really was an odd comfort to Lina all this time that Johnnie loved her. Johnnie intended to kill her, yes; but he did not want to kill her. Johnnie was looking just as miserable in these days as Lina herself was feeling. The idea of killing her plainly depressed him very much indeed. He would do it with tears in his eyes.

But a man must live.

Lina quite understood Johnnie's feelings. And it certainly was a very great comfort to her that he was not indifferent to the idea of her death.

It seemed a pity, however, when neither Lina nor

Johnnie at all desired Lina's death, that Lina should have to die.

Well, Lina had not got to die. She had only to go to Johnnie, tell him she knew he was in financial trouble, and . . .

But Lina never went.

And Lina never went either to Joyce, to Isobel, or to Lady Newsham. She did exactly what she had sworn so indignantly she would never do, and waited on at Dell-field, wondering dejectedly whether she would take the chance of Johnnie's killing her or whether she would drag out a wretched existence in safety away from Johnnie. Or even whether, if Johnnie did not do something soon, she would not kill herself and have a little peace.

9

"To the left," said Lina.

"No, darling," Johnnie retorted. "Straight on here. Left at the next fork." He drove straight on.

"Nonsense!" Lina snapped. "You know you never remember. Why on earth can't you listen to me? Very well; go on; I don't care."

Johnnie did not answer. He drove on, frowning.

Lina glanced at him. Johnnie was angry.

She began to feel uneasy. It had been foolish to snap at Johnnie, *now*. Johnnie might resent it. He always had resented her snapping at him. Now it might goad him into . . .

How could she have been so foolish?

"I'm sorry I spoke like that, Johnnie. I expect you're quite right, really."

Johnnie did not answer. He was still frowning. He *was* angry.

Lina began to feel afraid.

The road was a deserted one: not much more than a lane. The main road, which they had left, took a left-angled turn. It was only a small road that went straight on. She knew Johnnie should have kept on the main road, to the left. Why had he not done so?

There was not a person in sight. Few cars came along this little road. If Johnnie wanted to . . .

Johnnie *did* want to.

Lina was suddenly as convinced of that as if Johnnie himself had told her. Johnnie had brought her here, on this deserted road, expressly to . . .

A car accident.

She turned white with terror. Little beads of sweat pricked her forehead, under her hat. She dragged off her gloves, and clutched at the sides of the bucket seat on which she sat, as if to hold herself on to life.

She dared not glance again at Johnnie. She was too terrified of what she might see in his face.

How could a person kill another person in a car and make it look like an accident? How could a driver kill his passenger without risk to himself?

Oh, God, why had she not run away when she had the chance? Why had she gone on dallying and dithering, trying to persuade herself that she was safe for the time being, that there was no hurry? There had been hurry: frantic hurry. And she had refused to see it. Refused! And now it was too late. Johnnie was going to kill her on this deserted road, and not a soul to help her.

She and Johnnie were cut off once more on a desert island of murder. But this time it was her murder.

What could she do?

What would Johnnie do?

Supposing he leant across her, opened the door, and

with all his strength threw her out of it, so that she fell on her head in the road . . . and then he came back with the car, and drove over her . . . and left her . . .

Frantically she tried to decide what she would do if Johnnie did that. There was a strap on the upright to which the door was hinged. She would cling to that. And to the handle. Cling like death.

But supposing that was not Johnnie's plan. Supposing he——

"Don't want your window up on such a lovely day, monkeyface, do you?" said Johnnie, and leaned across her.

"No!" Lina shrieked. She grabbed at the strap and clung to it. "*No!* Don't! Leave it!"

Johnnie could not answer for the moment. He was busy steering the car in a left turn on to the main road. When he was clear he said:

"All right, all right. No need to scream about it. I only thought you'd like the window open." He added: "There you are, you see. I was right. You'd forgotten that short cut. It saves about two miles."

Johnnie had been right. Lina had forgotten the short cut.

She sat huddled on her seat like a sack of straw, utterly played out.

10

"Oh, God," Lina babbled on her knees, "let him do it quickly. I can't stand it any longer. I don't want to live any more: I want to be dead. Do make him kill me and get it over. Only be *quick!* And please, please let it be painless."

And yet, when her hysteria was over, Lina would re-

member that she simply must not allow Johnnie to kill
her. It would be a fatal thing for him to do. Johnnie
could never help getting into the most dreadful trouble
without her. Johnnie had been her job in life. She must
go on with it.

Lina was beginning to alternate between hysteria and
a strange calmness which surprised herself more than the
hysterics did.

She hardly did anything with Johnnie now.

It is all very well to decide, in moments of despair,
that one would rather be out of life than in it; but when
it comes to the point of offering another person opportunities for helping one out of it, the results are rather
different.

Lina hardly ever went in the car with Johnnie now.
Only when she could not possibly avoid it, and then she
sat beside him in a perfect ecstasy of terror until the des-
tination was reached, when she would get out dazed and
trembling. Lina still did not know quite how it could be
done, but she was certain that there must be plenty of
ways in which the driver of a car can kill his passenger if
he has the mind to it.

In the end she and Johnnie did not go away for a holiday at all, because whatever places or surroundings were
suggested, Lina instantly saw possibilities of death in
them. Lina's imagination had never been so vivid before.

Water was taboo; cliffs, rocks, and mountains were
taboo; fits of such panic seized her at times that it almost
came to food being taboo—certainly any food with which
Johnnie might conceivably have tampered in advance.
And with food, drink. Automatically now Lina first
sniffed at, and then very cautiously tasted, any drink
which Johnnie handed to her, even if the bottle was un-

corked under her eyes, or she saw Johnnie help himself from the same jug.

And still she could not make up her mind whether to run away from Johnnie or not.

Gradually she sank into apathy over it all.

Gradually it became not so much that she could not make up her mind, as that she ceased even to try to make up her mind. As the weeks went by, and the knowledge of Johnnie's intention became slowly less of a recurrent shock and more a part of her life, Lina found herself more and more fascinated by fate. She saw herself drifting, swept on by forces stronger than herself. The power of decision was less taken from her than relinquished by her. She did not want to decide.

Each morning she thought, dully: will he try to kill me to-day? Shall I be dead by to-night? She did not think she very much minded if she was.

Death did not frighten her, now. Death, even if it was oblivion, would be better than life like this. In her bedroom or the garden she would sit for hours alone, thinking about Johnnie and death, trudging the same circle of thought over and over and over again.

Only in Johnnie's presence did she rouse herself. Johnnie must not suspect. Away from him, she gave her fate-hynotized brooding full rein. If Johnnie had come to her during those moments with murder in his face, Lina really did not know whether she would struggle or submit.

And yet she still took no step towards buying back her life from him.

Lina knew she was weak. She knew she had been, in a way, weak all her life. Only for Johnnie had she been strong. And now, even as regarded Johnnie, her strength had gone.

Should she let Johnnie kill her or not?

11

In the end Lina's mind was made up for her.

After all these years she awoke to the realization that she was going to have a baby.

At all costs Johnnie must not be allowed to reproduce himself. Lina crushed ruthlessly down the new urge to live that her condition had induced. At *all* costs.

An illegal operation hardly entered her mind; suicide was terrible; Johnnie's way was the easiest of all.

Lina felt much calmer when her decision had been made at last. So much of her married life had been spent in beating from one side of the cage to the other. It would be peaceful just to sit and wait.

12

Isobel pushed her chair a little back from the tea table, crossed her large legs, and lit a cigarette.

"Now we can talk," she said.

"Yes," said Lina.

It was delightfully restful in Isobel's cottage garden. A clump of Michaelmas daisies caught her eye, and she dreamily absorbed their colour. Lina concentrated now on anything that gave her pleasure, getting as near to the heart of it as she could, as if storing up memories against a prison-future. She would never see Michaelmas daisies again. It was important to extract as much from them now as they had to give.

Isobel was looking at her curiously. "Something on your mind, isn't there?"

Lina gave herself a little shake. "No. Why?"

"I've noticed you've seemed a little queer this summer."

I'd begun to think you must be offended with me for some reason or other."

"Good gracious, no." Lina, the least demonstrative of women, sketched a little gesture of reassurance and friendliness. "No, I was just admiring those daisies."

"Oh, I see. Yes, you've an eye for colour. Well, anyhow, how's Johnnie? I don't seem to have seen him for weeks."

"Johnnie's quite well." Lina paused. She had come to Isobel's to talk about Johnnie, but she did not know quite how to introduce her subject.

Fortunately Isobel helped her. "You're a lucky woman, Lina. And you've got the sense to know it."

"How, lucky?"

"Having a husband like Johnnie."

"Oh! Yes, Johnnie's wonderful, isn't he?"

"He ought to have been Irish, with all that charm and blarney. Little did I think any man would ever get anything out of *me* against my will."

"Isobel! What do you mean?"

"Oh, it's nothing really. Just something I didn't mean to tell him, and he got it out of me."

Lina drew a quick breath. "What?"

"Nothing that would interest you, my dear woman," Isobel retorted, with a touch of resentment. "It was connected with the subject I'm not allowed even to name, to you."

"Don't be so silly, Isobel." Lina's heart had begun to beat faster. Isobel herself had offered her the very topic she had come to probe. "What did Johnnie get out of you?"

"Oh, it wasn't anything important, really. I don't know why I mentioned it." Miss Sedbusk flicked the ash from her cigarette onto the grass.

Lina could have shaken her. "Tell me, Isobel. I want to know. Why on earth make such a mystery about it?"

"My dear woman, I'm making no mystery. I'll tell you, if you really want to know."

"I do want to know. I keep on saying so."

"All right; don't get peeved. But it isn't of the least importance. The important thing is that Johnnie got it out of me at all. There's a certain alkali, a substance in daily use everywhere, one of the commonest things you could imagine, which happens to be an exceedingly powerful poison. But hardly anyone knows that it is. It's far too common to be put on the poison list, you see. Besides, that would only be advertising the fact that it is poisonous. So those who do know, don't say. It's sort of hushed up."

"Ah," Lina breathed.

"Because the really dangerous thing is that this stuff is practically undetectable by analysis after death. Not like arsenic, which can be identified years afterwards. So you can see that, if everyone knew about it, one half of the world would probably be busy all the time poisoning the other half—and getting away with it. There aren't even any symptoms worth mentioning, you see. It acts on the heart; and the heart simply stops beating, and that's all there is to it. So we who do know what the stuff is, keep very mum about it. We don't tell even our closest friends. Of course, it wouldn't matter, so far as they're concerned. The point is that they might pass it on."

Lina's mouth had gone very dry. She had to work her tongue in it before she could speak. "And Johnnie—got it out of you?"

"He did," said Isobel cheerfully. "Curse him!"

Lina stared at her feet. Her whole energies were concentrated in clasping her hands so tightly in her lap that Isobel should not see them shaking.

"Not," added Isobel, with a laugh, "that there's much danger of Johnnie passing it on, because he flatly refused to believe me."

Lina succeeded in looking inquiring.

"I tell you, he flatly refused to believe me. Simply said I must have got my facts wrong. Anything as common as that couldn't possibly be poisonous. I told him," snorted Miss Sedbusk, "that my facts are *never* wrong."

Lina found her voice again. "What is this stuff?" she asked, a little faintly.

"Oh, no," retorted Isobel. "One in the family's quite enough. I'm not going to tell you too. And if you're a friend, you won't ask Johnnie. It's much better for people not to know a thing like that."

"Perhaps it is." Lina could feel her skin moving oddly under her clothes. "Well, is—whatever it is, painful?"

"Not in the least. In fact," said Miss Sedbusk heartily, "I should think it must be a most pleasant death."

13

Lina was worried.

She was worried lest Johnnie might do something silly. A person in full health cannot just drop dead without a lot of fuss and bother afterwards. There would have to be an inquest and (she could not help shuddering) a post-mortem. Johnnie was always so childishly confident that he might not choose his moment carefully enough. Lina did wish she could advise him about it openly.

Because if only Johnnie was careful, there would never possibly be any suspicion. Quite apart from the stuff being undetectable, nobody would ever suspect Johnnie of murder. Johnnie, of all people, so popular, so well connected, such an important person now in the district and the county. No, Johnnie was perfectly safe, if only he was careful.

But Lina could not feel sure that Johnnie would be careful. She would have to see to that herself, as she always had.

After a good deal of thought, she did two things. She went to the public library in Bournemouth and read up the diseases of the heart; then she called in her doctor and complained of the symptoms she had learned. She was sounded and examined and was really overjoyed to be told that her heart was not altogether as healthy as it might be, though there was no possible danger so long as she did not strain it quite outrageously. That, at any rate, was something.

The other thing she did was to write a letter to Isobel, which she gave to her personally.

DEAR ISOBEL:

After consideration I have decided to write and tell you that I have made up my mind to commit suicide. When you open this, I shall have done it. I am writing to you, because you are the most sensible person I know, and won't think it necessary to tell the whole world what is purely a private affair of my own. And particularly don't ever tell Johnnie; it would upset him terribly. The reason I am telling you is just in case any trouble occurs about it afterwards, but I don't think there will be, as I am going to use the stuff we talked about (I did get its name out of Johnnie, but he never realized that he was telling me). I'm going to have a baby, and I can't face it.

With love,
LINA AYSGARTH.

She wrote on the envelope, "To be opened in the event of my death."

"Getting quite morbid, aren't you?" said Miss Sedbusk.

But Lina did not feel that she was getting morbid.

On the contrary, she felt an odd exaltation. The question of her death had now taken on so much larger a front. It was now no longer whether weak-kneed Lina Aysgarth would let her husband kill her or not. She was going to die, in a way, for the benefit of society in general. She did not feel a martyr, but she did definitely think she was being rather noble. She tried not to remember that if she had not been going to have a baby she would probably have let Johnnie kill her just the same. She would have acted the rabbit to his snake.

But it was difficult to think of Johnnie as a snake. Johnnie was the person she was sorry for now. Poor Johnnie was having a wretched time. He could hardly bear to part with her, Lina knew, and yet he could see no alternative. Well, that was Johnnie's punishment after all. Johnnie should not have taken up betting again. Lina really felt thankful that Johnnie was going to rid her at last of the hated responsibility that had been weighing her down so long.

Poor Johnnie! Lina was very tender with Johnnie these last days. She was so very sorry for him.

She knew so well what difficulty he must be having in maintaining the quibble which his strange mind had evolved. Isobel had shown her what that quibble was. Johnnie was not going to poison his wife. Good heavens, no! But Isobel Sedbusk had told him a quite incredible thing, which he simply knew could not be true. That stuff poisonous? What nonsense! Why, he would actually feed some of it to his own so-much-loved wife, just to *prove* that Isobel was wrong. Of course Isobel was wrong!

But it was a difficult fiction to sustain. Far more difficult than in the case of her father or Beaky. There must be times when even Johnnie's twisted soul had to recognize the fact that he was contemplating pure, unvarnished murder at last.

It did distress Lina still that Johnnie's first real murder should be her own. But it also gave her a certain sardonic amusement to reflect in the calm, detached attitude which she now felt towards the affair, that she herself was an accessory to it.

"Accessory Before the Fact."

Lina wondered whether anyone else had ever been an accessory before the fact to her own murder.

14

In the middle of November Lina caught influenza. It was a fairly mild variety that prevailed that year, but temperatures were running high and Lina looked forward to at least a week in bed.

The last two months had been rather harassing. Calm though she had remained in general, there had been moments of agony when she did not want to die at all; and other moments of despair when she was within a step of asking Johnnie for heaven's sake to give her the stuff and get it over, since she could bear the suspense no longer.

On the whole, however, she had kept her head. Poor Johnnie at least, she was sure, had suspected nothing.

She had even given him a cheque for the insurance, and the double insurance at that, in the most completely casual way.

But all her preparations had been made so long ago,

and the exaltation was beginning to wear thin. For three months she had been ready to die: and Johnnie would not kill her.

On the third day of her illness Johnnie came into her bedroom to see her, in the middle of the morning. He was carrying a glass of milk-and-soda on a little tray. Lina turned her head on the pillows and smiled at him.

Johnnie stood just inside the door, looking at her. His face worked.

The smile faded from Lina's lips. A single stab, like an electric shock, ran through her whole body. She knew, beyond a doubt, that the moment had come.

"Monkeyface, I—I've brought you this."

In an instant Lina's mind had mechanically reviewed the situation, and found it safe. Johnnie had not been silly. People did die of influenza.

She jerked herself up on one elbow in bed. She must be quick: quick to act, before she could think, and be afraid. The thin silk nightgown slipped down over her shoulder.

"Give it me."

But Johnnie hesitated. There were tears in his eyes, just as Lina had foreseen.

She stretched out her hand. "Give it me, Johnnie."

Johnnie sidled up towards the bed.

Lina snatched the glass and drained it. It tasted quite ordinary. Could she have made a mistake, after all?

But Johnnie was looking down at her in a way which showed that she had made no mistake.

She wiped her lips carefully on her handkerchief and lifted her face to Johnnie.

"Kiss me, Johnnie."

Johnnie was staring at her now with an expression of

absolute horror. It was as if he had not realized at all what he was doing until he had done it.

"Kiss me!"

She locked her arms round his neck and held him, for a few seconds, strained against her.

"Now go, darling."

"Monkeyface, I—I——"

"*Go*, darling." She did not want Johnnie to see her die. Johnnie went.

Lina listened to his slow, shambling footsteps going down the stairs, so unlike Johnnie's usual brisk tread.

The tears came into her own eyes. Johnnie would miss her terribly.

He had gone into the morning room. He would stay there, waiting.

Lina could hardly believe she was going to die. After she had lived so vividly. After she had liked life, in spite of what it had brought her, so much.

What would death be like? She was not exactly frightened of it. But . . .

But it did seem a pity that she had to die.

A tear trickled slowly down her cheek onto the pillow.

It did seem a pity that she had to die, when she would have liked so much to live.

THE END